Carole J Hall and her husband have raised four children. During that time, she worked in Architectural drafting and design and built with her husband using their own labour several new houses in three states of Australia. She is proud of the fact that all the children have been successful in their lives. Then she and her husband sailed the world in their Bavaria forty-seven-foot yacht unassisted calling into ports around the world, working in countries that they were allowed to support their travels over nearly five years. She feels that after going through storms and checking into countries where no English is spoken at all, bartered over the price of a tomato in the pacific islands nothing can frighten her, weather or man! Her support base is her children. She has now retired to write in the last home she designed, and now longer goes cruising coastal or over oceans.

To my husband Kevin who sailed most of the oceans and seas with me.

Carole J Hall

The Little Girls Club

Austin Macauley Publishers™
London • Cambridge • New York • Sharjah

This is a work of fiction. Names, characters, businesses, places, events, locales, and incidents are either the products of the author's imagination or used in a fictitious manner. Any resemblance to actual persons, living or dead, or actual events is purely coincidental.

A CIP catalogue record for this title is available from the British Library.

ISBN 9781035811786 (Paperback)
ISBN 9781035811793 (ePub e-book)

www.austinmacauley.com

First Published 2023
Austin Macauley Publishers Ltd®
1 Canada Square
Canary Wharf
London
E14 5AA

Table of Contents

List of Persons in This Book
By C.J. Hall

Tristan Keith Paravoni	
Lydia Isabella Paravoni	Wife
Lydia Isabella Paravoni	Mother
Kelvin James Paravoni	Father
Derek and Marion Smith	Friends
Nicole and Beau Harris	Children
Mogo Steven Montgomery	Hitman
Phillip Harris	Police
Jonathon Mitchell	Lawyer
Marty Mitchell	Lawyer
Mendez	Detective
Derek Smith	Lawyer
Brian Smith	Lawyer
Marilyn Thomas	Marion's Mother
Bill Thomas	Marion's Father
Carson	Fisherman
Tom	Boat Builder
Mary O'Hara	Neighbour
Arthur McDonald	Christina's Father
Bruiser	Bad Boys Club
Paul Hervey	Police Superintendent
Helen Hervey	Wife
Troy Bennet and Hunter Hervey	Sons
Barry Nicholson	Constable
Roger Dixon	Constable
Alan Davis	Constable

Bret McMillan	Constable
Stan Marshall	Pilot
Gail Hargrave	Nurse and Teacher
Trevor	Salesman
Mal	Mechanic

Chapter 1
Christina

The shiny black Bentley cruised down the highway. The driver who loved this fine piece of machinery slowed to turn into their destination. Turning into the driveway of their friends, the Bentley became almost silent as it came off the bitumen onto the concrete driveway.

The house was a low, long, dark brick, ranch style with a steel roof of green giving it a cool welcome look on a hot day.

As they approached the side way of the house, Tristan felt uneasy and glanced at his lovely wife who must as felt the same by the look on her face that seemed to be fearful.

The driveway passed the side of the house where there was an open carport, and instead of their friend's car, there a large black van with both back doors wide open blocking their normal view of the back patio that led to the rear entry of the house. From there, a high hedge went from the carport into a large semicircle forming a backyard situation to hide the view to farm sheds that housed the equipment for their small acreage.

Then a gasp from them both as they saw their friend's wheelchair upturned on the side of the driveway at the rear of the property.

"Maybe that van is delivering a new chair for Marion," Christina whispered.

"Hope so." He returned with a worried look.

Marion was confined to the chair because of a serious car accident a few years ago. The purpose of their visit to Marion was to bring their newborn baby to visit their friends as Marion would find it difficult to visit them.

The baby boy stirred in the back of the car in his capsule, but no sound came from him.

Tristan turned the Bentley in front of the farm sheds in a U-turn that left the big car facing outwards towards the front gate ready to leave after the visit as he always did, the thought being that if there was another visitor, they could not block him in. The hedge then blocked the Bentley from view as well.

Christina emerged from the Bentley. "I will go ahead and see what is happening," she said quietly and headed for the gap in the hedge that was just wide enough to pass through to the back door of the house.

"Right behind you, I will get the baby in a minute, want to see what is going on here first," he replied.

As she started to pass through the gap, two shots were fired and she fell back on her husband's chest, and he followed her to the ground grabbing her shoulders, so her head would not hit the concrete edge then seeing the two bullet holes in her forehead.

In shock, he could not utter a sound. He was low enough to look under the base of the hedge and saw a policeman heading towards them. He was stunned.

Looking from his wife with two bullet holes in her shattered head now laying in his arms, to the policeman, and although hidden behind the hedge, thought he was about to die also. He thought of his baby son. He was about to be discovered behind the thick hedge and die and he had no defence at all.

A call came from the house and the policeman turned back towards the shouting. Then, on his way back to the house, threw a handgun with an almighty swing up on the roof of the house. The gun hit the steel roof and then slid down the steel.

He did not see it hit a pipe go into the air and land into the hole of the rainwater tank, Tristan saw it disappear with a clunk into the water. "No evidence," the policeman chuckled.

Tristan knew he was hidden by the hedge and so was the car. Now that the policemen had turned towards the house, he pulled out his phone and dialled the emergency number, and voice lowered, pleaded for an ambulance.

Louder noise came from the rear of the house near the black van. There was more than one policeman that came into view, and they were struggling with a body bag complete with body, that they tossed with a loud thump into the back of the van. Two more men appeared with another body bag tossed in on the first one.

The first two that came out went back into the house and returned with a third body bag and that also went through the back doors of the van. The big doors were then slammed shut. Six men piled into the front of the van. Tristan hoped those body bags did not contain Marion, Derek and her son. Then heard the wail of the ambulance. Then the van drove off at a slow speed and out of sight for Tristan.

An ambulance turned into the driveway only seconds later and the men in the large black van, now on the road, were aware of this and watched it enter and drive along the concrete drive and out of sight behind the hedge. One of the men was a bit concerned and asked the other, "What happened back there? I heard a couple of shots in the back yard."

"No problems," came the answer. "Shot a dog, someone must have heard that and rang the ambo's."

The paramedics stopped close to Tristan and Christina. Both jumped out. One looked at the other and they nodded. "Domestic violence," one said quietly.

"For sure," the other replied.

They approached Tristan carefully. Looking at the bullet wounds, they were sure they had this covered and there was no saving this woman.

"I am Ben, and this is Tim," the taller of the men said.

"Want to hop in the back with her?" Ben asked.

Tristan replied, "Can't; the baby is in the car. I will have to take care of him first and come to the hospital later."

The two paramedics looked at each other once again. Perhaps they were wrong. Why would he shoot his wife with a baby in the car, if he owned that car, he could pay someone else to do it and have the perfect alibi!

"Feel like telling us what happened," one of them asked.

"You may not believe it," Tristan answered.

"Give us a shot," was the reply.

Tristan told them how they were coming to visit their friends and they felt something was wrong. Christina went in to see what was going on and a policeman in the backyard shot her twice. How he thought he was coming for him then but a noise from the house made him turn away.

He threw his gun up on the roof then joined the others and they drove away. "You must have seen them as you drove in as soon as they left!"

The paramedics looked at each other and nodded. Yes, they had seen a large black van.

"When we get to the hospital, the police must be notified as it is a gunshot wound, so if you can be there as soon as possible please as they will want to interview you."

"I will be," Tristan said. "May even go straight to the police station first."

“Have you been in the house?” The paramedic asked. “Is there anyone in there.”

“No. I have not been near the house,” Tristan said. “I could not leave my wife and I cannot think of anything else now. Must get the baby to my mother’s immediately.”

The paramedics went cautiously into the house, quick scan over the place, no bodies. However, looked like quite a bit of blood round and they would report that.

With the body of Christina loaded in the ambulance, it slowly and silently drove out of sight around the hedge past the house to the front gate and turned on to the highway.

Tristan got into his car and followed, numb with what was happening and unable to comprehend how his life had taken such a tragic turn. His now motherless son in the back behind the seat in his capsule woke up for his feed and nappy change. He willed himself not to cry or sob as he must drive safely for his little son, his mother’s place not that far away. How was he going to tell her what had happened?

When he arrived at his mothers’ house, he could not hold back any longer. Clicking the buckles on the capsule, lifting it out of the car and picking up the baby’s bag with formula and all the things that baby’s need carefully packed inside by Christina, the tears flowed as he opened the front door of his mother’s house.

She was in the kitchen as usual always cooking something and turned when she heard the front door open. His mother was smiling as usual to see her only child and the capsule in his hand. This meant she would see her grandchild as well. “The first of many I hope,” she reminded them. Looking for Christina, she happened to look at her son’s face and her smiling stopped, and a shocked face took its place.

“You had better sit, my darling, and tell me what he happened.”

Carefully placing the capsule on the floor and the baby’s bag on the kitchen bench, he collapsed on a chair at the table, and said, “Can you feed baby please, he is overdue.” The tears kept flowing.

His mother did as she was asked. Lydia Isabella Paravoni was a good woman, excellent and loving mother. Giving birth to Tristan later in life was a wonderful surprise for her and Kelvin Keith Paravoni, his dad. They were determined not to spoil the child but give him good values to keep him safe, and become a kind and useful human that cared for others. They did just that.

While she fed baby James Tristan Keith Paravoni, she carefully watched her son as he went into the lounge room and sat on the lounge with his hands covering his face trying to stop the sobbing so he could explain to his mother what happened, what he had seen and ask her what he should do.

Baby was fed, changed and put in the bassinette she kept there for when they paid a visit along with spare stroller and other things to wait until he was old enough to need them. After all, he was not yet two weeks old.

She went and sat opposite her son in a large armchair and waited until he began to speak.

She did not have to wait long as he first explained that he had to go to a police station or maybe the hospital to identify his wife. He then began the story of what happened between sobs but basically did very well. His mother took in every word.

When he asked his mothers' advice, she said, "First thing is, go to your lawyer as you need legal advice before you talk to the police. He will or should go with you to the station. You realise that these days they may call this domestic violence." He nodded his head.

"It obviously is not but you know the husband is always the guilty one."

"Thank you, I will do that first. Then maybe the hospital and then the police station as that could take a while. Making statements and answering questions in a police station could take hours."

He had known his lawyer for many years, mainly import or export actions Tristan felt if Jonathon could not handle this, he would know someone who could. Tristan rang him first and said to his receptionist this was an emergency and could he fit him in as soon as possible. She put him on hold and when Glenda returned quickly, she told him to come in immediately as Jonathon could always see him in an emergency. Grateful, he hung up the phone. Kissed his mother and headed for the car.

On arrival, Glenda said "Oh! Tristan, you look very stressed," and showed him straight into Johnathon's office.

Johnathon stood to greet him and on sight said, "Sit down, Tris." Grabbed his arm and steered him to a chair. "What the hell is going on?"

Tristan felt he was out of tears and told the story as best he could. He then told Jonathon that he had to go to the hospital and identify Christina, and on to the police station to make a statement before they come to get him. Then asked if he could defend him or come to the police station and try to help him out.

Jonathon replied that he would come to the hospital as support to identify Christina and on to the police station to find out the situation. He also explained that this was not his main legal field, however his brother was a Defence lawyer and a very good one. "Marty is the best and before we leave, I will give him a call."

While Tristan was identifying Christina, Jonathon beside him rang his brother, Marty. He relayed the message to Tristan. "Marty is in court, but that is ok. I can inform him what is going on and he can see you early tomorrow morning. Now I have to give you his number so get out your mobile. Here I will put it in for you as you look a bit shaky. I have given him yours, so now you can both be in touch all the time."

"His answering machine will tell you when he is in court, and he will get back to you as soon as he comes out. Hopefully, happy because he won his case! I will take you to the police station," said Jonathon. "They know me there and may make things easier for you."

"I am so grateful to you," said Tristan.

"You will get my bill," replied Jonathon trying to lighten the situation.

Jonathon pulled into the police station's car park and pulled into a reserved car park. "I am allowed to park here," he said. "It is for guys like us always someone in trouble and needs help."

They entered the station. Jonathon had a few words to the fellow at the information desk and told Tristan to wait as someone was on the way.

Detective Martinez introduced himself and asked them to follow him to an interview room. He opened the door and signalled to enter.

It was a small white painted room. There was a table and two chairs one side, one the other. There was also a window looking out into a large room with desks, some manned with men in uniform and some not and a row of doors leading off the other side of the room. Tristan was aware of it all and realised that the window was so outsiders could see if there was any trouble in the interview room.

Martinez pointed at the two chairs and immediately said, "So you're the domestic violence case; why did you shoot your wife?"

Jonathon interrupted with "Don't answer that, Tristan."

But Tristan could not answer it as a man had come into view in police uniform that he recognised as the one who shot his wife. He started screaming but no one could understand what he was saying, so Jonathon rose and said, "My client is obviously distressed, so I am taking him for treatment, and we will return another day when he is well enough."

Martinez stood aside and did not argue while Jonathon pulled his client to his feet and out of the room and out to the car. Tristan was still talking rubbish and Johnathon could not understand a word he said.

Jonathon waited patiently in the car while Tristan calmed down a bit, then quietly said, "They all start accusing men like that, if they catch them off guard, they can get a quick confession and case closed. Lots of 'brownie' points for that."

That calmed Tristan down and he quietly responded, "That was not the problem." He took a deep breath and continued, "I saw the policeman that shot Christina."

Jonathon was aghast; he could not believe what he was hearing. "I am taking you back to your mother's, so you do not have to worry about anything until you talk to Marty."

He took him back to his mother's and sat him on the lounge. His mother was feeding the baby. All was quiet. He whispered to Tristan's mother and she nodded, seems she had a sedative she could give him to see him through the night.

Johnathon stayed and looked at the baby. "Had they named him?" He asked.

Lydia nodded. "They called him James," she answered. "James Tristan Kelvin."

"That is a good strong name."

Jonathon smiled. He ran is hand over the baby's head. "So tiny; he must be 10 days old now."

"Yes, today. He is such a good baby; so contented, so easy to look after."

"I will help you get Tristan into bed and see he is settled before I go."

"Thank you," Lydia replied as she put the baby into his bassinette.

Jonathon waited until Tristan was asleep and he left a worried man. He could not wait to ring his brother and hoped that Marty had some answers or direction of where to go. He hoped he could sleep that night with a head full of questions with no answers.

Chapter 2
Phillip Harris

Phillip Harris left the family home when eighteen to join the Airforce. Glad to leave his mean father and complacent mother. His older siblings had left a few years ago to get away from them both. He was grateful, however, that he had never been beaten or abused. His father, a gambler, used to take his mother's allowance, and he did not think she received much, so he had to do without the many things he dreamed of having.

That was about to change when he joined the Airforce, he promised himself. At first, he wanted to be a pilot but changed his mind when he realised that planes crash and not much chance of survival.

He then found the answer. He would become an aircraft engineer to keep these guys who flew the planes safe in the air, so they could protect the country he lived in as he planned to live in style. He was tall, very handsome, and charming; he could be or do anything he wanted.

Now he was free.

He had the knack of becoming very popular with the staff he worked with and the other departments as well. Was not long before he heard, "Hey, Phil, how's it going," wherever he went on the base.

Off duty was the same. At the local discos, taverns or club bars, the girls always tried to gain his attention and he would give that to them as it meant a bed mate for the night. Of course, his friends used to go everywhere with him so they could get a woman that was left out in the cold, and they could have company for that night as well. Phil was the most popular fellow on the base.

He learned quickly about how fighter planes were put together. In two years, he could tell the problem the plane had and how to fix it fast. He could fix interior problems, wing, engine and undercarriage problems, then started on the electronics. Radios, radars, all the cockpits' instruments and controls were no problem. The pilots that flew them trusted him and often if another mechanic had fixed their fighter jet, they would ask their friend Phil to check it. But the crew got used to that and made jokes about it in the end.

All worked together and they would ask Phil if they were on the right track with the repair they had been trusted with. Sometimes this pulled Phil off the job he had been tasked to do but they were his friends and his mates, so it was no trouble for him and, also this meant the guys in the air were safe.

He was building up quite a bank account as he rarely paid for anything. Drinks were given to him, food bought in for him, sent into the base by the wives of his friends who would tell their husbands that Phil was single and he needs to eat good food, and the food on the base really was not good enough.

He never put a foot out of place. If he saw one of their wives alone with a trolley full of shopping and one or two little ones, he would stop and get out of his car or walk over to give her a hand. The wife would put the toddlers in their seat belt while he loaded all the shopping in the car for her. He always received a grateful thank you and the good deed information was passed on to the husband.

He also helped the mates by helping paint the nursery for a new arrival or help with moving in or out, and if new furniture or a fridge was arriving, he was always on the other end of a bed or settee. Yes, he was a friend to all. He never paid undue attention to any wife; they trusted him as well.

All this was for his own gain, not to be lifelong friends. His bank account was still growing.

Phil was a happy man. So happy he thought, he could get away with something like getting a free battery for his car. No problem. One arrived that night and the Airforce paid for it. Other small things appeared as soon as he mentioned it. In the end, his wages went into the bank, and he never touched it.

He then decided he should invest it on big interest or buy shares. He had now come up the ranks and had worked his way up the ladder of success. His superiors felt he was a valued asset, so they started to send him overseas on repair missions that could take up to three months away working on their planes. Of course, that meant more money for living away allowance, overtime and he applied for anything he could think of.

He had great success with shares, and interest and the money rolled in he was doing very well, and he was only twenty-two. Plenty of drinks, food, women and friends who would do anything for him.

The money was in banks overseas, but he also had a small bank account locally just in case.

He decided at the age of twenty-five years, he should take a wife. She could live on the base with him, and he could have a house instead of his small unit that he had since he joined the Airforce. The bonus would be that he still spent months overseas so the future wife would be here taking care of everything.

Not interested in the local girls, he wanted something special. Certainly, younger than him and preferably not have been messing around with men like him. Straight out of school would be nice and he could train her not to want anything expensive and do as he commanded.

Not far from the Airforce base was a high school, he knew that from the men who worked with him at the base and had daughters attending that one. He sat in his car watching them head for home through the double gates of the school yard out onto the footpath.

He watched for about three weeks and was concerned he could be accused of being a stalker, so stopped doing this for a week or so. On his first afternoon when returned, he saw what he was looking for.

She came out of the gates with her friends, happily strolling along, laughing at what they were saying. Taller than her friends, long blue-black hair, perfect body shape. He would love to see her out of her uniform in more ways than one. Now how to meet her. That did not take long.

Next day, he was there on the footpath trying to work out how he could start a conversation. No chance this day, she was surrounded by her friends giggling and playing around.

It took two days before she was separated from her friends long enough for him to step in for a chat.

"Hi," he said. "Wondering if you can help me. I am looking for Honey View Street. Do you know where that is?"

"Sure," she replied, "I live in that street." She proceeded to explain how to get there. Of course, he knew where it was, but pretended he did not.

"Is it ok if I tag along, that way I will not get lost again."

"Sure, no problem." She signalled to her friends that he was to follow them and four of them headed off in the right direction. The others gradually left, turning off at various streets. Just the two of them left, giving him the chance to get acquainted.

He asked what grade she was in so he could calculate her age. He thought she was seventeen, so that was good. He volunteered that he was in the Airforce. She was impressed. The small talk continued until they arrived at her gate and he asked if he could walk her home the next day. The answer to his delight was in the affirmative.

A romance came into being.

He had told her he was twenty years old, but her parents, Marilyn and Bill Thomas, did not believe it and disapproved of the association. Marion was too young and still at school. She had no independence or experience in life. She was smart enough to continue her studies. It had to end. They tried hard to break them up.

Unfortunately for them, eight weeks later, Phillip and Marion announced she was pregnant.

Her parents of strict Catholic religion wanted them married, however she was not able until she was eighteen years old. They had to wait a few months and then the wedding took place.

Phillip carted his new bride around the Airforce base showing off his beautiful bride. She was truly beautiful. They would have the most handsome children ever to be born.

Phil saw she had the right diet and medical attention. He hated it when he was sent overseas, he wanted to be beside her to see all was well. Their babies would be special and eye catching from the day they were born, with his good looks and her beauty. They would have black eyes like their mother and blue-black hair like hers as well.

He organised that he would be home with his wife when the time had come.

He was home for the birth and was first to cast his eyes on his newborn daughter. He did not like what he saw. This could not be his child, it was so ugly, so revolting. Totally bald and yellow face, yellow eyes, huge ears. He walked out of the hospital. Marion had dozed off and did not see his reaction.

When Marion came home, he showed no interest in the child, and when one year later, she gave him a son, he was the same. Marion was told, "That is it no more ugly bastards." He left the room.

As they grew, he ignored them and only did anything for them that Marion asked, and no more. Left the room as soon as he could. Marion was devastated at his reaction to his children.

It was good that he was abroad most of the time now, so she did not have to put up with him. She wanted to leave him, but her parents did not believe in divorce, and she had been determined to marry him against their wishes.

A few days later, she was walking them down to the shops and decided that she would go into the coffee shop for a rare treat. Sitting the children up as the table near a couple of Airforce men in uniform, she went to order her coffee when she overheard the two men talking, "Well, I see good old Phil is overseas again."

The other replied, "Yeah, time to lock up your daughters in Taiwan."

Marion stood still listening to them laughing. She skipped the coffee and took the children home. It had never occurred to her that he would be unfaithful to her. What a fool she was.

Luck was with her. A few minutes later, the phone rung and it was her mother who rarely rang her daughter after her marriage, only to ask how the grandchildren were on birthdays and Christmas. Marion's mother had never seen the children as she considered it too far to travel.

Her mother started with, "I have bad news, your grandmother died, and your grandfather is ill."

Marion replied, "Should I go and look after granddad, I can do that now as Philip is overseas again."

Her mother hesitated. Then said, "Well, that could solve a lot of problems. He will need care and I cannot do it with your father, how he is, when could you come?"

"Well, I should be there for the funeral for grandma, so in a couple of days."

"Well, see you then," she said and hung up.

Her grandfather lived in the Bay over one thousand miles south of her. She hoped her little car would make it or maybe take the train. She would have no money for repairs if it did. No, I will drive, she thought to herself and started looking for something to put clothes in and guessing what the children would need.

Marion called the children to her and told them of a great adventure they were going to have. She asked them to get their favourite things and put them in the car. They were so excited and happy, and she was glad about that. She left a note for Phillip telling him she had left him and not coming back.

Car packed with everything she could think of and enough room for the children in the back in their seat belts. She left late in the afternoon so the children could be fed before they got too restless and would sleep in the back. She would drive late into the night until she had to sleep as well.

The children, Beau and Nicole, were enjoying the trip and were excited to meet great grandad and he was overjoyed to meet his two great grandchildren. The funeral was short, and they all went back to her granddad's house to settle in.

The house was large and had four bedrooms so plenty of room. A large, fenced backyard that Marion could remember playing in when she was young. He also had a dog, and that created much happiness for Beau and Nicole. The dog seemed very happy to see them as well as he went and collected a ball for them to throw to him, they did and to their delight, he chased it and returned with it for more game.

Marion did not waste time getting granddad's medication under control, his diet sorted, and she took her role as his nurse very seriously. Granddad loved the attention and the children.

Marion needed money as soon as she could as she knew when Phillip came home, she would be cut off immediately. She wanted to work part-time as soon as possible. She had the ideal position within a week.

When she felt confident in herself, Marion went to a divorce lawyer. She explained her position and she could escape only because of her grandfather needing her help.

Her lawyer had lots of questions about her husband. He was quite certain that his position in the Airforce would be a good paying position and he could not understand why he gave her so little. Marion explained that she had seen his bank statement and only had twenty thousand in it. Her lawyer doubted it.

"Must have something stashed somewhere," he replied. "I do not know how you managed on keeping house on that meager amount. Well, we just have to wait until he returns from abroad and see what he has to say for himself. Let me know as soon as you hear from him."

She did not have to wait long. He was back the week earlier than she expected. "Get back here now," he threatened.

"No, my grandfather needs me, and I cannot live with your attitude towards the children."

"You better or else, I will see you get nothing and then you will wish you were dead." He slammed the phone down. As soon as he did, she rang her lawyer, who asked for his full name and the details of his employment so he could contact him.

Seems he was too late; seems Phillip Harris was no longer in the Airforce. His time was up a few weeks ago, he stayed on to finish the work he had started before returning home at the base.

They had no contact and no forwarding address.

Derek called Marion in to the office. She hurried in to see what he had found out.

Marion hesitated outside the office of 'Smith Brothers Lawyers', afraid that it would be not good news.

What they did not know for many years that he was already sitting in the Police Academy studying the law and going to climb the ladder of success as he did not want to be the average 'Cop'. He wanted to start at 'Sergeant' but that was not possible, so he worked and was smart, and got to that place quicker than most.

When Phillip worked for a while in one of the local stations, he then asked for a transfer to the Bay and that was granted. He was clever and once again, all his colleges thought he was just the best fellow around.

Out to make extra money, he dabbled in drugs and prostitution.

He had two goals in mind that he wanted to gain as soon as possible. One was to go to the shooting range and get more accurate and knowledgeable with guns. He went almost every time he was off duty. The other goal was to find someone with a boat.

Here he took notice of anyone who was accurate with their score and used them to give him as much information as possible. He never wore his uniform at the range. He was after an unregistered gun and was willing to pay anything for it. He did not want anyone to know that he was a police officer.

At the range this day, he met and was able to receive a lot of information from a fellow called 'Mogo'.

Seems 'Mogo' was in the army and angry that he had trained to kill and never got a chance to show off his skills on the enemy.

"How about just the bad guys, would that be ok?" Phil asked.

"Oh! Yeah. I would be happy to knock off drug dealers, kiddy fiddlers, Bikie. Blokes who love domestic violence or cruelty to animals, show them to me!"

"You know I am a police officer, Mogo."

"Yeah, I figured that, and I will not hold that against you." 'Mogo' smiled.

"Well," said Phil, "I think I can help you with that. Got a phone number?"

"Yeah, just out of curiosity would I get paid for that, you know reward money?"

"Of course," said Phil. "Well paid."

Seems also that 'Mogo' still had good contacts with his old Army mates.

"Well," said Phil, "how about obtaining an unregistered pistol?"

"Can do," replied 'Mogo'. "All my guns are untraceable, and I have some good ones."

A price was agreed on and Phil thought it was cheap.

"Take a few days," Mogo said.

"I can wait." Phil grinned.

Two weeks it took for the pistol to arrive and passed on to Phil.

"How about knocking off a couple of drug dealers for me."

"Love to."

"Let you know in a few days," said Phil. "I will meet up with you and give you all the details. Also I will help you with this one."

Phil drove his car to the marina. He was looking for a smalltime crook that could be conned into anything. He wore his uniform because that would intimidate the young fellow he was looking for.

Carson McDonald was not on the dock but out in the bay on the deck of his boat.

Phil tooted his car horn long enough for Carson to look up and then Phil waved him in.

Carson arrived in his dinghy. He thought that he could not be in too much trouble as he had been doing a couple of small drug runs for him when he was not out fishing.

"Got a job for you," Phil said.

"Ok, boss," Carson replied.

"Now this time it is legal, and I will explain it to you, so you know what you must do. Right!"

Carson relaxed and was ready to listen.

Phillip started the story. "One of my constable's family has had a terrible accident and four members of his family were killed. Now they have always stated that they would like a burial at sea. I am asking you to do it."

"There will be four body bags so you will not see the people and there will be three mourners plus my constable. They will put the bodies on board and weights to sink them to the bottom," he paused. "Do you understand?"

"I certainly can, and I can do that," replied Carson. "What day and time and do I get paid?"

"You will be well paid, more than the cost of your fuel and plenty left over," replied Harris.

"Arrangements are still being made, but in the next few days so, better clear the decks."

He had researched Marion and her new husband and those ugly kids. Shame she was in a wheelchair, but she deserved it. *Make no difference to me, I'm going to get that bitch.*

Back in his car, he thought about it. "This will be easy," he said to himself. He went back to his station. He rounded up four of his devoted constables and organised a meeting in a board room, the small one out the back. He explained to them about the drug dealers and how he wanted to rid society of them. No fuss, no media reports and no glory for the job we are about to do.

"These mongrels who are killing our kids and pretending to be an honest family, even to the stage that one is in a wheelchair. Seems she feels safe in the chair as no-one wants to check her out or search her for fear of discrimination. I will be there to help you out because I know what they look like. There will be no mistakes. Tomorrow is Saturday and they will be there organising Sunday's drug run."

Out in the carpool, there was a very large black van. He went to his superior and asked about it, what was it used for, and he had never seen it leave the area.

Seems it was purchased for a special round up of bank robbers. Twin cab serviced and washed and detailed regularly so if needed in a hurry, it was ready. "Yes, you can have it, just do the paperwork for it," his superior said. He liked Phillip Harris. *Good man*, he thought to himself.

Saturday at noon, all of them piled in the van at the station. Phil checked the fuel situation, and it was ok.

Mogo took his own car so he could go earlier and check the place out. No great activity was expected as it was family lunch time.

Mogo parked in front of the neighbours and walked in on the concrete driveway. Two constables in uniform ran in front him and pushed out the car that was in the carport. The black van went slowly passed him and reversed into the carport the two front doors opened, the men got out.

Mogo joined them and the four men entered the house. Phillip stayed outside to guard the place and see they were not interrupted. He also opened the black vans back doors to the cargo section.

Mogo went in first with the uniforms right behind him. Mogo pulled his gun and shot Derek and Beau, 'pop' 'pop' 'pop' 'pop'. "There was supposed to be four people here," he said quietly, hard to hear above Marion screaming. The men ran through the house and Mogo turned to see if they had the other one, Marion seeing him turn, took the advantage of taking off in her wheelchair through the back door to the carport.

The black van blocked her way out so no trouble for Phillip to catch her, but she managed in her panic to get through. He had to hurry then and caught her on the lawn, pushed her chair over and as she fell, she looked up and saw his face and fainted.

He grabbed her by her long jet-black hair and dragged her back to the house, threw her on her dead husband and son. She never saw who fired the shots that killed her.

Phillip asked where the other one was. "Not in the house," he was told.

"Well, let's get out of here," Phil said. "Put them in their bags and load them up."

Phillip went out of the back door and lit a cigarette. On the second puff, he pulled his pistol out and checked it. Then he saw a blonde angel come through a gap in the hedge. "That's a shame," he said as he put two bullets in her head.

He made a move forward to see if there was anyone else there but there was a call from the house to help put the bodies in the van. He threw the pistol up on the house roof. He did not see it land, just heard the thud as it hit the roof.

Mogo strolled back down the driveway back to his car near the neighbours and drove off. He would collect his reward money later.

Back at the station, Detective Mendez went to the staff room coffee machine. He met Sargent Phillip Harris there. "Hey," Phillip Harris said, "what was all that carry on in the interview room."

"That was our wife killer from this afternoon," said Mendez.

"The one from out of town, I heard about that. Shot her twice in the head?"

"Yep," came the answer.

"You know," Phillip said, "I cannot understand it; the boys came back and said they don't think it was. They reconned, there was no evidence that it was."

"You want me to double check that?" Mendez said. "I might find something to get him on."

"Yeah could be helpful," replied Phillip. "Don't want to have to frame him," he chuckled.

Chapter 3
Marion

Marion went ahead with her life, caring for her grandfather who she adored. The children seemed to be happy, and their past life forgotten. She never heard from Phillip but felt that he was not about to let her get out on his grip.

She was in contact with Derek often for any news as he should have to pay something for his children.

One day, Derek called her on the phone as asked her to call in after his work. She was at his office door at the right time, but he did not take her into his office. Instead, he asked if it was ok to transfer her case to his brother. "He is a better divorce lawyer than me I think."

"But I am happy with you," she replied.

"Well, the problem is that you are my client so it cannot really be ethical to ask you out to dinner."

She smiled. "Well, if that is the problem, I will be happy to see your brother."

"Well, then best we see him as he is waiting to take over, and then I can ask you!"

Marion told her grandfather she had a date that night. "About time," he replied.

The romance blossomed. Marion was truly beautiful. Derek not so handsome but so caring and loving.

Marion's grandfather took a sudden turn for the worst and died suddenly, much to her and Beau's distress, but Nicole was inconsolable.

One month after the funeral, Derek asked her father, Bill Thomas, if it was too soon to ask Marion to marry him as she really needed someone to totally care for her; Nicole and Beau approved. They really got on so well with Derek and trusted him.

They started looking for a family home and found it. Out of town was this lovely acreage with a long low ranch style home on it. A little renovation to get up to exactly how they wanted it. Plenty of room for the children as well.

It was further from town than they planned.

They decided to throw a very large party to welcome all their friends, three hundred of them. Among their guests were Tristan Paravoni and friend, Brenda, also Christina and her father's pilot, Paul. They never met that night.

Marion was delighted to see Christina who had come a long way to be there. Christina lived with her parents on a very large cattle station five hundred miles west. Her father had their pilot Paul, fly her into the Bay for the occasion and was to wait to return her home after.

Marion and Christina went to the same schools in the Bay, Marion went home every night after school Christina boarded at the school. They were the best of friends and pen pals after their schooling. Christina was relieved when Marion left her husband. She often wrote to her telling her the unhappy life she was leading.

Christina had been at her and Derek's wedding. They looked so happy and Nicole and Beau were just so proud of their beautiful mother. Derek in his wedding suit looked resplendent and could not stop grinning throughout the ceremony.

Marion's children were now nine and ten years old, so the property was the perfect time for them.

The years flew by, and the happiness remained in the family until, while Marion was heading to work along their country road, she was 'T-boned' at the first set of lights going into town. The car hit the driver's side so bad that it threw the car onto its side.

Paramedics and rescue services took three hours to get her out of the car. She was whisked off to hospital and straight into surgery.

The car that hit her ran a red light, the car was stolen, and the driver had left the scene of the accident. The hit and run accident were reported in every newspaper and witnesses who had seen the accident were asked to get in touch with the police as soon as possible. The owner of the car had reported the theft the night before. Her car was also an insurance write off.

The operation was considered a success. They had saved her legs; her other body injuries were healing, and this included her face the plastic surgeon had taken care of. The scars would fade. He had taken great care of her beautiful face and pleased with the result. "You will not be able to see any of these scars in two months." He was right, no trace at all.

At their wedding, Derek realised that Marion's mother did not seem to know Nicole or Beau. He asked her why and was told the truth. She was sorry that she had not been there when they were born or for Christmas or birthdays. She hated Phillip, she made that quite clear. She should not have taken it out on the children. "If you would let me, I would love to make it up to them."

He then asked Marion about it. Same answers. Derek then asked if he could take them to visit their grandmother now and again while Marion was working. "That would be nice," she said, "as long as she does not mind."

Every Saturday morning, he took Nicole and Beau to visit their grandmother. A bond was soon formed with grandma and her grandchildren. Granddad soon softened and joined his wife with the pleasure of having Nicole and Beau visit them once a week.

She baked them cookies and fussed over Derek; thankful he had made the move she could not bring herself to do. While grandma made them lunch, Derek chatted with Bill, their granddad.

After Marion's accident, she stepped into help. Derek was very grateful. Marilyn took the children home so Derek could spend all his free time with Marion in the hospital. His brother, Brian, took most of his clients just meeting with Derek during hospital visits to catch him up with Derek's clients.

Marion had tried to learn to walk again. It was not good her legs could not hold her up.

The physiotherapist worked hard on her trying everything she knew but apart from only being able to stand a minute or two, it was futile. At least she had her legs, and she could stand long enough to kiss her husband and feel tall beside him. She went home with a wheelchair.

The family had settled in nicely, even though Marilyn and Bill did not want to part with them. They loved Nicole and Beau dearly and did regret the time wasted that they never saw them.

Time went by and soon both the children were in high school. They had many friends and coped with their mother's disability by knowing how to help her in anything she found difficult.

Chapter 4
Marilyn and Bill

Marilyn and Bill rang Marion to ask if Nicole could stay another night. Nicole had been to her friend's birthday party that afternoon and seemed tired after her happy day with her friend from school.

No answer, but no problem; they all must be out on the property, and they never take their phones there in case they lose one out there where you would be unlikely to find it. Worse still one of their cattle could step on it.

She would try them later around bedtime.

No answer. Must be out late, or maybe they were on their way to pick up Nicole.

They let Nicole stay up later than usual as her parents just may turn up late. In the end, she was so tired, they put the teenager to bed.

At the same time, Derek's brother was on the phone to them. He often worked back on a Saturday night. Sunday was his main day off. No answer. As it was an important matter about one of Derek's clients, he tried a few times, gave up and thought he would just go and visit them early in the morning.

Marty did arrive early. No sign of anyone. He thought that Beau would be riding his new quad bike to check the cattle. No, it was still in the shed.

He went into the house calling out to them all as he entered. No answer.

At that time, he heard a car arriving and thinking it was them as it sounded like a four-wheel drive, he went out to see. It was Bill and Marilyn with Nicole.

"Have you seen them," Marty Smith called out.

"No, we have just arrived," replied Bill. "Wait, I will try their phones again." Both phones rang out. "I wonder why Marion's wheelchair is near the drive. Maybe she has a new one," he answered himself.

"Maybe we should go inside and wait for them," Marilyn said. "I cannot leave Nicole on her own and we have the time."

"Well, I don't," said Marty. "I need some answers for Derek's client. He has been trying to contact him too."

Nicole ran into the house; she had something to show her grandma.

Then the screaming started. The three of them rushed in the back door thinking she had hurt herself.

They saw Nicole standing in the lounge pointing to blood on the floor.

Marilyn when she saw this took over Nicole, put her arms around her and sheltered her from the sight. then took her out to the car. She did not need to see anything like this at her age, not at any age. She only saw the blood because it was on her attempt at knitting, and she wanted to show her grandma.

Bill was on the phone to the police. "Should we look around for bodies," he said to Marty. "Maybe but this is a crime scene so we would have to be careful."

They walked along the concrete drive and there was nothing to see in that area.

"Stay on the concrete," warned Marty. "Do not put your footprints on the soil or you could end up a suspect."

The police seemed to be forever getting there. Two constables arrived and introduced themselves and asked what the trouble was. The three of them tried to explain their situation with phone calls not answered and Nicole being returned from yesterday's party. They then took them inside to show them the blood on the floor.

"Best we call into the station about this. The detectives and forensic need to be notified for a start."

Marilyn told them that she felt they did not need her or Nicole at this stage so she would go home with her granddaughter and wait to see what they should do. If they would be so kind as to tell her husband, Bill Thomas, any procedure that was needed. Her daughter, Nicole's mother, was missing. She would co-operate with the police or try to help in anyway. Hopefully, they would be found alive.

What about Beau? Where was he? Can you look for him?

She drove off with a heavy heart and on the verge of tears. Bill would be dropped home by Marty when he had given his information to the constables.

At their house, she asked Nicole to go to bed and rest. Nicole refused and her grandma understood that Nicole wanted to know as much as she did where was her mother, stepfather and brother, so she let her rest on the couch so as soon as there was any news, Nicole would hear everything at the same time as her grandma.

There had been no news for hours. "Three people who have lost blood just do not disappear," she said to Bill. "I am going to the police station to find out what is going on."

"I am sure they are doing all they can. They have search parties out in all directions and have put a call out for any car that sees anything to get back to the station as soon as possible."

"I am going down there," she said. "Who is the policeman in charge, there must be someone in charge."

"Oh, I think the man in charge is Detective Mendez."

"Ok," she said. "Can you watch Nicole for me, she is so upset. This is just awful for her well."

Marilyn headed out to the car and took great care in driving to the station. It was not that far away but she did not want to have an accident on the way.

She entered the station and went to the information desk, and asked for Detective Mendez.

"You will find him upstairs," the policewoman said and pointed the way.

"Thank you," and followed where she pointed.

Marilyn climbed the stairs watching where she put her feet so she would not fall. As she neared the top she looked up. To her horror, she saw Phillip Harris crossing the floor. She knew what had happened to her daughter and grandson and Derek at that moment. She turned immediately, hoping he did not see her and slowly made her way down the stairs again.

Keeping calm, she proceeded to her car, had trouble in getting her key, in the lock, took deep breaths and finally drove out of the police car park. Driving very carefully and right on the speed limit so as not to be pulled over. She never had been pulled over for anything but best to be sure. She finally made it to their house and parked the car in the driveway. She waited a minute to think how to tell Bill and the best way to handle this.

When she told Bill, he went pale. She asked him what he thought they should do. "I think, we best just disappear as soon as possible."

She agreed and explained that they had to protect Nicole as if he has killed his ex-wife and son, he would be looking for his daughter and them. Her suggestion was to immediately load everything into their caravan. "If we go into the garage from the house with our clothes and some food, no one will see us load up. He may not know we have a van and if we leave at night, the neighbours will possibly not see us."

She told him to get Nicole and tell her we are going away with the caravan until they find her parents. Telling her it is too stressful living, and they will ring us if anything is found.

Bill was happy to do this, he agreed with everything Marilyn had said. "I think we should head interstate. We can ring on a public phone and see if anything has happened, we really should not use our mobiles. Maybe we should turn them off and get new ones with different numbers. I don't know how it works these days."

While they were taking flight, Mogo received a parcel that a courier delivered into his hands. He opened it to find three hundred thousand dollars in cash and a note that said:

'Sorry it was not four grand, that may be later, Phil.'

Mogo put the note in a drawer. "You never know," he said to himself.

About the same time, Carson had a fellow row out to his boat, also a courier, and his note said

'For burial at sea, five thousand each, total fifteen thousand cash. Thanks, Phil.'

Carson put the note back in with the cash and hid it in his boat.

The three young constables each were given five thousand cash in an envelope. Phillip Harris gave them that the next day and he said, "Well done and thanks." The whole deal as far as Phil was concerned was cheap, he had made that much from his dealings locally that month.

Bill and Marilyn were interstate at a caravan park planning their next move. Nicole was asleep.

Chapter 5
Tristan

Tristan slept well thanks to his mother's sedative. He was back on the couch in the lounge. His baby had been fed by his mother and was back in his cot.

He sat there with his head in his hands and thought of his life and how could it go wrong like this.

Tristan was three years old when he first climbed under a car with his dad. Not allowed to until his mummy had made him a pair of overalls like his dad's to keep his clothes clean. Like the inside of the car, the underneath was just as interesting. He could not get enough of cars.

When his dad came home from work, he had to wait for him to change into his overalls before they could start on the car his dad was renovating for some friend. There was always a different make of car coming in and they were all special to his dad and him. Tristan was not happy until he had grease on him like his dad, he would show his mother when they went into dinner. "Are you training him to be a used car salesman?" She laughed.

Tristan was a top student when he first started school and his mother used to keep him up with the schoolwork by teaching him lots of reading and arithmetic at home when he got in the door and while he was waiting for his dad to come home from work.

By the time he went to high school, he could pull an engine down and wash the parts, then hand each part to his father in the right order. He knew Mal, the car painter, and Marc, the guy who owned the car aligner, so the chassis was straight, and the doors shut perfectly. He also knew the motor trimmer who recovered the seats and put new overhead linings and door trims, new carpet or floor or other coverings as well.

His mother still tutored him at home, and he was getting top grades. Now when he came home and after his extra schoolwork, he would have everything ready for when his dad came home to start work with him, and sometimes his father would ask his advice.

"Hey, Tristan," he would say, "should we try another colour on this one."

Tristan replied, "Don't think so, best stick with the original, that always works."

One day, his dad came home with the biggest grin on his face. The grin that he usually had when they had returned a car to its owner knowing it was perfect.

"Guess what I bought today, and it is all ours," he chuckled away knowing his secret would delight Tristan, but maybe not his mother.

"Has to be another vehicle, something special, and ours as well, we get to keep it," said Tristan with excitement in his voice.

"Yes, it is ours and it is a Lamborghini." His father's eyes got big with watching Tristan's face.

"I have never seen one but know of them," said Tristan excitedly.

"Ours comes Saturday morning by special delivery."

He ran to his father's car book collection to find a photo. "Wow," his dad heard him in the study.

"What model?" He called out. His father said it was an old one and needed repairs, but they could both learn a lot from this one and added he bought it for a song.

As his father said, it arrived Saturday morning on a car carrier. One look at it and Tristan knew that this was his future, no doubt about that. H started working on the car as it was being unloaded, making notes of what materials and parts to start this project and in general getting in the way of his father and the delivery driver. The Lamborghini was a Countach 1974 model.

His mother dragged him inside to bed later than usual, but he would have been right with his father until dawn if he could. His dad came in at the same time as they had missed their dinner, they were both hungry as well.

Sunday was a repeat of Saturday and on Monday, Tristan and his dad reluctantly went off to work and school.

So, life went back to normal until the car was finished and they were reluctantly going to sell it. Both hoping they would make a good profit and Tristan had been on the internet to see if they could get another one. No more around however, he found a Porsche 911.

They made enough profit to buy the Porsche and Tristan started looking for another one before the Porsche was delivered.

Tristan was fifteen years old at this time. He was riding his bike home from school when something went wrong with his bike, it seemed out of control. Dismounting. as he guessed, a flat tyre.

He was passing the marina when this happened and started pushing his bicycle along to get home. Beside the marina was a large shed, the door was partly open. Hoping to leave his bike there so he could get home for a repair kit faster and not ruin his tyre, he left the bike at the door and went inside.

"About time you got here," a voice boomed out. "The broom is over there so, get cracking."

Not sure what to do, he grabbed the broom and started sweeping the floor where there were timber shavings all over the place.

He still had not seen anyone but somewhere in this shed was a grumpy old man. He kept sweeping hoping the kid who should have been here would turn up. No such luck.

At the rear of the shed was an enormous frame of a yacht. Just the frame and lots of planks of timber, so Tristan presumed that the booming voice was in there somewhere. Took him a while to finished sweeping up the shavings and he ended up with a great heap. Looking around he saw a large bin, so he went and looked over the edge. He found that it was half full of shavings, so he picked up the load he had swept up and piled it in with the other lot.

He looked back at the yacht frame just in time to see a grey beard emerge from it, followed by two sparkling blue eyes and a bald head.

"Hey, you were not who I was expecting, where's the other youngster? Hang on, I will be right with you young fellow."

The old fellow climbed out of the frame and joined him on the floor. "Job well done, hang on I'll get the cash." Tristan could not believe what he was hearing or seeing. No chance to get a word in either.

The old fellow disappeared into the room marked 'Office' and reappeared with some dollars in his hand. He counted some out and handed them to Tristan. "That ok, I'll see you next Wednesday, not waiting for the other boy he should have been here before you."

Tristan finally got a word in. "I only came in to see if I could leave my bike here while I went home to get my repair kit."

"Really?" The old guy asked. "Well, we can fix that right here; I'll get everything ready. Won't take a minute." He disappeared into the office again.

While he was out of sight, Tristan looked around the place. An interesting wooden box was not far from him. Two steps to the right and he could see there was an engine in it. On closer look, he could see it was a Perkins diesel. He had seen one before somewhere.

On his return from the office, the old guy said, "By the way, I am Tom, nice to meet you know what's your handle?" They shook hands.

"Tristan," said, "can I ask you about the Perkins? Will it go into the boat you are building?"

"Right," he said. "Now, Tristan, what do you know about boats?"

"Nothing really, I am into cars with my dad."

"If you want to know about yachts, I will teach you, but there is a lot of learning to do," he said. "They are nothing like cars. Noisy things running up and down the highway. Yachts are quite slow and much more fun. Learning about sea life and the ocean, how to read the sky and the wind."

"Navigation is a challenge and the excitement of reaching your destination is beyond anything else. So, if you want to try it, we will talk next Wednesday."

Tristan rode his bicycle home with a busy mind so much to think about. He could not wait until he told his mum and dad about Tom. He had his first job and money in his hand; he was on top of the world. He thought life could not get any better.

Tristan explained all of this adventure to his mum and then again to his dad. They were both so proud of him and when he asked then if he should learn to sail with Tom, they both answered that he should learn anything that would help him to understand things and that knowledge was power, and possibly money! They all laughed about this.

Now Tristan leads a very busy and happy life. By the time, he was eighteen, he was importing cars and becoming a very competent sailor. He also had a very nice bank account. He was a very happy young man.

Tom had eight investors in his boat 'Lady Madelaine', named after his late wife the deal of this was, they could all go sailing together because she was one hundred and twenty feet long. They all had their own cabin and if there was not going to be all eight on board the day, they went out on the ocean they were able to invite others on board.

Two of the eight had died and the next one was very ill, so looked like they were down to five. They had a special agreement between them that no one was able to leave their part of the boat to anyone until the last of them passed away and the survivor could leave it to whoever he pleased.

This way, there could be no one else to own a share and if the others did not like them, there could be trouble. They had owned the boat for decades, so no finance company was involved. As all these men were in the same age group it was not surprising that they were going to fall off the perch around the same time.

Tristan's friends often joined the crew and loved the day out racing 'Lady Madelaine' around the buoys careful not to run over the smaller boats. She was a handful and such a large size that she had to be moored out in the Bay. She had a large dinghy that could seat eight and that was used to ferry them ashore. The dinghy's name was 'Sand shoes'.

At the age of twenty-three, Tristen was advised by his accountant that he should expand his business of importing and exporting cars. He should not be renting a part of Tom's shed now that the last yacht was finished and sold. He should have his own property or the 'tax man' could send him broke.

Tom used the profit from the sale of the yacht he was building when Tristan met him, to keep himself and to pay a 'Boat boy' to live on and maintain 'Lady Madelaine'. He chose Tony Karina who was doing an excellent job. He was always on board when they took the Lady Madelaine out into the ocean so that he could see that everything was operational, needed care or maintenance. He was on board every night cooking his dinner and cleaning the galley, so it really shone brightly. He loved that yacht, no doubt about that. And he loved sailing.

Tristan was out looking for a new place to buy for a showroom. He had advanced the business so much he needed something in the town, so more people could see what he was offering. His phone rang and his distressed mother was blubbering on the other end of her phone. "Ok, Mum, I am coming home. Don't try to talk, I am not far away. Sit down and wait. Be there in a minute."

He turned the car and headed home. He was there in record time, hoping he did not get into any trouble with the police. He made it into the driveway of his mother's place.

"Oh! My darling," she said. "Daddy died."

Tristan looked at her in disbelief. He took her hand and led her in the house and sat her on a chair.

"Heart attack," she stammered. "They tried so hard to save him." He held her to him and let her cry.

He could not believe his beloved father was gone. He wondered what he was to do now. First thought was to take care of his mother. She was so distressed, but that was to be expected. His next thought was he could not leave her alone and he needed to go to the hospital where his father's body was at this time.

He thought of Mary next door. She was one his mother's many friends and the one he could contact immediately. She lived next door.

Mary O'Hara was home. He had called out over the fence to her, and she answered at once.

"Is something wrong over there?" Mary called out.

"Yes," he replied. "Can you come over quickly."

"On my way," she called back and headed to the side fence where they had a gate that they shared between the properties. Tristan's dad had put the gate in many years ago to save them walking out into the street to join each other for a chat over a cup of tea. Lydia had gone through the gate in an emergency with Mary's son when he broke his leg.

She cared for Mary's daughter while Mary went in the ambulance with her son. Otherwise, they just got together for a general talk most days.

Tristan quickly told Mary what had happened as he knew it. Mary went quickly to his mother and held her in her arms.

"Off you go," she said to Tristan. "Do whatever you have to do, I will stay with Lydia until you get back."

He drove down to the hospital quietly thinking about how life would be without his father. He relied heavily on him for advice on just about everything, although not so much lately as he felt he was in such a good position financially and confident in his business; he knew he could manage without him.

He had to know; he had no choice.

The visit to the hospital was dreadful. The staff were kind and helpful, but they could not bring him back. He drove home with great sadness in his heart and the awful thing to do now was to bury the man he loved so much.

It was late when he returned home. Mary greeted him with words of sorrow at his loss. His mother was asleep out of exhaustion and a sedative. He was glad he did not have to face her after such a stressful day. His mother's sadness after the hospital visit was too much to face.

He could grieve on his own all night tonight before he had to look into her sad eyes and comfort her. He knew that his father had left her well off financially, but he could have done that. It was the fact that now she faced loneliness that he could not help her with. So many years beside his father gone. He consoled himself that she had many caring friends, and they were all there for her at the funeral.

Tristan was surprised how many people turned out for the funeral. He was grateful for their nice comments about his dad, the nice speeches and comforting words to his mother.

He then had to get back to work. He was again looking for a showroom for his imported cars and on the internet looking for more cars to import. He was very busy but made sure he was with his mother at dinner time to tell her of that day's activities. During this time, he found out that his mother was originally trained as an accountant.

She gave it up when she married his father to devote her life to him. Tristan thought she was just an office girl or receptionist in an office. She then revealed that she was behind his father's financial management so that they always had money if they needed it.

"I always kept your father informed on how much we had in the bank so that he knew how much he could spend on the cars. He always told me how much he thought the car repair would cost so I could see that the amount he required was in our car account. Then I managed our savings account, watching the interest available from the bank for how long the investment was."

"There was also a house keeping account. So easy when you only have one wage to manage. When I was an accountant, I managed possibly over one hundred business accounts and had to advise them. I also had help when I became too busy! Too busy was when tax time came around. Hopefully, all my clients had listened to my advice. They would have that money put aside."

"You know when I get this new showroom, I may have a job for you."

"I may accept that." She smiled.

Another two days of searching and he found the showroom he wanted.

All glass front, a workshop behind it and a very nice two-bedroom unit upstairs. Perfect. He could possibly move his mother into that. He raced home to his mother at dinner time so excited that he had good news for her, and they could talk about the move, the future, and how he could grow his business.

He had rented the boat building shed at very low rent. That allowed him to save so he had most of the money to buy the showroom. He told his mother about how he had to only borrow a small amount and repayments were about the same as the rent for the boat shed.

"Have you taken out the loan yet?" She asked.

"No, I have an appointment in the morning."

"Cancel it." She smiled.

"Why?" He asked.

"Because I can lend you that and still have enough money to live on. In fact, I will give it to you. It will be yours one day anyway, and I think your father would want me to."

Tristan was stunned. He never dreamed that they had all that money.

He looked at her in disbelief. She smiled at him and said, "That is the advantage of being an accountant."

"Ok," he said. "I will make it up to you somehow." He reached across and gave her a hug.

He did not tell his mother, but he had the property purchased in his name and Lydia's as well. Easily done with just getting her signature on the paperwork by her trusting what he said and not reading what it said.

Tristan set his showroom up with four cars; the rest were kept out the back in the workshop ready to go or if requested by a client.

The four cars were a Bugatti Veyron 2005, a 2008 BMW 13. Next to them was a Jaguar E type 1966 and a Lamborghini Miura 1966. His car detailer had moved in and started polishing them, making sure not one speck of dust was in sight. They paid big money for perfection.

Before he left for his mother's that night for dinner, he had sold the 1966 Jaguar E type.

Then the next day as he advertised, 'If I haven't got what you want, I can get you one'.

A fellow walked in and asked if he could get him a 2014 Chevrolet Corvette. "Actually, I have one out the back," smiled Tristan. "Can you come back in an hour, and I will have it ready for you to look at."

He came back one hour later and grinned at the car he desired. Seems price did not matter. He was a used car dealer and wanted it to attract customers out the front of his yard and he could drive it home at night to impress the neighbours.

It was not long before Tristan was very well known for his expensive foreign cars. The range of people wanting them was more than he could comprehend.

To allow him more time, he hired his mother to take care of the finances. She was going very well with this, and he was so pleased with her ability. As she also had her social life, she worked part time.

He hired a salesman so he could research more cars, spend more time importing and exporting cars. He had now a worldwide reputation of finding cars others found impossible to locate and difficult to repair internationally. Thanks to the internet, and his knowledge of how to work it.

His workshop had men who could work magic on old cars like a 1960 Lotus Seven or a 1948 Citron CV. Even a Chrysler Airflow 1934. He valued these men and paid them well; they all took great pride in their workmanship. They all got on together and they all were so fond of his mother. Christmas parties were great fun and good work was recognised with a bonus.

Then the day came that Tristan got bowled over. Unexpectedly, bowled over.

He was in the showroom and saw a car drive up out the front but took no notice. It was until he looked up and saw an angel helping an older man into the showroom. He stared at her and she spoke with a soft melodic voice.

"Can you help my daddy; he wants a Rolls Royce," she said.

The older fellow said, "My daughter heard you can do this."

"I certainly think I can," Tristan said, and noticed she was looking at him. "I have located a few of them for my clients." He smiled at her and she winked back. This startled him.

"Well, I am Arthur McDonald, and this is my daughter Christina."

"I am Tristan Paravoni," Tristan said. "Do you have a model or the year of a model I can get you, Sir."

"I want a brand new one," Arthur McDonald replied.

"Oh," Tristan said. "No problem with that. I have photos and prices in my office if you would like to see them. I can give you a copy to take home with you as well."

"No, Christina does all of that stuff, I will leave it with her. May I have a look around at these beauties in the showroom?"

"Of course," Tristan smiled. "I will get my salesman to show you the workings of them, and why people like them so much."

Christina followed him to the office. He wished she had led the way so he could get another look at her.

His first words were, "What was the wink about?"

"Just wanted to let you know I was not with a sugar daddy." She smiled. "Hope you are single." The grin got wider.

"Not had time for romance," he said.

"My problem," she said, "is no available single men where I come from."

They took care of the Rolls Royce first and then sat about chatting and telling each other their life story. Every now and again, they would glance at her father to see if he was still looking at the cars in the showroom. Suddenly, her father went out of sight. He suspected that his salesman was entertaining him out in the workshop so the two of them could spend more time together.

Her father finally returned. "Very interesting out the back," he said. "Those guys really know what they are doing, and happy in their work."

Christina stepped towards her father, and said, "Your car may be a while being imported."

Tristan chipped in saying, "Main problem is that it comes on a ship, that's not the hold up. It means we have to wait longer for the space on the ship as a Rolls has to have a meter of space all around it and other cars only have 600mm or that may mean two feet for you, Sir."

Arthur McDonald grinned. "That is correct. Ok, Christina, let's go. I will get Paul to fly you in here every now and again. His wife can go shopping and you can keep in touch with Tristan and see where my car is."

They left and Tristan felt she took a part of him with her.

The romance blossomed. They wanted desperately to marry but Christina was her fathers' full-time carer. Tristan decided he should have a meeting with her father. Arthur knew what they wanted and unknown to them had made arrangements of his own.

Tristan started the conference by asking Arthur if he could marry Christina.

"Yes," said Arthur. "Do you think I could not see this romance blossoming? So now you have officially asked me for my daughter's hand, I shall fill you both in. I have employed a housekeeper to be here full-time, so Christina does not have to permanently live here. The new lady starts Monday, so Christina can organise the wedding."

"I have also asked Paul to leave his house on this property and move in here with myself and the housekeeper. I suppose I should tell you that the housekeeper is Paul's wife," he chuckled at this. "So now to you, Christina. I would like Paul to fly you out here once a week for the day to keep my bookwork up and order supplies also two days a week when our cattle stock is getting low, or we have any problems."

"Done," said Christina. "Ok, Tristan?"

"Fine with me," he answered. "Now let us set a wedding date and you had better furnish the unit over the showroom to start our life in. Now can Paul fly us back to the Bay if that is ok?"

Probably the most beautiful and largest wedding the Bay had ever seen.

Christina and Lydia became very close. They were great friends and confidants. Dinner together with Tristan was on every night that Tristan was home and often just the two women would eat together if Tristan was away buying cars.

On weekends, they would try to go sailing and now took Lydia. Turns out she was very good crew.

Christina did not want Lydia to ever feel lonely even though she had many friends. Often Mary next door would join the two of them when Tristan was away. Life seemed ideal.

A very unexpected pregnancy shocked Christina and she confided in Lydia so she could ask how to tell Tristan.

"Just go up and tell him," Lydia said. "He will be as excited as I am." Her eyes were glowing. "I am going to be a grandmama!"

Back in their unit, Christina made his favourite dinner and candles on the table; everything looked lovely.

"I have something to tell you," she said shyly.

"Uh oh!" Grinned Tristan. When she told him, he was so delighted and excited, he started making plans immediately.

Nine months later to the day, they felt their happiness was complete and so was Lydia's. Tristan cradled his son and felt his life could not get better. Both he and Christina knew that Marion, Christina's best friend, wanted to see their son as soon as he was born, and as it was difficult for her to get to them, or the hospital they arranged the day to see her.

Why did they pick that day? He shook his head and came back to reality hearing his little son cry.

His mother was by the baby's side within two seconds.

Chapter 6
Mendez

Mendez sat in his chair by the desk with his elbows on the table and his head in his hands. He was thinking that this was a real puzzle. Three people missing, possibly four, with a little blood on the lounge floor, and no violence as such as the furniture seemed to be in place. Nothing broken or askew. Then the beautiful blonde lady, new mother, dead on the concrete driveway half hidden by a hedge.

Makes no sense. The husband such a nice guy, new baby son, why? So distressed could not even complete the interview. There was no disturbed earth near the driveway showing a struggle with her or anyone. No marks on his Bentley inside or out. He had really given the car a good check over and waiting for forensics to give a report. Makes no sense at all.

Mendez then decided. He called up to get a car brought around to the front of the station. It was early in the morning, but he thought that Tristan Paravoni should be up and available to give him some sort of a statement. The car arrived and he was notified. He had the address and did not think it would take long to get there. He made good time and went in the front gate and up to the door. He hesitated for a second and then pushed the bell.

After a few seconds, Lydia opened the door. He hesitated as he thought he may have the wrong address. When she asked who he was, and he responded, she introduced herself and asked him to come into the lounge.

Tristan was on the lounge cradling his little son. He saw the detective and bowed his head over the baby. He was pleased it was not the sergeant from the station. Mendez at this point was concerned about what Phillip Harris had said 'I may have to frame him'. This man would not shoot his wife. He was certain of that.

Mendez introduced himself and asked if he could talk to him. Tristan nodded and held the baby closer.

Lydia stood by and offered to take the baby from him. Tristan shook his head. So, Lydia just stood by.

Lydia asked if she should ring his lawyer and turned to Mendez for an answer.

Mendez replied that this was just a quiet talk between them. No statement would be taken until Tristan was at the station.

Mendez spoke quietly and thought this was not the time or place to take a statement.

He asked if Tristan was able to tell him what happened in his own words, and as he had not read him his rights, he would not take notes, he could not enter any of this in court. His mother would be a witness to this.

Tristan started the story and he tried to get his words correct and describe how he caught his wife, as she fell against him, held his wife as best he could, worried about his baby in the car and terrified that he would be discovered behind the hedge by the police sergeant that shot his wife. The police sergeant had the gun in his hand as he approached him. Then he told him how yelling came from the house, and he saw at least four police dragging out three body bags from the house and four of them jumped into the front of the van in the carport after they shut the back doors of the van and left.

He never mentioned the gun. If he was faced with, that he would say he just forgot. The sergeant must have got in the drivers' seat as he did not see him.

Tristan asked Mendez, "Can I ask you some questions?"

"Sure," Mendez said. "I will see if I can answer them."

"Is it true my friends, Derek and Marion Smith, are missing. The ambos said there was blood on the floor in the house. I never went in the house. Also why was Marion's wheelchair out in the yard? What about the two children, are they ok?"

"We are all working on that case, they have not been found yet, I believe that according to Derek Smiths' brother that the daughter was with the grandparents. We cannot verify that as the grandparents do not seem to be home. We have been leaving messages telling them that there has been no news to tell them. They wanted to be kept updated. I think that is Marion Smith's mother, and the missing boy is her grandson and Marion's son."

"That is correct," said Tristan. "Marion needs her wheelchair; she cannot walk more than two steps."

Mendez did not tell him that there were drag marks near the wheelchair that went into the house. Forensics are on to that. "I don't like to tell you, but I feel that whatever happened they will not be alive to tell us unfortunately, but we must keep searching for as long as there is hope."

The tears once again started to roll down Tristan's face, so Mendez thought it was time to leave. "I will get you when you are able to come down to the station to make a statement. Let me know when you are coming as I want to do this statement nobody else."

As Mendez left the house, he thanked Lydia and wished her well. He thought to himself there was no way that Tristan Paravoni committed domestic violence. He is a good man.

On the way back to the station, he had a frightening thought about Marion Smith's parents. He wondered why he had not been able to contact them at all just to keep them up to date on where they were looking now or forensic reports. Had they met the same fate?

He went to the front desk and asked the policewoman there if she knew anything of that family, had they been in or had she seen them. The policewoman said, "You mean Marion Smith's mother, Marilyn Thomas?"

"Yes," he said. "I thought she may have come in for updates on her missing family."

"Well, she did, and she asked about you. I told her you were upstairs and directed her to the stairs. She followed the directions of my finger pointing and I watched her starting to climb the stairs but then the phone rang, and I had to leave to answer the phone. I did not see her return down the stairs."

"Thanks for that," he said. "I will follow that up."

When he returned upstairs to his desk, he asked to see the sergeant and asked if he had seen them or interviewed them. Phillip Harris said, "No," and left it at that. "Any news on them?" He asked.

"No" was again the reply and then Harris walked away.

Then he checked with everyone that was at the office desks. Seemed no one knew anything about it and Marilyn Thomas had not been seen. For that matter Bill Thomas and the granddaughter, Nicole Harris, had not been see either. He was worried about that.

Phillip Harris had it in his mind that he had forgotten about them so, had better get something arranged to get rid of them. *The bastards. They must still be in town, and I presume in the same house*. He set off to make sure of all of that and nothing had changed. Then another thought about maybe that ugly girl kid is with them. He could never call her his daughter, made him feel sick even thinking about it. *Will not forget about them now*, he thought.

He made a call to Mogo.

Mendez went to the house of Marilyn and Bill Thomas. The house was locked, but not the garage. He entered the garage and the door into the house was not locked so entered the house. At first there seemed to be nothing out of place but then in the kitchen, he noticed that the refrigerator door was propped open, and it was totally empty.

So, he went onto the bedroom. All of them were in disarray like they had been sorting out clothes and not sure what to pack. Were they on the run he thought? A voice called out and gave him a start. He went back into the kitchen and through to the lounge to find a very old man with a rake in his hand. "Who are you?" He asked.

The old fellow replied, "Who are you is more like it, what are you doing in Bill's house?"

"I am Detective Mendez," he replied. "I take it you know Marilyn and Bill Thomas and why do you have a rake in your hand."

"Thought you were an intruder," the old fellow said. "I live over the road, and I look after this place when they go away."

"Were you going to hit me with the rake?" Mendez asked.

"Too right," the old fellow said.

"Well, you can put it down, it's ok. Now how do you know they have gone away?"

"Because they left with their caravan at midnight last night. Then they left me a note with ten dollars attached for fuel to mow the grass like I always do. Must be going for a while as he usually leaves me two dollars and I never use it all." Then as an afterthought he said, "Do you have a warrant?"

"Don't need one," Mendez said. "Place is unlocked and it is now part of a crime scene."

"Oh! Am I in trouble?"

"No of course not, you have been very helpful, so you can take your rake home. I have all the information I need for the moment."

"Ok, but if I can help, I live in the blue house over the road." Then turned and wandered off.

Mendez went back to his unmarked police car and opened the door. As he got in, he wondered if he should report what he had just found out. *If Marilyn came to see me and going up the stairs changed her mind, something must have triggered that. News of her daughter should have been most important.*

He got out of the car again and headed for the blue house. The old fellow met him at the gate before he made it to the door. "One question," Mendez said. "Do you know if they had their granddaughter with them when they left?"

"Well, I know they went and collected her from a birthday party the afternoon before. I did see her this morning out in the yard, and I also saw Marilyn go out in the car for a while, but not for long and Nicole went out to greet her at the car when she returned. Nicole was in the yard again later before dinner time and no one came to pick her up," he paused. "She is a dear little girl and always calls out to me if she sees me."

"Thank you for that information. I will pass it on at the station, now we know she is safe, we were wondering where she was."

Back in the car, he thought these sticky beaks were so helpful sometimes. He drove back to the station, checked with the desk and was told, "No news on the Smith family."

"Well, I know that the daughter is safe with the grandparents so that is good, but do not know where that is as they are not at home. He never said a word about the caravan."

When Mendez went upstairs, he reported to his team and Phillip Harris that the girl was last seen with her grandparents. He did not elaborate. He was told that they had a team of twenty out searching for the three missing people.

Phillip Harris decided that he had to frame Paravoni for all the murders. The blonde and the three friends. The best way was to get another murder committed, and it had to be someone close to him like his wife. His brain went into overdrive, and he came up with Paravoni's mother. She would be an easy target for Mogo.

She was at home minding the baby. So, he rang Mogo again. He had a special mobile phone for Mogo and a separate sim card. Last time Mogo did not answer. He tried him later but still no answer. Not happy, he tried again. Mogo answered.

He said, "Where have you been?"

Mogo answered, "Had to do a job for your bikie mate, you know the one that pays you to keep his bikie mates safe. You will read about in the paper 'drive by shooting'; easy job. Pay's good, He knows so many bad guys, it is a pleasure to get rid of them."

"Well, I got another job that will pay you well," Harris said. "Can't tell you over the phone so how about a coffee at the shop in the quiet. I knock off at six tonight so see you there," and hung up.

The coffee shop was down a filthy rodent ridden lane with rubbish everywhere in a way that the average person would not want to enter. It made coffee for the homeless, the drug users and dealers, prostitutes, and any other low lifes you could imagine. Phillip Harris was known there so his narks had somewhere to meet him and money was exchanged to them, and money went the other way from the Madams of the brothels so that Phillip would not shut them down.

Harris was their protector as he was for illicit bookmaking and other things the general public did not know about. The coffee was good, and the menu consisted of meat pies and cheese sandwiches. Enough to fill the hole in your belly. Phillip and Mogo never ate there but enjoyed the coffee and the secrecy of their hideaway.

They met at six and like a pair of spies, sat at the back of the coffee shop so they could see who may come in. There was a back way out they knew about as well.

"New job, same money," Harris said.

"Spill it then," said Mogo.

"I need you to knock off an old lady. Backbone of a drug ring. She covers herself by being a lovely kind grandma who cares for a baby. Does the dealing from the baby's stroller and it has a bag under it, and a bag hooked on the handle like most strollers, drugs under the carriage. Money in the bag on the handle."

"Now I do not want you to touch the pram. That will be my job and I will get the credit for it. You will end up with the money in it. Now here is the address. So, check it out and do it as soon as you can."

Mogo drank the rest of his coffee and left. Harris lingered sipping and enjoying the rest of his. No hurry to get back to his studio apartment. He was smiling.

Mogo went past the address on the way home, easily found. He noted the neighbour's houses and saw the cars pull into the driveways as they all come home for the night after work. He knew that this time of day was not good. Next morning early, he was there to see all the neighbours head out to their work to get paid so they could pay their mortgage.

He parked up the street so he could see the house he was watching, and all seemed to go quiet at around ten in the morning; the time to strike. It was a weekday next day so that would be the right time. He noted that the house had a yellow letterbox, a carport joined to the side of the house and a door into the house from the carport. Also, a front door on the front of the house.

He also noted there was a gate in the side fence to gain access to the house next door. There was no car next door unless it was in the garage out the back of the house in the back yard. There was a red car in the carport.

The next morning, Lydia received a phone call from one of her friends regarding the usual lunchtime get together once a month. Lydia said that there was too much going on and with the death of her daughter in law, she thought it would not be right. Margery would not take no for an answer.

"Don't do this to us," she said. "We want to support you and comfort you and I am sure Tristan would want you to let us do that."

"I know," said Lydia. "Tristan is not here; he had to go to his lawyer this morning to start and make a statement to police, and I have the baby."

"Oh! You poor thing," Margery replied. "But we all think it would give you a breather and we can help." Lydia did not know what to do; her friends would help her, she had known them all since Tristan was born. Margery continued, "Can someone mind the baby just for a couple of hours and I will pick you up and deliver you home. Just a couple of hours is all we ask. The others will be so disappointed if you will not come."

"Ok," Lydia said. "I will ask Mary next door and will ring you if she cannot."

"So just come we can at least have a cup of tea."

She rang Mary next door with her request and Mary said, "I would be delighted to mind the baby, I would just love to do that; I will be straight over." Lydia heard the side gate open and click shut. Then she went to get dressed ready to meet Margery. The baby had been fed and if he should wake early there was more formula in the fridge.

There was a bag packed with nappies and spare bottles in the kitchen should Mary need anything. Also, a change of baby clothes and a spare little blanket in case he should dribble or vomit on himself as babies do. She would only be a couple of hours.

Mary came in and gave her a hug. Lydia explained the situation and Mary said, "So you should go, it will do you good."

The car arrived out the front of the house and gave a toot.

Lydia scurried out to Margery, and they set off. They had just rounded the corner of the street into the next street when Mogo arrived from the other end of the street and pulled up in the driveway of Lydia's house behind her red car in the carport. He knew she was home as her car was there.

He slipped off his shoes and in his heavy woolen socks, approached the door in the carport that went into the house. He always took off his shoes as too many men had been caught by leaving footprints, as now they can tell what sort of shoes and track them down that way.

Mary was at the sink in the kitchen. The baby was in his bassinette at the wall opposite the kitchen sink so Mary could reach him quickly if need be.

Mogo entered the lounge and two steps later, he saw Mary at the sink. "Short grey wavy hair just over five feet tall," Phillip Harris had said. Right. 'Pop' 'Pop' and she fell dead on the floor.

As he turned, he heard the baby murmur in his bassinette. "Christ, what am I going to do about you?"

He remembered that there was a baby involved but did not expect it to be here or so tiny. He was worried about it. Poor little thing. It could starve to death if no one was due to come and see that woman. He thought about it again and decided that the only thing to do was take it home and deal with it then. Looking around the room and saw a large soft blue bag.

He went to see what was in it and found all the things Lydia had packed that Mary may need. He then went to the refrigerator and found more bottles of made-up formula. Then, on the bench, a large tin of what he presumed was more formula to make up later. He disengaged the bassinette from the stand it was on and raced it out to the car.

Then returned for all the other things, looking about for anything else. He saw a small pile of clothes and on inspection, found they were newly wash baby clothes, so grabbed them as well. He started the car and slowly backed out of the drive into the street, no one to be seen, so cruised along the street and turned for home, a plan in his mind for his darling wife that he adored.

Chapter 7
Mogo

Born Stephen Simon Montgomery after his grandparents, he was a much loved, only child. His parents were rather well off, so he wanted for nothing from the day he was born. His parents were also only children and had planned to have a larger family but for medical reasons that was not going to happen. When he was two years old, his dad bought him a water pistol and showed him how to use it.

Dad had to fill it with water so he would not make too much mess. He loved to squirt people with it and most tolerant people would laugh and encourage him to do it again. However, his dad said to him later that afternoon when there was no-one around. "If you ever shoot anyone, remember men always leave a trail behind."

Mogo did not understand that until later in life and then he never forgot it. "Never leave a trail," he would say to himself even playing with water pistols.

He could not say his full name of Montgomery, he managed to say Mogo so that stayed with him into adulthood and beyond.

There were two family pets that were part of the family before Steven was born. Mogo loved his cat and dog. They were his playmates and companions' day and night. At nighttime, the cat would sleep in the bottom of his bassinette and later his bed. The Labrador would be with him in the yard of a day and beside his bed on the floor at night.

He never pointed his water pistol at them. One day, his dad thought it would be funny to squirt the dog. Young Steven was distraught. His dad said he was sorry and never did it again.

The cat passed away when it was eighteen years old, and Mogo was sixteen years old. Dreadfully upset, His parents bought him a kitten and that eased the pain. He soon loved that kitten as much as the last one. His dog died when Mogo was eighteen years old.

He did not want another dog; he was happy with just the cat. This was because he had grown to love guns. He and his dad had joined a gun club and went to the rifle range once or twice a week to practice their skills. His dad had told his mother that Steven could end up at the Olympic games and be a gold medalist the way he was so accurate with his targets. But Steven had other ideas.

He joined the army where he expected to learn more about guns that anything else. His parents were quite happy with this they thought he could, and he did learn many skills and a trade as well. The Army was happy with him too. Mogo graduated up the ladder of success. At the age of twenty-six, he received the ghastly news that his parents had burned to death in a house fire.

Neighbours had rescued the cat and were caring for it and wanted to keep her. He agreed and soon after when his time was up, retired from the Army with honours as a sergeant major.

Civilian life was not what he remembered. He did visit the neighbours to see how the cat was. He also saw the new house that had been built in its place where his parents had died. He felt the cat remembered him. She was being well cared for so best leave her with them. They were so happy about that.

He had his Army pay, he never spent it. His parents had often sent him money for Christmas and birthdays. He could afford to by himself somewhere nice to live. He found it on the beachfront, a modern, two-bedroom on the third floor. Ocean view, nice beach, perfect.

The Bay was a tourist town as well so lots of coffee shops and restaurants on the beach front.

He then found a letter from a lawyer in his mailbox. Seems the lawyer was looking for him, found out he was in the army they had given him the postal address for Steven Montgomery. Curious as to what he wanted, he called them and was asked to come into the office.

He entered the office of Jonathon Mitchell. "Please take a seat," Jonathon said and pointed to a very comfortable chair.

"First, I want to say how sorry I am at the loss of your parents. They were good people, and I was their lawyer for many years. I have asked you in because they left a will, and you are the only heir."

It had never occurred to him that his parents had a lawyer or left a will. He was eighteen when he left home not even interested in that type of thing.

Jonathon continued after letting Mogo think about what was about to happen to him. It may be a shock. You had to let people have time to take it in. "So, I have to tell you that your parents had looked after your future." He paused again. "They owned their house, and it was well insured. The new house is yours and their life insurance policy is quiet substantial." Jonathon paused again.

"Let me understand this," said Mogo. "You mean that lovely new house in my parent's block is now mine."

"That's correct. The insurance company contacted me as was in their will and as the house was insured and all paid, they said they would get a builder to build a house similar to the one that was there. I said ok. So, they went ahead. I have paperwork for you to sign then you can have your brand-new house. You can keep it or sell it."

Jonathon continued after another pause. "The amount of cash from your parents, life insurance, is five hundred thousand, or half a million, and we can invest it for you in a short-term investment if you are not sure what to do with it immediately. Let me say that I admire you parents greatly, they have certainly thought carefully of how to set you up for your future."

Mogo was stunned and could not answer for a few minutes.

Then he said, "How about I live in the house, and you invest the money less your fees."

"No fees," said Jonathon. "Your parents took care of that when they made their wills. You just have to sign on the dotted line for your money and release the house insurance company as you plan to take possession, there is quite a few papers to sign. I have the time now if you want to, or you can inspect the house before you do sign. I have to say as your parents' representative, I did inspect the house and I can assure you it is very nice and well built, passed council inspections and has a certificate of occupation."

"I will take your word for it and get these papers signed."

Mogo walked out of his office quite dizzy, still trying to take in what had happened.

He loved the house. He went straight to it and could not wait to put the key in the door. He still had a nice bank account from buying the apartment, he could buy whatever furniture he wanted within reason of course. He would keep that apartment; it was furnished so no expense there.

As soon as he had looked at the house, he went to the hardware shop and bought himself a shovel.

During his Army time, he had sent his father parts of guns. His father had collected these parts at the post office and when he got home, he would assemble those guns carefully and all those parts were untraceable. When he had a complete gun, be it anything from a pistol to a sniper rifle it would be placed in a steel box and a padlock attached.

When he had been sent all the parts for ten completely untraceable guns, he buried the box with the padlock on right against the back fence of the property; the key was placed in the bank in a security box and Mogo was sent the number.

The idea was that the two of them could go out in the bush and practice shooting accuracy so when they went to the gun club they would do very well indeed.

That never happened due to his mother's love of scented candles.

Mogo lived happily in the new house, not much furniture as he only needed a refrigerator, bed comfortable chair and a television. He did not cook much preferring the local café where it was served to him, and he did not have to use the new dishwasher that came installed in the new house. Mogo took the shovel and dug along the back fence.

He was concerned that the builders' may have found the steel box. He found it after thirty minutes of digging. He reburied it and next time he went to town, he checked the key was still in the bank. It was. He left it there.

It was one of those so called balmy evenings when he chose to eat 'Al fresco' at the local café. Sitting in the street under a canopy was very pleasant and he was happy enough with his life.

Then everything changed as he saw a vision coming down the street. She was so lovely in her knee length floral dress swirling around her perfect legs. He could not stop staring as she came nearer the café. His thoughts were how great it would be if she stopped for dinner there too. He could keep looking at her while he ate his dinner.

She did stop and she went into the café. He could still watch her. He was on his own at the table, the other outside tables were full. His had three empty chairs. She must have ordered because she came into the doorway looking for a seat. He saw that and signalled at the three empty chairs. She came across towards him. "Are these taken," she whispered.

"No," he stuttered.

"May I join you? I don't like to eat alone."

"Pleased do," he answered. "My name is Steven."

She introduced herself, "And my name is Felicity."

"Pleased to meet you," he said.

"What work do you do?" She caught him off guard with that question.

"Um, well I work for the government."

"Doing what?" She asked.

"Can't tell you really," he lied. "I am sworn to secrecy."

"Like a spy?" She asked.

"Sort of but I can't tell you, but I can tell you that sometimes I am away for a night or up to a week."

She sat beside him, did not leave a spare chair between them as he thought she would. Her perfume wafted across his nose, and he thought he would pass out with pleasure.

"What do you do?" He asked.

"Nothing yet, I am looking for work."

"You could try here; they are always looking for staff."

"Thanks, I will try after I have eaten. I do not care what I do as long it is legal." She laughed.

She chatted away and he could not hear enough of what she had to say. He looked at her slight frame in a floral cotton dress and the straw floppy hat on her head with flowers that looked real in it. He told her that he usually eats there every night saves him cooking and the meals are good.

He was there next night and looking in the same direction he saw that vision appear along the footpath in a different, longer floral dress and no hat today, but very pretty sandals on her feet. She joined him without asking. He was delighted. So far, he discovered that she had just moved to the Bay from interstate. She was there to get away from an overbearing aunt who was her guardian. She could do that now she was twenty-one years old.

He told her of his army life and how he had lost his parents and he was still recovering that as they were such special people.

She sympathised with him, and her heart went out to him. He was not the most handsome of men but had a good heart and a strong build, was caring and gentle. She knew that by the way he spoke of his cat and dog that he grew up with. *Surely, I cannot be falling for this guy*, she thought.

The evening meetings went on for weeks and in the end, she invited him out for dinner. He took that well, a bit embarrassed that he had not asked her first.

Mogo had two dates in his life but when it came to the bedroom, he failed dismally. He was afraid she would be the same. Maybe it was that he respected women and because they were not married, it bothered him and he could not perform.

He asked her to marry him after two months of evening dinners at the café.

She said, "Yes I will because I am totally in love with you."

He smiled at her. "I love you too so much, I can hardly stand it."

She planned the wedding and he paid for it. A simple ceremony and fifteen guests. Very private and delightful.

They went on a weekend honeymoon that gave them time to furnish the house how she liked it. Felicity was easily pleased. He never told her about his unit on the beach front.

He was nervous about the wedding night. He failed again but Felicity said, "We have the rest of our lives to get this right. I haven't done this before either." They both laughed; he relaxed with her attitude. It only took three days to get it right.

They settled in their house. He had organised her a bank account, so she always had money to keep house and buy anything she needed. The amount would increase annually because of inflation. His bank account was growing fast, thanks to the money from Phillip Harris and the half a million left to him from his parents. In fact, his bank account was very healthy.

They had wanted to start a family but no luck after years of trying. They went to the adoption bureau to put their name down and were told there was a ten year wait. They gave up and decided to get a puppy instead, and added a kitten.

Mogo decided to join the gun club again. They welcomed him back. On his third visit, he met up with Phillip Harris, sergeant of police.

That is what led to him driving along with a baby in the back of his car. Bloody Phillip Harris.

I will not tell him about the baby, he thought. *My plan should work.* He pulled up in front of his house and he thought about this again. I am not really kidnapping this baby or stealing it, really, I am just saving its life. He satisfied himself with this.

He left the baby in the car and hurried into the house. Felicity emerged from the kitchen to greet him.

"Sit down, my darling, I have to talk to you quickly as I have done something wrong."

"What is it?" Concern filling her face.

"Well, you know years ago we went to the Adoption bureau to see if we could adopt a child," he said. She nodded. "Well, I went back to see them and signed all the papers and forged your signature."

"What!" She said alarmed now.

"They rang me today and said that they had a baby for us if we still wanted one."

Tears filed her eyes. "What did you tell them?"

"I said yes, of course."

"When can we have the baby?"

"Now, the baby is in the car, that is the urgent bit; can't leave it there."

She was stunned and crying. He told her to just sit there, and he would get the baby and all the things that went with it. He went to the car. The baby was just waking up. He gently lifted the bassinette out of the car and took it in. He took the baby out and placed it in her arms.

She gently pulled the blanket back and smiled, all, she could say was "Oh." The baby opened its eyes and looked at her.

Mogo returned with the soft blue bag and the other things. Putting the bottles of formula in the refrigerator and tin of formula on the kitchen bench.

He sat opposite his wife and looked at her, such happiness in anyone's eyes he had never seen before.

"You will make the loveliest mother. My little earth mother," he said smiling.

He had to make some explanations about this situation before she could ask questions. "Honey, the Adoption people will call you and come out to see how you are going and said if anything is a problem, go to the doctor. You will have to work out the formula by the instructions on the tin."

She smiled up at him and said, "Boy or girl?"

"Well, you had better check," he said, "and then you must think of a name. I have the papers to register a birth."

"A boy! You have a son."

"And the name?" He asked.

"Well, when we were thinking we could have a child and you said that if it was a boy, you liked the name Christian, and Leigh for a girl."

"So, we shall call him Christian if that is ok with you?" He asked.

"Yes, Christian it is."

The rest of the night they made great plans for the future of the three of them.

Chapter 8
Lydia

Margery brought Lydia home and dropped her off in the street. She said, "Wait, I will come in with you and see Mary. I want to thank her for caring for baby James so you could get a break. The funeral is after next weekend so you will be busy, and you will have Christina's father to care for as well."

Margery got out of the driver's side and joined Lydia as she opened the front gate.

As they headed for the front door, Lydia retrieved her front door key from her handbag.

She opened the door with Margery a step behind her. Margery called out to Mary but, no answer.

"She must be in the kitchen," said Lydia. "I will go and see."

At first sight, she could not see Mary dead on the floor but as she approached the kitchen sink, she saw her. Margery was still in the lounge and heard the agony in the scream from Lydia.

Margery bolted into the kitchen, seeing the problem, pulled out her mobile and rang the ambulance and the police. She then took Lydia into her arms and shook her a bit to stop the screaming.

"Lydia, Lydia," she said. "Where is the baby?" Lydia suddenly became silent as she heard Margery.

"In his bassinette," she sobbed.

"I will have to check," said Margery. But there was no baby James in his bassinette.

Margery was relieved to hear sirens coming in their direction. Help was coming. Thank God.

Lydia was searching all the rooms in panic. No baby, she kept crying out. Impossible, he must be here somewhere.

The paramedics arrived and took one look at Lydia, whispered in low tones as to what they would do and gave her a strong sedative and held her hand until she went to sleep. They then loaded her onto a stretcher and with sirens blasting, raced her off to hospital as shock is one of the greatest killers of humans.

Margery seeing the state of Lydia, rang Tristan and he went straight to the hospital to see his mother, not knowing that they could not find his baby.

Lydia was still unconscious two days later and missed Christina's funeral. Lydia also missed the funeral of her neighbour and dear friend, Mary. The police had called in extra men to look for the baby.

Tristan was distraught that he had lost his wife and the police were now searching for a possible double murderer and missing baby. His mother was in the hospital about to be transferred to another section for mental health, where counselling was full-time care.

Arthur McDonald was by his side. Worried about Tristan and upset over the loss of his daughter and what happened to his grandson that he had only held once in his arms.

The police were at their wits' end. They had five definite murders on their hands three missing people and a baby to find, dead or alive.

Chapter 9
The Lady Madelaine

The Lady Madelaine was anchored out in the Bay, too big for the Marina to handle.

The property of old Tom who built her with the financial assistance of seven of his friends, all of them had since passed away. She was the largest privately owned yacht in the district, and Tom still managed to get a crew whenever he wanted to go out for the weekend or the day. Tristan was always with him on weekends, or he did not go out.

He was delighted that Tristan had more time on Saturdays as most of his foreign car purchases were made during the week. He and Tristan were very close, and he was quite distressed to hear of his loss of wife and child.

Tristan had moved his mother in with him at the unit above the showroom so that he could keep his eye on her. They managed very well together, supporting each other.

Tristan's business had grown because Arthur McDonald had boosted it, in an unusual way.

He was basically a cattle baron and dealt with the Arab countries for many years supplying beef to them. He also bred and kept enough sheep for the Royal family's over there as well. Arthur also was most welcome when he visited the Royals as he often went over to see that they were happy with his product.

At his last visit, one of the Royals minders approached Arthur, and in very good English asked that the King would like a car like her Majesty the English Queen had. They did not know how to get one of these cars or what they were called.

Arthur McDonald informed him that he would take care of that and could have his son-in-law find one and deliver it to them whenever they wished. The minder was delighted with this as it would increase his standing with the Royal family.

When he returned home, he went to see Tristan and explained the situation. Tristan did not find this a problem. The Queen drove lots of cars but she does love her Land Rover Discovery. "If I get a brochure and a photo of the Queen in it, would that make them happy?"

Arthur McDonald smiled. "Get them for me and I will return and give them to the king."

The King was pleased, and the interpreter said, "This what he wants exactly. Can your Mr Tristan get us one as soon as he can." A deal was done. Turns out the King was so happy with his new car, he ordered twelve more new Land Rover Discoveries for his family, also a Bentley and a Rolls Royce.

Tristan said, "He would be so wealthy now he may never have to work again," and laughed out loud. That laugh was music to everyone's ears as no one had laughed around here for a while.

Phillip Harris was not happy. He could not see to pin anything on Paravoni. His other problem was that Police Superintendent Hervey, wanted to know why more progress had not been made. Harris was pissed off that all he was doing to Paravoni was making him unhappy and not putting him in jail. If he could nail him, he would be a hero and maybe get a promotion.

He met with Mogo again in the coffee shop. "I have another job for you," he said. "There is an old guy called Tom, don't know him by any other name, no one does. Now I have found out he is a paedophile. Been locked up before over it but only gets a couple of months because although, he destroyed the lives of about thirty kids, the judge let him off as it was a long time ago and he is old now."

"That's bullshit," said Mogo. "Same price for the job?"

"I suppose so, but don't get the wrong this time!"

Mogo left the café thinking about how he could go about this. First, a disguise so no one could identify him as someone who hired a small speed boat. Then find out where to hire one, and how much cash he would have to take with him. The boat hire would have to be near the water as he supposed they usually were, as usually if you hired a boat that meant you did not have one, so no means of getting your own one to the water.

Did he need to hire a flat-out speed boat or a fishing boat with a big engine that would make a quick getaway. *If it is a windless day, I could look just like a fisherman with a sloppy hat and maybe could blend in better.*

He returned to his secret unit and went through his rifles that were in the steel box. He had transferred them there as soon as he moved into the house and decided not to tell anyone about the unit. He had chosen his favourite sniper rifle made for killing men.

He watched the weather reports for a calm weather weekend hopefully on a Saturday, so it would be certain the Lady Madelaine would be on the water in the Bay and the perpetrator would be on board. He did not have long to wait. Good weather next Saturday, and his ideas were put into place. Dressed as the average fisherman complete with fishing basket and bait, he hired the boat, no questions asked and headed in the direction of the Lady Madelaine.

In the cockpit were a few young men so he would have to wait until an old man appeared on deck. This did not take long and an old fellow with safety lines headed up to the bow.

His first shot hit the mark and obviously fateful. He thought the next shot had missed as the boat lurched a bit to port. He headed back to the rental boat dock, left the boat and left the scene. No one sighted him he was sure of that as well.

Felicity would be at home with the baby they had now named Christian. From the moment she held that baby, she never left his side. She would sing to him and rock the bassinette until he slept. Felicity never watched TV much but now. it was never turned on. She never read the paper saying, "There was too much bad stuff, and most of it not true."

Felicity would take him for walks around the block or to the shops so he would get fresh air. Never spoke to anyone except an old neighbour she had made friends with and probably never watched the news anyway. He was a dear old fellow, and she would tell Mogo how he was going and how his garden was growing. He also said if she needed advice on plants, he would help her. Felicity was very happy in her new role as mother.

Mogo made a quick phone call from the café. It was not long before Phillip Harris arrived, but he had another fellow with him. He was introduced to Bruiser, the leader of a very nasty 'Bad Boys' bikie gang. This gang was known for their abuse to women even to the fact that they had female sex slaves, mostly underage girls, and all supposed to be very attractive. Drugs were the other vice of choice.

Phillip Harris was paid to look the other way and very handsomely too. Money changed hands always to Harris almost daily. Mogo knew that Harris had money overseas as he had advised Mogo to do the same. The best banks at the best interest, written down for him to do the same. Mogo thought seriously about it and had planned to follow this in the near future.

In the meantime, he was happy with the fact that the money that flowed to his wife weekly was not even using the bank interest. He recently had bought her a new little car and paid for driving lessons and her driving license as she may need that in an emergency with the baby.

Mogo looked at Bruiser wondering what this meeting was about. Finally, Harris started to fill him in. Bruiser wanted to eliminate someone in his gang and the other members were not to know he had anything to do with it.

"Why would they think you did it?" Mogo asked.

Bruiser did not seem to want to answer that.

"I need to know so I can plan this job," said Mogo. "Just a couple of details."

"Alright," Bruiser said. "It was about a girl. She is fourteen and that was ok, but he decided he wanted her for himself permanently and I said none of that. These girls are for sharing and anyway, he said he would tell my missus if I did not let this one go. He went on to explain these girls may have a contact if she leaves and then we could all end up in strife."

"Ok, I can follow that," said Mogo. He wanted to punch his face in now. The bastards. He would knock off this one with pleasure and then take out Bruiser too. Then thought better of it.

"Right, got an address or description, anything to help identify him."

"Well, it is like this I will not be anywhere near the bay next weekend. I got to go interstate and flying there. So, do you think you could do it then?"

"Possibly," said Mogo.

"What's the money?"

Bruiser smiled. "Same as Harris; one hundred K. That enough?"

Mogo wondered just how much he was really prepared to pay; however Harris spoke up and said, "He is good for it. I will give it to you and he can fix me up that is a better way, the least they know about you the better. You do not want to get known as a friend to the bikies."

"Let me think on this," Mogo said. The other two watched him, it was like you could hear his brain ticking over. He then spoke quietly and said, "Do you know where I can find him this weekend?"

"Yeah, he will be on duty at the club house as I will be away, he is second in command."

"Any good way to identify him?" Mogo asked.

"Sure," was the reply. "Billy, the bastard is six foot six inches tall, big, long ginger beard. Only one in the club that looks like that." He grinned. "Can't miss him."

"Ok, got to go and sort this out. I will let Harris know how it went." Mogo got up to leave.

Phillip Harris piped up, "Not so fast, Mogo. Bruiser, will you piss off, I need a word with Mogo."

Mogo was not to too sure of this so as soon as Bruiser left, asked if there was a problem.

"No," Harris replied. "Just a question." He paused for a second then said, "How come you only put one bullet in the old guys' head?"

"Did I not wipe him out?" Mogo was worried.

"You sure did, but why only one bullet?"

"I did fire two but a ripple on the water after the first threw me out a bit. Conditions have to be just right for that distance," Mogo replied. "At least I did not have any breeze to adjust for but don't know where that ripple came from."

"You always said two to make sure."

"Well, I did fire two but the other one went wild," said Mogo.

"Ok, mate, I will send your fee tonight if you will be home," and turned to walk away.

"No, leave it until tomorrow. I won't be there, I have some research to do."

They parted company.

Mogo wandered off to check on Bruiser's club. He knew where it was and checking on the colours so he would not be making a mistake. Then he wanted to see the other club to see what the 'Bull-dogs Bikie club' leather vests looked like, so he could wear one and look like the enemy. After checking everything he wanted to know, he returned to the unit.

The unit came with a garage and in his garage was his Harley Davison, probably the fanciest one anyone ever had. He bought it when he was in the army and would never part with it. No-one knew about it either. Even his army friends did not know in case one of them wanted to try it out, and he was afraid they may damage it.

He took his car to get a vest of the 'Bull-dogs Bikie Club' and an 'opportunity' shop to pick up second-hand clothes to go with it. Then returned to the unit to lay it all out and select a pistol to do the job. He cleaned the gun and fitted the bullets, so all was ready for the weekend.

Once again, Tristan was in mourning. Old Tom was dead, shot by someone in a passing boat. He was down below in the cabin making sure everything was secure and safe for the day's sail. He was not there to help Tom and that saddened him. Lydia was again comforting Tristan as he did for her. Just as well they had each other. Tom's funeral was next week. "When will all this carnage stop?" Lydia asked.

Mojo went home to his wife and the baby, Christian. He loved them both dearly and wished he could spend every minute with them both. It was so good to watch Felicity with the baby and he loved that little child that he felt he saved from death. He was about to do a risky job this weekend. Not sure of the time or how it would go but he would do his best as he must care for these two who meant everything to him.

Early morning, he went for a drive in his car and then parked it and walked the rest of the way passed the 'Bad Boys club', where the big red-headed, tall guy was in caretaker mode. No sight or sound from the club. He looked over the gate, it was close to the building that was the club house not one movement or bikie in sight. Presuming that all were not there or asleep, he thought it would be that way most mornings.

He checked the gate to see if it was opened or locked. There was a padlock, but it was not closed. The fence and gate were very close to the club house.

Happy that he had enough information, he left the car in the garage and took the Harley Davison out early the next morning. Dressed in the clothes he thought appropriate and the other clubs' vest, Sunday would be even better than Saturday morning, not that he thought that any of them would be at church.

His pistol in his pocket, he left the silencer off as it may hinder him pulling it out of his pocket if he needed it fast. He loved his guns, but this was a favourite because it was very accurate for short distances and light too; a woman could use it if need be.

He stopped the bike outside the gate, dismounted and saw the padlock was in the same state so he pulled it off and threw it on the ground. Hoping the sound would cause someone to appear. No-one. So, he went three long strides to the door. He quietly tried it to see if it was unlocked. He was wondering if this was a trap, or something set up to get him.

There was not a sound so, he pushed the door open and went in. He could not believe it; there asleep in a big lounge chair was Bill, the bastard, with a young girl asleep on his lap. He quickly pulled out the gun and bang, bang, the big ginger headed bastard was dead. The girl on his knee stirred and woke up, Mogo turned and strolled out.

A few seconds later as he mounted his bike at the front gate, he heard the screaming. So, the fourteen year old was awake, he thought. Hope she saw the 'Bull-Dogs' vest. Could start a bikie war. Hope they shoot each other, the whole lot of them, bunch of low lifes. Those poor little girls and bloody Harris is not looking after them, Just the money.

A few days after that weekend and old Tom's funeral, Tristan received a phone call from his lawyer, Jonathon Mitchell, to tell him that he should call in as soon as he can. Thinking that it was something to do with Christina's death, he made an appointment for that afternoon.

He entered his lawyer's office and was immediately shown into Jonathon and a chair to sit down on. Glenda, the office lady, asked if he would like a tea or coffee, and he replied, "That would be lovely. I could do with a coffee."

Johnathon sat down at his desk and said, "I am sorry that you have lost your friend, Tom. I know you were very close, and he helped you through some very difficult times. So, this does not surprise me. I have Tom's will here and as he had no living relatives, I am not surprised that his money went to charities. He knew you were not short on money so, he left you the Lady Madelaine and the boat shed. In his will, he mentions that he knew you loved the yacht and could see that she was well taken care of. This, I hope, includes young Tony who does so well at keeping her in good condition now."

"How wonderful of Tom, I will take very good care of her and keep Tony on board to keep her maintenance up. Seems like I will have to do a lot more sailing now she is my boat."

"Who shot him?" Tristan asked.

"Wouldn't I love to know. A great old man, helpful, good to you and Lydia and anyone who needed him. What a bastard to kill him for no reason. You know it was a sniper rifle, someone was out to get him, and no-one knows why; makes no sense. Same as Mary, who would do nobody any harm."

"The only difference is Mary got two shots to the head and Tom only one." He did not mention Christina in case he upset Tristan, but Tristan did mention it.

"Yes, two in Christina's head, I will never forget. Shame they never found our friends, Marion and Derek. I really hope they are just in hiding from whoever was after them. What about Beau?"

"And then Marion's parents, Bill and Marilyn, and her daughter, Nicole," said Jonathon "Derek was just a great fellow. Really good and helpful lawyer, I knew him well."

Chapter 10
Paul Harvey

Paul Harvey was the superintendent of police that covered Philip Harris' police station area, and he called him in.

"Ok. Phillip," he said. "We have a problem in your area and not much is being done would you care to explain." He smiled at Phillip hoping to put him at ease so he could get the most information as he could.

"I presume you are talking about the murders and disappearance of people in our area during the last few weeks."

"Yes," Paul said.

"Well, as far as I know, the first was a domestic violence offence by the husband. Although, as three people have disappeared from that address, two adults and one child, we do not know if they were murdered or just escaped the scene of the domestic violence. However, there was blood and forensics seems to think that there were only two blood types and the two blood types were unrelated to each other."

"The other missing people we know nothing of just that they do not seem to be home. They are the parents and the daughter of the third possible victim," Phillip volunteered. "This makes it seem possible that Tristan Paravoni murdered the two males, and he and the missing female planned to go off together so, he shot his wife, and he could be free."

"So, the other people thought they would be next, so took off with their caravan?"

"What caravan?" Harris looked shocked.

"Oh!" Paul Harvey said. "Why did you not know about the caravan?"

"Someone at the station mentioned a caravan," Phillip lied.

"This story you just told me does not make any sense. Now go back and find out what is going wrong and come back with the truth," Paul Harvey snapped.

"While you are there, find out about the burial at sea." Paul was getting very cross now.

Phillip scurried out of his office not wanting to hear any more about the burial at sea. He wondered where that information came from. He knew the young constables would not say one-word about it as they knew they were paid to shut up. So, must have been that slimy little Carson. Well, he is gone next, no more rumours from him. *But, on second thought, I may use him one more time and then get rid of him.*

Paul Harvey sat in his chair and thought about what could have happened with these cases. He had spoken to Mendez about the situation the night before when he could not get hold of Harris. Mendez came to Paul' s office; he seemed to have a different view of the whole situation. Mendez told him that he found impossible to believe that Paravoni had murdered his wife.

Too much of it said that he did not. The fact that he was so distressed about his wife being shot and he was behind his wife, he held her while she fell to the ground. That was where the paramedics found him, on the ground holding her head so it would not hit the ground. By the way, at first glance the paramedics said, they thought it was domestic violence.

However the way he was sitting and holding her, also, the new-born baby in the car. Talking to him and assessing what was going on around them, they saw no gun, no disturbed ground. They do this when they think it is domestic violence as he could still have had a gun on him and then they could get shot as well. They also treated him at the scene as he had to drive the baby to his mother's, and they were worried about him on the road.

There was no other person at the scene or any evidence of it. Mendez also told him of the missing woman's mother and daughter had fled with her father in the middle of the night so no-one would see them. However, the old guy opposite does not sleep well and saw them take off with the caravan in tow. No idea what direction as they turned the corner at the next block so could have gone anywhere.

He presumed the granddaughter was with them as he saw her being called into the house around seven thirty. Mendez then described inside the house where food was out of the pantry and clothes sorted out all over the bed.

While he was talking to Paul, he mentioned that a fellow who had been watching the news found out about three missing people. Mendez had stopped on his way home that night for a quick beer. He very rarely did that because he would be in trouble with his wife. At the bar, a fellow who knew him, by sight only, went up to him and told him that he saw the news and he had been talking to a fellow later in the evening who told him he had just had to do a burial at sea.

He said he had to have a couple of still drinks after that. I had just been watching that on the television. Would that have anything to do with that? Mendez asked if he knew any more about it. The reply was that no, he did not but thought it coincidental. Mendez asked if he knew who the fellow was. Again, the answer was negative.

Mendez told him that he was looking for a boat at the marina to see if he could get any more information. Paul thanked him for all that information and was hoping for more information when he had it. Mendez said that he would not stop working on it but was sure that Tristan Paravoni had not shot his wife; someone else is up to dirty tricks.

Mendez rang Reburger back half an hour later to inform him that a good friend of Paravoni had been shot while on his boat, but only one bullet this time so does not think it was related. Also, a member of a bikie gang had also been shot but he had no details but would get back to him as soon as he did have.

Paul Harvey hung up the phone so glad he had Mendez to inform him of what was happening in the Bay.

Back at the station, Mendez started looking at the forensics and information about the shooting on the Bay, must have been a sniper as no boat of any kind was seen near the yacht. By reports, there were lots of boats out in the bay because the water was so calm. There were enough people on board the yacht who saw Tom fall.

Paravoni was below securing the yacht for sailing, everyone on board confirmed that. The newest member of the crew was with him learning what to do. People who were on the Bay at that time were asked to come or ring the police station. Many did as they knew Tom and loved him for his attitude and advice on their boat.

He helped with safety and boat repairs. Nothing was seen to be out of place. He had called in to the hire boat company who told him that he had only one small fishing boat hired out that morning, returned a bit early, but he had his creel and fishing rods in a canvas bag. All seemed normal, no sign of a gun. Mendez then asked for a description.

The reply was blonde hair down to his shoulders, not wealthy as his clothes look well-worn and second hand. "However, no-one wears new clothes to go fishing. The fellow had a tanned skin look and mirrored sunglasses. Did not see his car. I do a bit of a check because I forgot to get his numberplate but he seemed really pleasant."

Mendez thanked him and left.

The call came in about a bikie had been shot in the Bad Boys Bikie club. He set off wondering when the murders would stop. When he arrived on that Sunday morning, he saw a distressed child about thirteen or fourteen years old. The paramedics were with her and that meant the victim was dead and they could not do any more for him.

Mendez asked to look at the body and was shown into the rear of the ambulance. The first thing he noticed was two shots in the head. How could you miss it, he thought? He returned out of the ambulance to talk to the paramedics.

"What do you two know about this, any information I can use."

"We are just settling his daughter and we are off to the hospital," one of the paramedics said.

"Ok," replied Mendez. "Can I speak to her then?"

"Yes, I suppose so, but take it easy on her."

"Hi, honey," Mendez said to the girl. "I am Detective Mendez. What is your name?"

"I am not telling you until you tell me who killed my boyfriend," she pouted. She repeated that again.

"Yeah, my boyfriend."

"Don't you mean your father?"

"Don't be so dumb, Billy is my boyfriend."

"Oh! I am sorry, my mistake," said Mendez.

"That's ok."

"Right, now what is your name, sweetie?"

"Karen and don't call me sweetie. I am Billy's sweetie, not yours."

"Right. Now who do I call to get you some help. Do you have a family or someone you are close to?"

Karen looked at him with a concerned face. "No. Billy was my family. Is he ok?"

"No, I don't think so, did you see what happened?"

"I don't know," she said. "I was asleep on his knee, he likes me to do that."

"So, what woke you up? Did you hear anything?"

"Yes, I think I heard bang, bang. I don't know but I saw a man from the 'Bull Dogs club' going out the door." She started to cry.

Mendez said, "I think you had better come with me. I don't want anything to happen to you. I will get you protection in case he comes back."

"You think he may come back because I don't think so, I am Billy's girlfriend."

"Yes, he may come back because you are a witness to what he did to Billy."

"Ok." She took his hand. Just like a little kid, he thought. Mendez figured something was wrong here.

Back to the police station and a few whispered words to a waiting policewoman, and he handed her over.

She took the policewoman's hand and they disappeared out the door to the carpark. Mendez heard a car take off onto the highway and speed away. Destination safety.

Mendez reported this to Paul Harvey before he wrote it up. The fact that there were two bullets in this guy's head meant the gunman was still around.

Chapter 11
Carson

Carson was a mackerel fisherman. He made the money to buy a boat from the proceedings of petty crime. He was a street kid with a drunken father and a drug addled mother. On the street he learned to trick, thieve, bash and blackmail. Often pulled into the police station for petty crime he never went to jail, and he never knew why.

He loved fishing so he spent time around boats of all descriptions but he loved the maceral boats best as they came in with piles and piles of fish on the back deck, and the dock was so busy unloading them and fish buyers were shouting and so much going on he found it so exciting. So, when the opportunity came up to buy a maceral boat, he found that his bank account would let him. It had a name, but he painted over it as soon as it was his.

It was a thirty-five foot boat with galley, large bed, electric toilet, good reliable engine and a genset that allowed him to use all household appliances to make his life enjoyable. The boat was never renamed he liked it that way, he felt anonymous.

He anchored out in the Bay as he did not want to pay the marina for a berth, and for privacy. He also took the opportunity to sneak into a vacant berth if a yacht left the marina. He would just wait until the marina staff left for the day and, off he would go and tie up in the vacated marina berth and have a night on the town.

He could also do his washing and shower as he had access to the facilities. He liked chasing the girls but, when they heard he had a boat they lost interest in him. He once thought it was his appearance or fishy smell. He was right on both assumptions.

Tristan Paravoni had a visitor in his showroom office. It was young Tony. He always had time for Tony, so stopped his car searching and settled in his office chair to listen what Tony had to say.

"Tristan," he said shyly. "Tristan, I know how much you love the Lady Madelaine and how sad you are about Tom. Just the best man ever. Well, I was wondering if you would agree to something."

"Go on," said Tristan.

Tony hesitated for a second before he continued. "I have managed to find seven guys who also love her as well. I was wondering if you would allow us to do what Tom and his friends did."

"You mean to buy her off me and, carry on sailing her and looking after her, passing her down the line to the last owner?" Tristan said, secretly smiling to himself; he loved the idea.

"Well, yes," said Tony. "If it is alright with you, I thought we could work out a price and take her over. I would still live on board and do the maintenance. My friends, and you know them all, will pay one-eighth each and get a solicitor to draw it up."

"Well," said Tristan. "I think that is a great idea, I would love that. Now let me think about a price."

He made a pretend face that he was thinking about the price then said, "I will tell you what. I reckon it is too hard to put a price on the Lady Madelaine. They do not make yachts like that anymore. So, I have a plan." He looked at Tony who was holding his breath.

"How about you eight young fellows get me another yacht. About forty-five feet long and a fiberglass one, so I will have the time to look after her; if I need help, I will call on you Tony. There is probably one in the marina for sale. My mother and I could handle that size, she is great crew!"

"Wow," said Tony. "I thought you would want over a million bucks because she is worth that easily!"

"Well," said Tristan. "I am glad you are happy with that. I know she is worth over a million, but I know also it is more important that she gets the care she needs. And I can call on you if I need to!"

"So, can you organise that, Tony? And I will organise Jonathon to do all the paperwork." As he picked up the phone, Tony ran out of the office. "One excited man," Tristan chuckled. He was just as happy.

Tristan explained the situation to Jonathon and asked him to take care of it. Tristan was happy to pay the bill.

"I think what you are doing is just great. I am sure they will find you a great smaller yacht that you can sail on your own or with Lydia. In fact, I may be invited sometimes," said Jonathon. "There will be no charge for this because it makes me happy to help."

It took three weeks for Tony and his friends to find the perfect yacht for Tristan, and when they did, he was delighted. Forty-five feet, white fiberglass, blue and timber trim, sail covers and Bimini top to shade the cockpit. Twin steering wheels at the helm. *Wow*, he thought, and down below every electronic piece of equipment ever invented.

From electronic charts to fridge freezer, genset, engine looked new, wonderful Captain's cabin, and the crew quarters were perfect. Tristan could not wait to take her for a sail.

Tony climbed on board and asked if he was happy with it. Of course, the look on Tristan's face was priceless.

"Oh!" Tony said, "I have fixed everything with Jonathon too. However, when we needed a signature, we could not find you. We guessed you were back overseas buying cars so put her in your mother's name. Hope that is ok."

"Yeah," said Tristan, his mind on other things.

Tristan was at home reading the newspaper, a rear treat for him. Relaxing in his favourite chair, he heard his mother enter the room and looked up.

"Sorry to interrupt, Tristan, but I was wondering where my car is."

"What car?" He asked. It had been so long since she had driven her car; he was surprised.

"My red Mustang, dear," she replied.

"Well, it is in the workshop with a protective cover on it. My Bentley is with it."

"Can I drive it tomorrow?" She asked.

"Oh, sure. The guys look after them both, so they are always ready to go," Tristan said.

He smiled at his mother. "This is great. I am so happy to hear you want to get out more."

"Well, Margery rang this morning, and asked if I would join the ladies for our usual lunch and I thought instead of her picking me up and returning me home, I should get back to normal and meet them there."

"Well, I am delighted." Tristan smiled.

"I think it is time I started doing the shopping by myself as well instead of Arthur taking me in his Rolls," she said. "But that is a nice car."

Arthur Macdonald had moved into the Bay after Christina died and was spending more time in town than his cattle station. His managers were going so well he was letting the youngsters take care of it.

Paul and his wife flew into the Bay every week to do shopping and keep him up to date on how the station management was going.

Arthur would miss taking Lydia shopping very week. It filled in his day.

Tristan was driving past the marina and noticed that something was not quite right with his new boat. He stopped and walked to the outer fence to see if he could tell what was different. The Lady Lydia was one of the outside docks and he could see her easily as he drove past. He drove into the marina's carpark and went to the office to let the know he was going in to check his boat.

He went through the gate using his own key and as he approached his new yacht, he could see what was going on.

On his dock was a very large machine. The machine was used to clean the docks that were used by the public to get to their boat. This machine was very large and overhanging his rigging. However, it cleaned all the dock, so they almost looked brand new. The water jets were very powerful and so were the chemicals.

There was a severe storm predicted for that night so, if the Lady Lydia started rocking around, she could hook up on the machine and do massive damage. Could even pull her mast down. He went back to the office and explained the situation and his worries.

The office staff immediately looked for a vacant berth he could change to. The only one available would be later in the day when another yacht not far along the same dock was going to be lifted out of the water by a ship travel lift to be cleaned underneath and other work done.

However, that was not happening until later in the afternoon if that was ok, could he come back then.

"No problem," Tristan said. "Do I need to come back into the office, will you all still be here?"

"No, we know what will be going on. I will note you have left dock 'A' berth twenty-three and moving to dock 'A' berth number forty-five. Just go ahead when the other yacht leaves. Forty-five berth is the same side as you so should be easy to just reverse out and go up there and turn in."

Tristan went back to his dock and walked along to the boat that was to be lifted out of the water. The owners were there and confirmed that they were leaving. In fact, they were about to leave.

Tristan went back to his car and went home. He worked out what he needed and decided everything would be on the boat and he should return at once to move, in case the storm should come in early. As he reached his car, Lydia drove up.

"I have to move your namesake, want to come for a very short trip." She just jumped into his car so fast, he could not believe it. On their way to the marina, he explained what was happening.

They boarded the yacht and he started reorganising his lines ready to tie up in the other dock.

All went well and they were back on the dock with the yacht secured with extra lines and checked before they left. Both very pleased with a job well done.

They did not see Carson watching them and getting ready to move into the dock that was now vacated.

Carson liked this berth because even though his boat had a higher superstructure, it was mostly hidden from the office windows by the machine on the dock. The office people had gone home anyway. He was not worried about the security cameras on the dock as he was not leaving through the gate that night. The storm was brewing on the horizon already. Looked like a good storm heading his way so felt lucky that other yacht had moved.

He was to take another drug run last night but the severe storm warnings rattled him so he would go tomorrow night. He had not given any signal to the distributer so he would not be expecting him tonight and Harris would never know.

Phillip Harris had contacted Mogo to meet him at the café. He arrived early and sat back and waited.

Mogo arrived at the café and saw Harris was already there. A quick look around and he joined him.

"I have another job for you. This mongrel is distributing cocaine from his boat that he has anchored in the bay, but he sneaks into the marina when he can for a pickup. He has a delivery coming tonight, and he will go down the coast with it. Get rid of him, money is the same."

"What is the boat like?" Mogo asked.

"The usual," Harris replied. "Blue and white, probably a bit of timber trim, you know they all look like that. However, I do know the dock number so you cannot go wrong. So, it is dock number twenty-three, got that?"

"Ok, well I will get going and check it out. When is he leaving and when will he return?"

"He went last night and will be back by now. Also, I bet he will be in the marina as there is a storm coming and the boats all shuffle about and leave for somewhere safer."

Mogo left the café and headed over to the marina. Everything looked calm and peaceful there. He checked the security cameras and the gates. To make sure that everything looked the same as last time he was there. It did. Back at his unit, he found a bunch of keys that he had collected over the years, and found the one that opened the security gate at the marina. He had stolen it from an unsuspecting yachtsman a few years ago.

Then for his disguise. A set of wet weather gear, that was yellow as yachtsmen seemed to like that style best. Maybe because they were easy to see in bad weather. He smiled to himself. He also pulled out his soft blue vinyl bag and put a few small things he thought he made need in it, and his favourite pistol with another of his favourites in case the situation changed.

He also took a walking stick so he would look like, in the camera, an old man with a limp. The hood on the coat fell well over his face. He headed for the gate and the key worked the rain was falling and getting very heavier by the second, he doubted the camera would pick up anything but a human shape.

Looking downward at the dock so he could see the berth numbers, he limped slowly along the dock to berth number twenty-three. White boat blue trim and timber bits across the back. That fits the description he thought. There was a light on below so, he drew his pistol and climbed on board. The boat was rocking with the waves and banging on the dock as the wind became stronger. He thought he was unnoticed until a voice called out, "Who's there?"

Mogo said nothing and then said, "I have a message for you."

"Well, come on down out of the rain."

Mogo opened the hatch and entered. A face appeared and two shots were fired into the forehead. Not sure, a third shot was fired as he saw no blood enter from the first shot. However, he missed and the bullet just made a hole in the cabin sole. Mogo looked at the situation.

There was an open hatch beside the dead man, and he could see in the bilge there was packets of white powder. His eyes opened wide. He had left the blue bag in the cockpit. He opened the main hatch and reached for it quickly, not easy as the boat was now heaving against the dock, rain stinging his face like sharp needles, and then slammed the hatch shut again.

Stepping down beside the open hatch in the cabin sole, he opened the bag and swiftly loaded twenty bags of the white powder and found a few more under the dead man that he had rolled over. Carson had dropped them when he was shot. Twenty-five bags altogether and each at least one kilo. Then dropped his gun on top of it and closed the bag.

He struggled with the bag to get out of the cabin and the cockpit as it was quite heavy. Mogo was a strong man but under the circumstances in a small enclosure on a rolling and heaving deck, it was not easy. He dropped the bag onto the dock below and went over the side with his walking stick. The wind was screaming in his ears as he staggered along, hanging on to that bag with all his might. It was bitterly cold as well and his fingers felt frozen.

When he arrived at the gate, his hands were shaking as he lowered the bag to his feet to open the gate. He put one foot on the bag to steady it on the dock. The gate opened easily so he was able to push the bag through with his foot, and he held onto the gate as he managed to get himself through while everything under his feet was moving in different directions, and the gate threatened to knock him off his feet it was swinging so violently.

Glad to pick up the bag again, he balanced himself on the dock and happy to get back on land again to reach the car and threw the heavily laden bag in the back seat as the rain poured in. Much rain got into the front of the car as he made it into safety and the shelter of the car. Despite the wet weather gear he was wearing, water leaked into his shirt and pants, making him uncomfortable and very cold.

The visibility was non-existent. He could not see through the windscreen. He knew exactly where he was so drove blind to the track that led to the road leading to the marina. Here he stopped to get his bearings. It was awful outside the car. He had never seen weather so bad. He just sat and felt the car rocking, the sheets of rainwater and the yowling wind.

He felt that the rain was easing a bit and he could sort of see through the windscreen, so headed off slowly and thought just as well he did not have that far to go. He would go slowly and safely.

When a boat gets a small hole in it hull, the water does not spurt up high, it just bubbles in and to hold your hand over it can virtually stop it from coming in. The bullet hole was doing just that, and the water had slowly reached the body of Carson.

The heaving of the boats and the dock had managed to do exactly what Tristan feared. The large steel machine that cleaned the docks with all the things that protruded from it and hoses hanging from it, had managed to get itself hooked under the safety rails of Carson's boat. As the boat moved around, it gradually brought the machine nearer to it.

As the water bubbled into the bilge of Carson's boat, the weight of the boat got heavier and pulled the machine on an angle, tipping it in the direction over the boat until it finally lost its balance and fell onto the cabin top that could not hold its weight. It smashed through the timber cabin top and went into the cabin below onto Carson's body. The weight of the large machine pushed the boat lower into the water.

With the weight of the machine and the water entering through the hull, also the rain pouring in it, did not take long for the Maceral fishing oat to sink to the bottom of the marina.

Mogo took advantage of a lull in the storm. He slowly crept along in his car towards his unit. This was not too bad as there was no traffic and the road lighting and lit up signs helped verify that he was going in the right direction. He was most relieved to arrive at his garage under his unit. Wearily, he got out of his car and went up his unit, dried off and lay on the couch.

He tried to think of nothing and just relax after the stress and struggle he had to go through to get back to warmth and safety.

After a while, he felt himself calming down and started to remember and analyse what he had done. He sat up suddenly; the bag was still in the car. Going down to get it out, he thought about who it would have belonged to. Harris was right about this fellow running drugs. What a bastard.

Who did he get them from was the question? He did not feel he should tell Harris about them or turn them over to Bruiser who would just make money out of them. He decided to just bring the bag up to his unit and wait to see what happened before he planned a decision.

When he was dried off, changed and felt up to moving, he headed to his house to see his little family. He drove into the storm again. It had not eased much so he was careful. He could not wait to see Felicity and baby again. Two days away was too long, but sometimes to make the money it had to be.

He opened the door and went in to find his love curled up asleep on the bed with Christian in her arms, both sound asleep. This gave him great joy and a happiness he had never known.

Felicity woke and saw him there watching. She smiled and held the baby up to him.

Felicity was delighted to see him as the storm outside was frightening. She now felt safe.

"He is getting so big now," said Mogo. "Teething and nearly walking, also trying to talk." He felt like the happiest man on earth.

The next day, when the storm abated, the damage bill would be millions. The marina had a pile up of boats that had been swept up on top of one another, docks that had sunk power lines dangerously hooked up on other boats. Yachts broken loose from their moorings, reports of deaths and injuries from sailors, and their friends trying to save their yachts and power boats from bashing themselves on the harbour wall.

What a mess, and nobody noticed Carson's boat or Carson, and the cleaning machine missing. So many other boats had been swept out to sea and rescue crews were being organised. The scene was a mess and waiting for backhoes, tip trucks and Bobcats with other machines to move in. Volunteers were on phones trying to find missing people, and two ambulances had already left and planning to return for more injured. People sitting around crying and others on the phone to their insurance companies.

Chapter 12
Troy and Hunter Harvey

Paul Harvey was a good man. He married a homely girl that had a son from a romance that broke up during her pregnancy. The baby boy never knew his father who just disappeared before the birth. His mother, Helen, as a lone parent had raised him to the age of five when she met Paul Harvey at a friend's birthday party.

Neither were looking for a partner as Paul had his work in the police force and she had her son and a part time job that she loved in day care. The friends at the birthday party had not set them up as they knew their situations. They introduced themselves to each other. It was like the song said 'Across a crowded room'. He saw her and just maneouvered himself through the guests, so he was beside her. "Having fun?" Paul whispered.

Helen smiled up at him and he thought his heart would burst. The conversation went on all night until the party ended, and he took her home. He took her to her front door and watched as she went safely inside the door. Before the door closed, he asked, "Coffee tomorrow?"

She nodded and smiled. "After work," Helen replied, and he nodded.

He called around after work and picked her up. They went to a pretty little coffee shop he knew, and they spent an hour chatting. Helen had to leave to pick up her son.

The courting went on for two months when he asked her to marry him. Helen said, "Yes."

Because they had so many friends, the wedding was quite large, but everyone joined in their happiness and made it a wonderful happy day, not only romantic but funny.

Paul and Helen with her son, Troy, settled into a happy family life. Paul never thought he would marry as he had seen so many failures. He made sure this would never happen to him with Helen and her son by his side. Their joy was complete when Helen told him one night in bed, that she was pregnant.

Seven months later, she gave him a son. They named him Hunter after her dad who had supported her during her pregnancy with Troy.

Hunter Harvey grew up to be an academic and studied law. Handy for Paul as he was able to learn from him. Troy, who loved the only father he had ever known, wanted to follow in his footsteps and be a policeman. Paul was delighted.

Hunter seemed to never leave the university and wanted to end up a professor. He was well on the way.

Troy, after going through police academy, applied to go to the Bay and with a brother to encourage him to study law, was now a senior constable and starting to work up the ladder towards his dad.

Paul was very proud of his boys and so was Helen.

Paul Harvey arrived early at his office. He took a phone call that he was not happy about. He already knew this from reading the paper. The story that made the headlines was about the severe storm that swept through the bay two months ago. Seems they just managed to retrieve the machine that fell off the dock onto the boat using a crane.

As the engine would have been rusted through because of the saltwater, there was no hurry to pull it out. Now that they had lifted it, the boat under it had to be salvaged. The boat was basically cut in half by the machine and in lifting the first half, they found the body in the second half. The body had two bullets in his forehead.

The body had been in the boat since the storm, and it would not be a nice job to rescue it. The ambulance and the coroner were all there. The body did not hold together very well, so mostly came out in pieces. A young constable was on duty to keep the public away.

Tristan also read the paper and read the article to his mother. Lydia became upset as she believed that the person that shot Christina did this. It had also occurred to Tristan but, he was trying not to think of it. The memories of Christina after all this time were still strong and stressful, and then he thought of his missing son. Was he dead or alive?

The fact that they had cleared his berth meant he may be able to get back to it in time, as the boat that had left it to go to the travel lift would want to return as soon as Tristan vacated his berth.

Phillip Harris also saw the paper. He had wondered where Carson had been for the last two months. He was trying to find him for an answer to what happened to the drug delivery. The drug dealer was very angry over the missing cocaine as he had paid big money for it, and he knew that Harris would not give it back. He was blaming Harris and threatening him over it.

Harris blamed Carson, although he had never failed before. Delivery was on time, and he had returned from the delivery because he had found a hidey-hole in the marina on the dock in the berth to shelter (He even knew the berth number). So, the dope must have been delivered. He had reported him as missing and put him down as a missing person of interest. Well, now he had been found and very dead so could not tell what had happened.

Mendez was on the job when the body was found. Forensics had come up with something that interested him. There was a bullet hole in the bottom of the Maceral boat. So, the body had two bullets and one in the boat. Mendez thought about it, and it puzzled him. One bullet in the boat hull to sink the boat, why?

One bullet hole would take quite a long time to sink it, long enough for someone to notice it and report it. However the storm was in action then. So, who was this guy? It was his boat, but he was not on the marina's list of boats berthed in the marina; however he did anchor out in the bay unless he was out fishing.

Most of the people in the immediate area knew him or of him as he caught maceral and sometimes lots of it. And sold it in the Bay. So now he was at a dead end. Mendez felt he was missing something, but what? He would go out into town, have a coffee, relax a bit and think about it.

Mendez returned to the station and decided he should ask some of the young constables who do a police beat now and again around town and seafront. The first two said they knew nothing at all about him or his boat. The third was a different story.

Young constable, Troy Harvey, came into Mendez office and sat down in front of him. Harvey was a Bennet, but his parents had changed his name by deed poll, so he felt entirely within the family. He was an intelligent young man and had a keen eye for who and what was around. Thanks to his brother, he knew a lot about the law as well.

Mendez asked him if he had read the paper that day and Troy told him that he had. Mendez asked him if he knew anything about it. Troy said that he did. Mendez said, "Tell me about it."

"I was sent to keep the public away from the scene when they found the body in the boat. Of course, I knew most of the people, they were just curious locals. They chatted away to me telling me about the guy named Carson and how well they knew him. I was happy to talk to them because the locals here are right into gossip and tried to fill me in with all their knowledge. I think most of it was correct."

"So, what were they telling you exactly?" Mendez said.

"They all knew he was a maceral fisherman and that he owned the boat; it had no name so no one could identify it with him. His name was Carson and that was all no other name known, no one knew if that was his family name or Christian name. It seems that he never wanted to pay for a berth so anchored out in the bay and after the marina office hours he would sneak into a vacant berth for the night."

"This gave him access to the marina facilities and fill his boat water tanks. Of course, he would leave before the office opened in the morning. There is a security camera over the gate and security patrol the docks in the night. There is only one man patrolling as no theft has happened there mainly because the cameras are there and none of them have been damaged."

"However, that night, no one was patrolling the docks because of the severe storm. All the locals wanted to talk about that. It was really bad according to them, bits of boats airborne, boats bashing together damage to the marina was unthinkable. Boats broke their lines and smashed into boats on other docks."

"The boats in the far corner near the front gate escaped all of this, they were safe, and it seems the boat in the corner called the 'Lady Lydia' had just moved in there a few hours before. Lucky."

"You have done well, Troy; anything to add?" Mendez asked.

"Well, yes and I don't know if I should say this or not," said Troy, hesitating.

"Better tell me," said Mendez, not knowing what was coming.

"Well, Sergeant Phillip Harris was there."

"That is not unusual," said Mendez.

"I know, but it was what he was doing that was strange."

"Go on," said Mendez.

"Well, he was messing around in that area like he was looking for something. He even lay flat on the deck with his head over the side and his arm was in the water feeling around under the dock. He was quite a while and I thought that he should not do that as forensics had not been there at this stage. He seemed very angry as when someone spoke to him, he told him to fuck off."

"When he got up, he headed off the dock and went towards the ambulance, they had just shut the doors and took off. More loud bad language. Then ran to his car and took off."

"That seems a bit odd, but why would you think that was odd. He was possibly looking for more information to pass on to me," said Mendez.

"Well, the guys at work were telling me that they helped him with a burial at sea and I think, in fact, I am sure that was the boat that did the burial at sea. I would not mention it but, they were paid well for the assistance, always joking about how they reckon they should get another job like that."

"I would like to know more about that, see what else you can find out."

"Ok," said Troy. "I will get back to you, may take a while."

"Good work, Troy, and thanks," Mendez said as Troy left the office.

Two weeks later, Troy found Mendez in his office on the phone. He waited until he finished his call and went in. Mendez looked up with a smile. "Good to see you at last, Troy, got anything for me yet?" He beckoned Troy to sit in the chair opposite.

"Think so." He sat in the comfortable chair and continued. "I have found out some interesting things that involve Sergeant Harris."

"That's interesting but somehow, I am not that surprised," replied Mendez.

"Ok, I managed to talk to one of the constables who said four of them helped him out on a job that was to be kept quiet. Seems that these fellows were told there was a drug ring that unfortunately involved a teenage boy who was happy to sell and deliver the drugs. As teenagers never get proper punishment and are let off with a smack on the wrist, they had to take him out too."

"They were told not to come armed as then they would not have anything on their conscious; a hitman would come in, that would do the job. There would be no acknowledgement of this happening or credit for getting rid of these drug dealers, they would just disappear. There were three of them, a man, woman and the teenage boy. They went in a black van and had four body bags to get them out of there. All they did was load them."

"I asked him if he should be telling me about this. He said that it was over three years ago so should not matter, but you will keep it quiet."

"Let me digest this," Mendez said. He sat back in his chair and closed his eyes.

"While you think about that, add to your thoughts the three bodies that had the burial at sea a day or so later."

"Just what I was thinking," Mendez said. "So, what about the young woman shot in the driveway."

"I asked him about that, and he knew nothing of it. However, he thought that a dog was shot, and Harris was the only one outside."

"Well done for what you have discovered. How to handle this, is the problem. Thanks for your work and I will get back to you. I think I must go higher with this. Your father is, Paul Harvey, isn't he?"

"That's right."

"I may call in to see him," said Mendez.

Mendez pulled out his mobile and made a time with Paul Harvey for the next day.

Mendez was welcomed into Paul Harvey's office the next morning.

"Take a seat," he said. "What do you have for me?"

"Well, Superintendent," answered Mendez. "Thanks to your son, I have found out something interesting but cannot go to the sergeant as it involves him."

Paul Harvey frowned. "In what way?"

"Have you seen Troy recently?" Mendez asked.

"No, I haven't. He often works when I am home and vice versa."

"Ok, I can understand that, so let me start off by asking if you know anything about the death of Christina Paravoni and her three missing friends. One of these a young boy, the son of her friends?"

"Yes, I know about that and also the missing woman's parents and her daughter," said Harvey.

"Right, I have some more information about this, which is it seems that Phillip Harris organised three or four of our young constables to aid him in taking out Paravoni's friends."

"What!" Harvey yelled. "That is impossible." Shaking his head in disbelief.

"Seems they were paid quite a sum for this. Now, they were told not to bring any arms at all, because there was a hitman to do the job. Then they had to put the bodies in body bags and load them into the black van that is usually in our car park at the station. I have checked this out and Phillip Harris did borrow the van for the day that Christina Paravoni died."

"So, who shot her?"

"Seems that the gunman left as soon as he fired the shots so, while they were loading, they heard a shot outside and as they left and were out on the main road, they saw an ambulance pass them and turn into the driveway they had just left. One of them asked about it and Harris told them he had shot a dog, maybe someone had heard the shot and rang an ambulance."

"They all got out of the van as soon as they arrived, and Phillip Harris drove away. The next day, three of them were to go on a burial at sea on a maceral boat, the same boat that they have just recovered from the water in the marina with the body of a fellow called Carson." Mendez paused for breath.

Paul Harvey pressed a button on his desk and a young woman appeared "Coffee for two; how do you take it, Mendez?"

Mendez told him and the young woman left.

"We could be here a while," said Harvey. "Now tell me how you found this information."

Mendez said simply, "Troy, your son. I suspected Harris a while ago, just that he was involved somehow as he kept pushing us to arrest Tristan Paravoni for the murder of his wife as a domestic issue. Tristan Paravoni is a good man and interviewing him, it was impossible for him to shoot his wife by the forensics information. Paravoni said there was a policeman in the yard, and he shot her then tossed the gun up on the roof of the house. No gun was found."

"Do you know the hitman who shot the ones in the house?"

"No, and forensics said no trace at all," Mendez said.

"Do you think that has anything to do with the woman's parents?"

"Yes, I do, because the mother came up the stairs as directed by our policewoman on desk duty, but Marilyn Thomas never arrived. I did see Harris in the area at the top of the stairs at that time. I am guessing as she was climbing up the stairs and saw him and went back down again. That night, they took off with the daughter and the caravan. Since then, I went to find any information on their disappearance and found that Phillip Harris has been keeping the record of the searching."

"Any connection between Harris and the Thomas family?" Harvey asked.

"I am on to that at the moment, I will let you know if I find anything," answered Mendez.

"Now, we have had a lot of drive by shootings lately, any tie in there?" Harvey asked.

"Looking at that too. Every shooting has two bullets to the head. The hitman must be an excellent marksman; two bullets close together and always in the forehead. There has only been two cases of three bullets. One in the boat where I think the hitman got Carson before the storm. CCTV shows an old fellow on a cane going up and down with a soft blue bag like the one yachtsman carry. He came out struggling with that bag looked like he was saving some of the boat's equipment before the storm."

"See the boat he went to?"

"No," said Mendez. "The CCTV only covers the gate."

"We have a lot to get through over this," said Harvey. "When I see Troy, I will have a word. You check out what you can at your end," said Harvey.

"One more thing," said Mendez. "I am troubled about Troy. I worry if this is what we think with Harris, if word gets about that he knows any of this, is he in danger?"

"Right," said Harvey. "Thanks."

Mendez left, he had work to do, and he felt good that the superintendent was on board with him. Harvey would also take good care of his son, Troy.

Paul Harvey was a worried man. He thought of his son, Troy, and was concerned that if Troy had spoken to another constable, putting Harris in the pooh Troy could end up on the hit list. He could not just tell his son to not go to work, but he could just tell him to watch his back. But he did not want to alarm him or have him try to find out more information.

However, he could find out more information if he just spoke to him about it. If Phillip Harris did have a hitman, what else did he have? He decided to also check out all the two shots to the head murders and see just what did add up. He also thought of trying to find out how much money it took for a young constable to shut his mouth on a crime.

Mendez went to the street that the Thomas family had lived. The house looked like they must have returned because it looked like they never left, so neat and tidy. He knocked on the door and a woman answered. He introduced himself as Detective Mendez and gave her his card. He asked her if Mrs Thomas was home.

"Who?" She asked.

"The people who own the house," he explained.

"I don't know who owns the house, we just rent it." She looked at him for a second. "You are not the usual policeman who calls in all the time. He wears a uniform. I don't like him, he is pushy."

"Sorry to hear that, Ma'am, we just think that family is missing. Did he tell you that?"

"No," she said. "He scared me, demanding information that I did not have."

"What did he want to know?" Mendez said.

"He wanted to know where they were. He wanted to know how I am renting this house and who the real estate agent is. Then he wants to know where my husband works and stuff like that."

Mendez thought she was going to cry.

"Can I come in and explain," Mendez said, and she opened the door and beckoned him in.

They sat in the lounge, and he told her that the family was missing, and we suspect that they will come to harm if we do not find them very soon. So, if she could give them any information that could help, he would be very grateful.

She smiled then. "You have asked so nicely so I will tell you the little I know. We have a friend who told us he had a friend who could possibly get us a house cheap to rent if we looked after it properly. Then we think they talked him into letting us rent it and we could bypass an agent and just pay the money in a bank account. So that is it."

She hesitated and he waited. "Do you want the bank and the account number?"

Mendez smiled and spoke. "That would be a great help."

They said goodbye on the front step, and he told her not to worry about the other policeman. He said to tell him you have given me all the information you have and refer him to me. I will also tell him.

He headed down the narrow front path to the gate, gave her another wave and went to his car.

He traced the bank account to Nicole Harris. Phillips Harris's daughter.

Mogo sat in the living room of his unit. He had just left the house he gave to Felicity and Christian. He loved them dearly. They were everything to him. He thought he worked hard planning to rid society of these grubs who beat women, abuse kids, drug dealers and sellers of the stuff. The risks and planning.

He knew it could not go on forever. The bank held most of his money. There were several accounts, mostly for Felicity to see never had to worry about money for her or Christian. He knew that it all had to end, so he had plans for that, but he had to be careful, he had a lot to do yet.

Paul Harvey had called his staff together for a meeting.

"We have information that Sergeant Harris is committing criminal activities. So far, we suspect that he had his ex-wife, her husband and his own son, shot by a hitman and at the same time, he shot Mrs Tristan Paravoni. We suspect he is hunting down the Thomas family who have his daughter, Nicole. I am concerned they could be the next victims."

"Detective Mendez of the Bay station is working on this, and I am sure we can help him. Now usually when we have a rogue cop amongst us, they have other things on the go as well. I want you to work on this and see if he is into other things, like drugs or prostitution or any protection money likely to be on the go. I really want you to start on this immediately as we feel he has found the Thomas family."

"They have his daughter, Nicole, and as he shot his son, we are afraid for her. Nicole will be a teenager now, if an attempt on her life at this age she may never recover. Any questions?" He waited while they had time to take in what he had told them.

One young fellow asked, "Is this contained to the Bay, State or National. Would he be likely to have an overseas bank account?"

"It could be possible keep thinking along those lines," Harvey answered.

"If any of you want to follow a trail of his activities, let me know and then we can organise assistance or whatever you may need. So, we have work to do, off you go for now and I will call another meeting next week."

As it happened, Phillip Harris had found some information that could lead him to his daughter. He had followed a trail but had never seen her at the destination he had waited at. She was still at school, and it was her year before university. Harris thought if he could not find her here, she could go to any university, and he would have to start all over again.

He had rang Mogo and told him he had one more job to take care of. Trying to think up a story that Mogo would make this teenager so bad that Mogo would be happy to shoot her.

He was quite surprised with Mogo when he shot Billy, the Bastard, that he never asked about the teenage girl on his knee when he shot him. She was only partly dressed in sparkling G-string and very little else. Maybe her age threw him, and he thought it was her father. The Bikie club often had jobs for him, and they were not the only ones. Mogo was getting very popular especially outside the Bay.

Mendez sat in his office thinking. It was quiet in there with no external noise so his brain could tick over in first gear. It occurred to him that he should interview Tristan Paravoni again now he had this new information.

Tristan Paravoni had not long from a visit with the Arab Royalty in Dubai. He had a slight problem there at the moment as one of the princes wanted him to marry one of his daughters. This was not on as far Tristan was concerned as the girl was not yet thirteen. The prince explained that this was the normal age for a princess to marry, or most girls for that matter.

No matter how many times Tristan put up an argument against this, the prince had an answer. Tristan knew it was only to get his cars at a discount price, but it was to Tristan an insult to his country and values. He also did not want to lose his business as that was the most profitable and easiest to handle. That was on his mind when Mendez turned up at his office.

Tristan welcomed him in. Showed him a seat and asked his mother, who was hovering around, to get Mendez a coffee.

Lydia said, "Of course, I will get the detective a coffee, would you care for some cake as well."

"That would be great. I haven't anything to eat today," Mendez replied.

They exchanged pleasantries while the coffee came. Lydia came with a sandwich and cake.

"How can I help you?" Tristan said.

"I am on the trail of something and I think you should know about it, and also you may be able to help in this."

"I will help you with anything you want to know."

"Well," said Mendez "We seem to have a bad guy amongst us." Tristan waited for him to go on. "I want you to repeat everything that you told us in your statement when you lost your wife."

"Oh! Christ," said Tristan. "Not again." He looked sad as Christina's image came to him. "Sorry, of course I will, what would you like to know?"

"That is ok, I am sorry for springing this on to you. I need you to tell me about the policeman in the yard that you saw and who shot Christina. Can you describe him again as you saw him, also exactly what did he do after the shooting?"

"Right, he was in the yard having a cigarette. I did not see him at first as Christina was in front of me. She fell back on me, and I held her as she came down to the ground. I was so low to the ground, I could see him under the hedge very clearly. He had on a hat and uniform of a sergeant and his gun was in one hand and a cigarette in the other."

"He dropped the cigarette and put it out by stamping his foot on it, he turned and threw the gun on the roof of the house. The gun slid down the roof and hit the gutter up in the air again, and hit the pipe into the water tank, it then bounced up in the air hit the waterpipe Then into the hole in the tank and splash."

Mendez said, "The gun went into the water tank?" He was amazed. "You never told us that."

"Yes, I must have," said Tristan.

"I read your statement before I came here, that was not in it." Mendez paused then said, "You know you were distressed, you had just lost Christina; I cannot blame you if you did not remember everything. So, hopefully we can find the gun now. May not be easy but if it is in there, we will find it. Now, one more thing." He pulled a photo out of his pocket and handed it to Tristan.

Tristan took the photo and the colour drained out of his face. "That's him," he whispered.

"Thank you," said Mendez. "I want you to keep quiet about this as we suspect him of more crimes. I would ask you another thing too. The Thomas family, did you know them at all?"

"Yes, they are Marion's parents," said Tristan. "There were a few parties and Christmas time. Such nice people and they loved Nicole and Beau. They would do anything for anyone. They never saw Nicole and Beau for years as they lived way up north. They are making up for that now. They have lost Beau though; they must be terribly upset."

"You know they have a caravan and gone away in it?"

"Yes," replied Tristan. "Why?"

"They took off with the caravan and have not been heard of since. We suspect that policeman you just identified wants to shoot Nicole and maybe her grandparents."

"What?" Tristan had to control himself. "Who is this guy?"

"You must not let on you know this, and I do trust you to be sensible. That policeman you just identified was Marion's first husband and the father of Beau and Nicole. We understand that he had a hitman shoot them while he was in the yard, and unfortunately you and Christina were in the wrong place at the wrong time."

"The Thomas Family fled and have not been heard of since. We now suspect that he knows where they are. If you have any idea where they may be hiding, you can tell me now and we will be able to protect them."

Tristan thought about this. "I know they had a favourite caravan spot in a free camp by a river. But it was in the outback, Nicole needs her school. They were always talking about it. The fishing and quiet. The swimming and the other caravans that came in for the night. They loved it."

"I will give you directions to get there as we went to spend a couple of days with them. Don't know the name of the river but the directions are good. It's a day's drive or more on the border. We stayed at the local hotel for the night. Just a small town not far from the river."

They shook hands and parted. Mendez with a mud map in his pocket, and the name of a small-town hotel.

He headed there the next day after informing Superintendent Paul Harvey, who was pleased that Mendez had found out more information already. It was a long drive and he settled in a motel the first night. He thought he would make it in less than three days, and he was right. Because it was a country run and he had to be careful to keep to the speed limit, as these country towns often had a police car sitting somewhere in the main street and would soon stop him for speeding.

He could not let that happen as he would have to give the name of the Bay Police station and Harris could hear of his trip out west. That could be a disaster for the Thomas family.

Late on the second day he arrived at the camping spot. There was a van there that fitted the description of the Thomas caravan. He approached the van as he felt they should be there as it was dinner time. There was a light on, so he knocked gently on the door. Hoping that he would not frighten them in any way.

Bill Thomas opened the door. "Can I help you?"

"I hope so," said Mendez. He introduced himself and then Marilyn Thomas suddenly appeared at the door.

"Detective Mendez, is that you from the Bay police station?" She asked.

"Yes," he replied quietly.

"Can you come in please? I was trying to see you a long time ago. Are you on your own?" She said.

"Yes," he replied.

He went in the van, and she showed him to a seat near the small table. "Thank you," he said.

"Yes, I am alone," he said. "I know you were trying to see me so; I have been looking for you for a long time, and thanks to Tristan Paravoni, I have found you at last."

"Would you like a coffee or drink of some kind?" She asked.

"Yes, that would be very nice," he said.

They sat around the table, just the three of them and a young girl sat on the bed nearer the rear of the van. Mendez smiled at her and said, "You must be Nicole." She shyly smiled back. "I am happy to see you here."

The silence was peaceful.

Marilyn started telling Mendez of how she had come to see him and as she was walking up the stairs where the policewoman directed her, she saw Phillip Harris. She was so afraid she turned and went down the stairs again. "I do not know what I would have done if the policewoman was still at the desk. How would I explain this turn around? However, she had gone off somewhere, so I was able to scurry out the door to the car. I was praying the car would start. I was terrified."

Mendez nodded and said, "I was wondering what happened and now I know. Can you tell me about Sergeant Harris why you were so afraid of him?"

Marilyn Thomas started from the beginning. How she hated the thought of her daughter getting married to him and what a dreadful life she had with Phillip Harris. Worse than that, she told him how he thought his two children were ugly and should be put down like dogs, he hated them. She believed he had killed her daughter and her son in law, also his own son. And that was why they had absconded with Nicole to keep her out of his sight.

Mendez looked across at the very pretty teenager with the long dark hair and big brown eyes, and asked himself how that man Harris could think that girl was ugly. He had a stunningly beautiful daughter. An old photo on the wall of the van caught his eye. It was a truly lovely woman smiling at the camera and it was obviously her mother. He noticed the rough-cut edge of the photo and guessed that was Harris cut out of the photo.

Marilyn interrupted his thoughts. "He was cruel to those two children and that is why I could not bring myself to go north to see them. It was best I kept away and not know what he did. I asked Marion to not tell me anything more about him and what he did as it gave me nightmares, and she would not leave him until she found out that he was unfaithful to her every time he went overseas. The other men were laughing about it. They did not know she was standing near them."

"He became very nasty and threatened her after she left him. We thought he would get over them as he did not care at all for the children."

"Well, I am here to tell you that Harris, at this moment does not know where you are. I would not tell him but if you feel unsafe because I have been here then move. I would ask you one favour; I would like you to ring me every month and tell me where you are. We are gathering information on him as we also suspect he had something to do with a few murders."

"Ring me from an untraceable number like a public phone and when we get him, I would need you to testify in court. If you would of course."

"Try and stop me," she said with a grin. They were happy he had called and to know they were on to Harris. They slept well that night and made the decision to move. They would ring Mendez once a month as requested.

Chapter 13
Barry Nicholson

Constable Barry Nicholson went through his cadetship with flying colours and a bright future. He loved his job and would rather work twenty-four seven than go home for a night.

Barry was honoured when Phillip Harris, his sergeant, asked him to be in on a job to eliminate a drug ring. He knew that it was hush hush and there would be no medals or recommendations for carrying out this job. He could not carry a gun, so he felt his safety was assured. He felt confident that he would do something for society to protect those who were hooked on drugs.

On the day he went in the black van to the site. It was a nice house in a country setting with a manicured hedge forming a back yard with a children's playhouse to one side. Quite a coverup, he thought. Whoever would have thought that a drug dealer, or dealers, lived here? They established that the family was in the dining room. Easy to find out if they do not know you are there.

There was three in the dining room. They waited for a sort time when a man arrived with a gun that looked straight out of the army. He went in first, six rapid shots and then confusion, seems one of them escaped. He saw the woman in a wheelchair try to get out the back door, but the sergeant was there and dragged her out of the chair by the hair and into the dining room and threw her on the two dead bodies.

Then they had to put them in the body bags and load them into the van. They were heavy even with the four of them. He knew that they were buried at sea because one of the others were involved in that. Brian Evans had gone on the boat trip. The three of them were not happy about that but there was a large supply of heavy spirits to drink and that made it bearable.

The next day, Phillip Harris gave him an envelope with five thousand dollars with the explanation that it was part of the reward money. This seemed plausible because he did not feel Harris could pay it out of his pocket.

Barry had heard a rumour that one of the four had made a bit of a confession about the execution of the drug dealers. He was always suspicious of the young boy getting the same treatment and the wheelchair victim getting treated so badly. He decided he should talk to the others but would have to be careful incase that was a hitman in Harris' employ.

Barry threw a few hints about that day when alone with one of them and could not be overheard. There was not much response from them. They would shrug their shoulders or say things like 'That's life'. Barry decided he should get one of them on their own again but in a different situation. He knew that Constable Roger Dixon went to the local hotel every night on his way home.

He did not know if he then drove himself home or was picked up. So, he thought he would check it out that afternoon. Barry was a single man with no family ties at all. His parents moved a long way from the Bay. Barry had a great unit with an ocean view to live in and a lot of friends that he would miss if he moved away.

So, he left work behind Roger and tailed him to the hotel. Seems Roger had a table reserved for him whenever he came into the hotel and his beer was delivered as soon as he sat down. It was a small table with two chairs so maybe going it alone or someone would join him there.

Could just be the one who would drive him home after a drink. Barry found a table with two chairs up the back of the room so he could watch him, but Roger could not see him unless he did a one-eighty turn to the left.

He watched Roger drink down two small beers and then a young woman came in and joined him. She plonked herself down in the chair quite unlady like. The dress and the makeup piled on, Barry thought, she could be a sex worker of some sort. Her clothes said this.

They huddled together whispering then got up together and left. Barry could not work out who she could be. He watched them leave and was tempted to follow but thought he would leave that for another day. Surely that could not be his wife.

When Barry saw Roger at the station where they worked the next day, he approached him and asked if he could have a word. He led Roger to one side and said, "I think we have a problem."

"You reckon, so what is it?" Roger said.

"Seems there is a rumour about Sergeant Harris," Barry said.

"What about him?" Roger replied.

"I am not sure," said Barry. "But something about the missing three people and the burial at sea."

"That's a lot of rot, take no notice about it," he said angrily. "And see if you can stop spreading the rumour idea around."

"Sure," said Barry. "I was in it though and I don't want to get into trouble."

"Keep your mouth shut and you will be fine."

Barry walked away. He felt he could not speak again about this as if he had that attitude, maybe he was up to something that involved this or worse. He decided that he would just keep an eye on him. Maybe following him next time if the woman turned up. Also, with Roger's attitude, he could get into trouble with him as well.

Roger was thoughtful; he did not like what Barry was saying and he did not want to get into strife as well. He saw the actions of that hitman and did not want to be a victim. So, he went to his sergeant and asked to speak to him on the side as he may know something that Phillip should know.

They went into small room out the back away from most of the office staff in the police station.

"Do you have a problem?" Phillip Harris asked.

"Could have, want your advice," said Roger.

"Go ahead then," said Harris.

Roger told him of the conversation with Barry. "He is a good guy but now he worries me."

"Glad you told me, and I will take action to stop any rumours, so you do not have to worry. Good man for letting me know."

Constable Alan Davis was a married man whose wife always worried that he would get shot. She wanted him to take an office job inside the police department. Especially now that they had twin sons, only six weeks old.

The job had bothered him. Seeing a hitman come in and just shoot three people. Doesn't matter what they have done. If the police department had the evidence, they should have had a fair trial. That is what the law was about. *Problem is if I say anything, I could meet the hitman under different circumstances.*

He had also heard a rumour about Sergeant Phillip Harris but not much information about what the rumour was about. He did not know if it was about the 'job' they did with the three drug runners as he had also been at the burial at sea. Nothing could come of that now as Carson and the boat are dead. He was sure, that part was ok.

The five thousand dollars in an envelope came at the right time, helped them get the house they now had. The boys were off to school now and he and his wife were delighted that she was pregnant again as she wanted a daughter. Scan showed it was a girl. So much happiness in the future to look forward to. Nothing could spoil that now.

Constable Bret McMillan overheard something that made him uneasy. The story was about Sergeant Harris and the missing people and the three people who went off in a caravan it bothered him. He wanted someone to talk about it with. He thought he should talk to Barry Nicholson, warn him, as they often socialised at work parties or get togethers. He really liked him. They seemed to chat away for hours about cars work where they would like to travel in their annual holidays.

Both single; they both had girlfriends now and again but apart from their names and where they had dinner that was it. Personal details were never spoken of. He was not sure how to approach Barry. He was pretty sure that Barry would know something about it. He decided to ask Barry to join him for lunch that day but Barry was out in one of the police cars that had to go to an accident.

He left a note on Bret's desk saying he needed to speak with him as soon as he could. Harris was passing his desk and saw Bret place the note on Barry's desk. Harris picked up the note and read it. He then asked Bret "What's so important?"

Bret was a quick thinker and replied, "My girlfriend wants to double date with us tomorrow and needs an answer as soon as possible so she can line her friend up."

"You young fellows had better not get up to any mischief," Harris said.

"Oh! Don't spoil our fun, Sarg," said Bret.

Harris did not answer, he just walked off satisfied that all was well.

Two days later, Barry and Bret met up over lunch. They both had a lot on their mind.

Bret was not sure how to start the conversation so, Barry did it for him. "Is this about Harris?" They talked through lunch time so had to make it quickly back to the station. Fortunately, nobody seemed to notice they were late back from lunch. They had plans to meet again that night and sort it out.

They both felt they could be in danger if Harris found out what they were doing. Who to turn to for advice? Who would not make the situation worse or report them to Harris? Was all this rumours? They wondered about that. Maybe someone had it in for Harris and the whole episode was legal and the money received was a part of the reward money. Maybe not.

Would the government pay a hitman to turn up and terminate three lives and be looking for a fourth person? Would the government approve of dragging a crippled woman by the hair into the house? They did not think so. They did not want to meet up with that hitman again, pretty ruthless.

They concluded that they should see a lawyer; Barry agreed. They settled on Marty Mitchell as he was a criminal lawyer, and at this stage, they figured they could be up on criminal charges.

Chapter 14
Alan Davis

Constable Alan Davis also heard the rumours. He did not want to believe that a rumour had started for no reason. Sergeant Phillip Harris was his idol. Harris had helped him raise money for a children's charity by having a BBQ at Alan's house. He managed to fill his backyard with people who donated a lot of money.

He was a good man. He could not let anything happen to Harris as he had promised that annually he would be available to that money raiser or any other that Alan was assisting in his charity work at any time. He would be happy to do it!

He wondered if Harris knew this was going on, if not, should he inform him about the rumours?

He headed to the large office that Harris had been allotted years ago, and he was there. He was sitting in his chair daydreaming when Alan quietly tapped on the door. Harris asked him in and pointed to a chair.

"What can I do for you, Alan? Another charity as I will be happy to help."

"No, Sir," Alan started and then seemed to lose his nerve; he could not utter another word.

"Alan, if you have a problem, I will do anything to help, you should know that."

Alan still could not speak, Harris thought he was going to cry.

"Alan, just a second and I will shut the door so no one can hear or see us while you tell me the problem. Is your family ok?"

"Yes, they are fine," he stuttered. "I have heard a rumour going around about you and I cannot believe it." He seemed to grow a bit of confidence then.

"What are they saying?" Harris said quietly. "Tell me everything you have heard, and I will put a stop to it."

"I heard that you had something to do with the shootings of the three people that disappeared, but I was there with you and so were the other three, we knew what we had to do, and we did it well. I am upset that they should be suspicious of you about anything. What you told us was correct. No publicity and I did not expect any cash but makes sense that if they were as bad as you said, there would be a reward."

"Not a large reward as there must have been a lot of organisation and people involved. I know you are a good honest man, and I am stunned that anyone could say anything else."

"Thank you, Alan, I am honoured that you think so highly of me. You are right I have done nothing wrong. Perhaps I have upset one of the others unknowingly, and they think I did something wrong. Now I want you to calm down, I will get on to this and fix it."

"I have many friends in high places that will believe me and gave me the information and instructions about those people. They will punish those who start untrue rumours. I did not find those drug dealers out by myself you know."

"Oh! I am so glad to hear that. Thank you, I will get back to work now." Alan left the room.

Harris called him back. When he returned, Harris said, "See if you can find out anything else about that rumour and who started it."

"Right," returned Alan. "I am on it, discreet enquiries?" He asked.

A nod from Harris sent him in the other direction.

Bret, Roger and Barry were the only targets Alan could get to know better as they were the only ones involved. They all were paid the same amount of money in cash.

Alan thought he should have a word to Roger first. He planned to ask if he had heard the rumours or anything that could make the sergeant look bad.

Roger thought about the questions that Alan was asking. Some did not make sense to him. They did a job and were paid for it by the reward money, and nothing was in the papers about it so what was the problem. Roger then thought about the morals and ethics of this and maybe it was wrong, and they should have asked for more proof of them being drug dealers, especially as one was a young boy.

Who was the fourth person they could not find? Questions tumbled through his mind, and he decided to look further into this. He told himself that Alan was ok with it and wondered about Barry and Bret. He thought he would have a chat with them both and separately as soon as he could.

Alan Davis entered the office of Phillip Harris about two hours after he spoke to him. "A word, Sir," he said.

"Come in," Harris replied. "That was quick. Don't tell me you have info already."

"No," said Alan, "but as I am playing detective, I saw Mendez screw up a bit of paper and throw it in the waste basket, so I retrieved it and it is a mud map, thought you may like to see it."

"Let's have a look then." He took it off Davis and studied it for a while. "This is a mud map alright but it is a long way from here," said Harris.

"Ok, if it is of no use, I will throw it back in the bin," said Davis.

"No, I will keep it and find out what it is all about, could be useful."

Alan headed back to the desk as he was on front desk duty for another four hours.

Harris looked at the map and wondered if it was anything to do with the Thomas family. The decided he had better follow it up. He had a couple of days off due soon so he would see if he could head off tomorrow.

As it happened, he left the next morning and headed west.

Two days later, he arrived and found that the Thomas family had been there but left yesterday. No-one knew where they were going or which direction as there was a three-way intersection down the track that led to the river so you could not see anyone turn when the arrived there. Harris checked this intersection as he left the campground and headed for home. "I will get those bastards one day," he muttered to himself.

Barry Nicholson and Bret McMillan met again over lunch a few days later. They were on about Harris, after their small talk had ended when Roger Dixon walked in and headed for their table. "Mind if I join you both?" He asked.

"Sure," they chorused together. "Grab a seat and pull it over."

Thinking that Roger had just happened to wander in and see them there, they went back to their small talk and rambled on about the weather and cars and anything they could think of except Harris.

Roger started up after a while and asked if they had heard rumours about Harris and the drug business elimination. Yes, they had heard about it and were wondering what it was about, and who started the rumours. Both men at the same time told him that they were not involved in starting the rumours but were very worried about it. Roger agreed.

Roger said, "We could be in trouble if this was not true and he paid us for a crime, because that is what it was."

"We think like you do, and we have decided to get ourselves a lawyer and we see him this afternoon," said Barry.

"Can I get onto this with you two or should I get my own lawyer?" Roger asked.

"Let's talk to our guy and ask him before we make any of those decisions," said Bret.

"What about Alan?" Roger asked.

"Seems he can see no wrong in Harris. They are close, and I do not want to involve him in our troubles as he thinks that it was all ok. The money got to him when he really needed it and Harris helps him with his charity work. Probably would be right to say he is in denial," said Bret.

"By the way, I would not tell him anything as it will get back and we are a bit afraid of the hitman, whoever he is," said Barry. "Anyway we will meet up at our lawyers the three of us and see what comes of this. See you after work this afternoon," said Bret.

"So, where did this rumour start and who started it," asked Roger.

"Not a clue," answered Bret. "Must be someone we do not know. Who else was involved in this? Does anyone of us know someone that may have been in it?"

They all sat at the little table thinking about this. After a while, Roger spoke again. "I know it it's a long shot, but Troy was at the marina when the boat was salvaged and the body was found. Now he is in our age group so, maybe he just happens to know something."

"You know you could be onto something there," said Barry. "He is a good cop ad would enquire about anything and everything while he was stationed there to keep the public away. To add to that, he would be discreet and no-one would know what he was up to. Do you think we could ask him about it?"

"Have to be careful with him as his dad is Superintendent Harvey," said Roger.

"Let's talk to our lawyer and get his opinion. We will not mention it unless he thinks it is ok," said Barry. They all agreed to meet up in time to get to the lawyer and see the results of the meeting. They would stay together after the meeting and talk about the results

Chapter 15
Felicity

Felicity was not the brightest of young women, but she knew right from wrong, and certainly preferred to always do the right thing.

When Mogo put that tiny baby in her arms, her heart went into melt down. She was so extraordinarily happy, a feeling she had never had before. The nearest to it was Mogo's proposal of marriage, and she knew she was right when she said yes. He was the most devoted man who gave her anything she wanted and loved her more than she ever thought could be possible. She was totally in love with him and knew that would never change.

Mogo was often away over night or for two days at the most. She had her new little car that she could drive anywhere. She was still expecting member of the adoption department to call in and see her, and check all was correct and she was looking after the baby properly. She decided to go and see them. She knew Mogo would be away for two days so now was the time.

She placed Christian in his pram and decided to go on public transport to go to the city as parking was almost impossible near the government buildings. The bus went to the door so barely a short walk into the building. That would be better.

So, she set off reasonably early so she could have lunch in the city, she loved to do that. Maybe after lunch, she could go shopping.

She found the right department and went to the desk for enquiries. The receptionist was very friendly and asked her a few questions about her adoption, then asked her to sit on the velvet lounge and she would get the officer concerned.

A middle-aged woman in a pale blue uniform with a brown-haired bun on her head and the name 'Miss Mangostein' printed neatly on her name tag on her chest appeared after a short wait. Christian slept soundly in his pram and was not due for his feed for two hours.

"Good morning," said Miss Mangostein. "I believe you have an enquiry about your adoption." She ignored the baby in the pram as though he was not there.

"Yes," Felicity replied. "I know I cannot find out who his parents were or anything like that, but I was wondering why no member of the adoption agency ever came out to see how he was or how I was going being a first time mother."

"Give me your full name and address so I can look into this as we always come and check on our adopted babies."

"My husband said that you do that, but no-one ever came," said Felicity. She felt as though she was going to cry and did not know why, except she felt this woman did not care about the babies and she was an annoying pest who had interrupted this woman's day.

"Ok, I will check it out and be back soon," she said and disappeared through a green door.

The receptionist smiled at Felicity and said, "Don't worry she will not be long. Just relax, we get a lot of nervous new mothers in here."

The blue uniform and brown hair bun appeared not long after and said, "We have no-one of your names on file. Are you sure little Christian came from this department?"

"Yes," said Felicity. "My husband said so."

"Then I will check again, I am sure there are no records of this child." Miss Mangostein disappeared again behind the green door. She was longer this time.

When she returned, she seemed to be a bit softer and a bit nicer to Felicity. Even showed interest in Christian by looking into the pram and gently touching his blanket, pulling it down so she could see all his little face.

"You certainly take good care of him," she spoke. "He looks very healthy, good size for his age and well dressed, you should be very proud of yourself." She also noted that although simply dressed, Felicity had good fashion sense and her clothes were not cheap.

"Now I must tell you that there is definitely no record of Christian here, although he has a birth certificate stating you as the mother and Mr Montgomery as his father. So, as you say you did not give birth to him, there must be a reason this certificate exists."

She took a deep breath and sat beside Felicity and gently took her hand. Felicity started to shake with fear. The blue uniform ignored that and continued.

"Do you think you husband has had an affair with another woman who did not want the child?"

Felicity stopped shaking the fear subsided, and she said, "No way! I trust him completely, he would never do that! If you knew my husband, you would know that as well."

"I only suggested that because another lady came in years ago and that turned out to be the case. She never knew he had been having an affair for years. The other woman did not want the child so gave it to him and his wife. He said he found it outside a church!"

Felicity smiled at this. "So that is not my case," she said, "and I know he is faithful to me."

"I have another suggestion, that is possible." She took a deep breath. "Do you think your husband could afford a surrogate to carry a child? This would be done by artificial insemination. Your husband the donor and a possible unknown woman who is paid quite well to carry his child."

Felicity thought about this suggestion. This was possible. "Yes, this is possible," she said to Miss Mangostein. "You know he said to me that he had made a mistake on the adoption papers. Something to do with my name. He asked me to forgive him. I would forgive him for anything; he is the sweetest man and loves Christian as much as he loves me."

"Cannot wait to take him fishing and teach him how to play football or tennis. Why these things I will never know, I suppose it is a boy thing." She smiled and relaxed. "Do we have to change the name on the birth certificate?"

"Not our department," was the answer.

"Well, I will be going," said Felicity. She had risen from the lounge and took hold of the pram. Smiling she turned and said, "Thank you for your help. I will talk to my husband about this, and I will forgive him for not telling me about the surrogate. I know he had good reason for not saying anything. Makes me love him even more, if that is possible."

She gave them a short wave as she left and headed out into the street, off to spend some time shopping, happy with her new knowledge that she had done the right thing.

Mogo came home that night and was greeted with the usual smiles, hugs and kisses. He had just finished a job for Bruiser, the bikie, and a follow on for Harris with a domestic violence bastard who bashed his wife daily after being at the pub. Harris had told him that if the wife will not leave him, then he must go as a few nights in the cells given by a magistrate would never save her life.

For Mogo to be in his wife's arms was heaven and he could see the love for him in her eyes.

After the greeting came coffee and then a catch up on what had happened while he was away. Because she thought he worked for a highly secretive government job, she never asked him about his work.

She broached the subject of going to the adoption agency. Mogo froze on the spot. He was too afraid to say anything and wondered what was coming. She told him several times that she loved him and would forgive him for his little lie. Then thanked him for paying for a surrogate so she could have Christian.

Then she added, "You know what? The lady there suggested you may have had an affair! I told her that was not possible as you loved me too much and you were an honourable man."

Mogo breathed a sigh of relief, and said, "Forgive me for not telling you but I never was sure that the surrogate would come through, and I am Christian's father even though I never touched another woman. That little room with the magazines is a nightmare!" They both laughed and hugged and then settled down while she made dinner.

Christian woke and Mogo picked him up and said to the baby, "You were worth it though." More laughter echoed through the house.

When Christian was about to go to school, Mogo had thoughts of giving up what he thought was his career.

He never wanted his boy to know what he did for a living. He could get away with a few lies with Felicity as she believed every word he said. His next move should be to set her up for life. He thought about the forty kilos of cocaine in his unit. It had been there for years so it should be safe to get rid of it now.

He would have to be careful as now money changing hands was carefully monitored by banks and the government. He was sure Harris was into drugs and prostitution so that would be a good place to start, or maybe Bruiser, the bikie, would be better. He should throw hints to both and see what happened. He had so much money at this stage, he sent a couple of million dollars to a bank in Switzerland in Christian's name. He would always be taken care of.

His solicitor knew of it and would never say anything until Mogo passed away. He also put another couple of million in Felicity's second bank account that she knew nothing of, and he had more in the English Channel Islands banks.

The taxation department was the problem. He paid tax but not the amount he should.

They did not even get the annual interest amount. Currently, people were responsible for sending in their own tax declaration information by computer. He did not have to see anyone. So, if they were not just looking up millionaires to check on, he felt he was pretty safe.

Felicity had more money than she could spend coming in weekly. Mogo did not mind as he knew she did not waste any on unnecessary stuff. Her wardrobe was not totally full of shoes or clothes and the house was nicely furnished with no clutter. Any money over went into her own bank account. He just wanted them safe if he died.

Tristan was in his office with his feet up on the desk thinking how good his life was financially, and in his way, he was happy, but he never forgot the baby he lost or his beautiful wife. He knew Christina was dead and that could never be altered but a baby body was never found, and he wondered if he was alive. If he was still alive, he would be in school now. This thought made him very sad.

Chapter 16
Arthur McDonald

A tap on the door and Arthur entered, closely behind him was Lydia. Arthur turned to Lydia and told her to wait outside. "Why?" Lydia asked.

"I have business with Tristan," he answered. She obeyed but stayed near the door.

"Tristan, may I have a word?" He asked.

"Anytime," answered Tristan.

Arthur came close to the desk and quietly asked, "May I have your permission to ask your mother to marry me?"

"Of course, call her in and ask her."

"Well, I had thought of a romantic dinner," said Arthur.

"Bugger that," said Tristan. "I want to hear her say yes."

"Ok then." He turned his head and saw her at the door and beckoned her in.

"Tristan wants to hear what you say when I ask you to marry me," said Arthur.

"That's not very romantic, this should be over dinner, but yes I will." She laughed.

"Sorry, just wanted to see my mother say yes!" Tristan said.

"Well," said Arthur. "I have booked a special table at a special restaurant for us, and I will put the ring on your finger then. Tristan, be quiet, you will not be there for that ceremony."

"Ok," said Tristan. "I will check that out tomorrow." He put his feet back on the desk as they walked out.

His phone rang and he went back to work. He had given his young and energetic salesman the day off. Sometimes he felt he worked too hard. His mind went back to Lydia and Arthur. About time he asked her. Drives her around town in the Rolls every week, just about lives with us. Yes, about time.

His mind went back to his baby son, and he picked up the phone and dialled Mendez.

Mendez answered the phone. "Yes, Mendez here."

"Tristan here, any news about the gun?"

"Funny you should call about that," said Mendez. "We did, and it is a police issue, so we are now tracking it."

"Well done," said Tristan. "Let us know what you find out." He hung up with some relief as now they would believe him after all these years.

The next day, there was much excitement in Tristan's life. A wedding to be planned a honeymoon to be organised and work was coming in fast, so busy.

Arthur had money, lots of it. He exported cattle and sheep to various countries that needed this to feed their growing population. He sold livestock and frozen meat to them all. Seemed that the livestock was most popular as refrigeration was a problem in these countries also, with livestock, they could sell it for breeding stock.

Arthur and his manager ran a tight and profitable business. These days most of it was on the internet but his manager was often on the ship to make sure the livestock arrived in good condition as they wanted no complaints about cattle cruelty or sheep mishandling.

His marriage to Lydia was a new light in his life since Christina died.

Tristan had confided in Arthur about the police reports and the fact that they had found the gun he saw the policeman with on the afternoon of her death. They were just trying to track down the gun now. They feel that it was one of their men from the Bay station so, were on to it.

Mogo sat in his unit thinking how to hide money in a different way. He had heaps in the unit as well. There was so much there he had not bothered or did not have the time to count it. He would rather be home with his family.

The drugs and how to cash them in was on his mind when the phone rang and it was Bruiser from the Bad Boys Club. He often rang with a job for Mogo, usually some small-time crook he wanted eliminated. Today was a bit different as the target was not to be spoken about on the phone and he would meet him at the coffee shop up the lane.

A time was set and they arrived a few minutes apart so as not to get the attention of anyone already there.

"The target is Phillip Harris," Bruiser whispered.

"What?" Mogo answered. "I work for him as you know so you want me to cut off my income?"

"Yeah, I suppose I do," said Bruiser. "But good reason. Harris is suspected of shooting that Paravoni woman now. They found the gun that he used on her; now you will be on the list of hitmen. the young cops will blab for sure and that is the end of you."

"Shit!" Mogo went pale. "I see what you mean. I suppose that I always use two bullets to the head means they will get me on other stuff as well."

"You had better believe it."

Mogo sat for a long time. He had to figure out a way to get Harris and should he raise the subject of the cocaine.

Bruiser sat beside him watching him think; he could almost hear his brain ticking over. What Mogo said next certainly brought him to attention.

"I have forty kilos of cocaine I can lay my hands on; are you interested?"

Bruiser was stunned. "Where did you get that?" Bruiser stuttered.

"Can't tell you that and you know better than to ask," Mogo snapped back.

"Sorry," said Bruiser.

They both sat there thinking for a while.

Mogo had to work out how to get Harris and quickly, because he was bound to get word of his pending assassination. His solution was to get him at his unit later in the night as he trusted Mogo and would open the door. Problem was he may answer the door at that late hour with a gun on his hand.

Unless he could think of something else in a hurry that would be the risk he would have to take.

Mogo approached the unit late that night, but it was a bit too late as there was no noise at all coming from the street or any other unit of the six-unit building. He really needed some noise of a television or music or cars going by that the noise could be mistaken for a car back firing. He wanted to use the pistol that was quickest to handle, lightest to use and with a silencer.

He went back to his unit and went through his arsenal of unregistered and untraceable guns. He was very proud of the way he kept them always ready for action. So, after a while, he had the one he wanted, he could hide it under his coat, and small and light enough for quick to draw and fire.

No one could beat his speed. His escape from the building and anyone who just happened to pass by to identify him should be home watching television at that time. If there was a problem, he could just make out like he was visiting Harris.

Bruiser was happy that he was about to get rid of Harris. This worked well for him as Harris was gradually taking over his turf and as he was a cop in a high place, there was nothing he could do about it. Happy that Harris had come under a cloud and Mogo would fix it for him.

Harris was also trying to take over the drug and prostitution area of Bruisers, not happy with expanding into Bruiser's protection rackets. Bruiser had expanded his young girl's project. He now purchased a motel with a restaurant and large pool also reception rooms. The elderly owners found it too much to keep up and sold it cheaply to retire.

No renovations or updates needed as it had been well cared for, the only addition was a steel fence around the swimming pool that blocked the view of the pool. Bruiser had taken to getting young homeless girls off the street. He had even put in for a government grant to throw people off the scent. The officials from the government had been out for inspections.

They were happy with the motel rooms and Bruiser explained that there would be only one girl to a room and there were thirty-five rooms. The government was happy to think that up to thirty-five young homeless girls would be off the street. The grant was approved. A large brightly coloured sign went up, 'The Little Girls'.

"We want the girls to throw off the homeless stigma and feel they were in a club like environment," Bruiser told the official and that was approved as well.

Homeless girls from twelve to sixteen years old were the only ones taken in. Once they hit seventeen, they were back on the streets. If they had been behaved as they were told to, they would be found a job in one of the brothels, and a place to stay. It started with 'bikies' only visitation place that they could come anytime.

That stopped when they started to hurt the girls. They were hitting them and Bruiser felt if the girls were being hurt, one might run back to the streets and tell someone about it. He felt the money was better if the girls had no marks or bruises on them. So, Bruiser then put it to the wealthy to pay big bucks for a visit to 'The Little Girls Club'.

The girls were dressed in the latest fashion with very short skirts and tiny tops and very small lacy underwear as well as stiletto shoes, sometimes fishnet stockings or other requests. Rooms nicely furnished, good food and a nurse to check them for sexual diseases or pregnancy. The nurse also gave them lessons in reading and writing on a Thursday afternoon. She was the nurse for the brothels that Bruiser ran and had been employed by him for over ten years.

Bruiser groomed the girls himself and any that were unsuccessful for the job were sent off and another taken to replace them. None of the wealthy men ever complained and often they stayed the night for the sum of five thousand dollars and as many girls in the room that night as he wanted. The girls were actually paid. The money went into a bank account for their future.

When the government officials were called in, the bank books were always displayed. The money paid in would be that of a low paid worker. There were regular inspections by appointment, so the girls were dressed in their school uniforms looking well cared for. Business was booming.

Bruiser took the call that said, "Mission accomplished." Bruiser smiled.

Bruiser hired two security guards. They were Italian young men who both had two Germen Shepard guard dogs, well trained and would most certainly savage an intruder. They patrolled the grounds of the ex-motel from six in the evening until six in the morning. They watched every car that came into the carpark at the back of the motel. It was fenced as the pool with steel sheeting around it and a lock at the gate.

All the expenses Bruiser had was less than the government was allotting him for the care of the girls so, the nurse, security guards and the dogs, also a friend of the nurse was in the motel restaurant to supply meals and food if required. Most of the food was re-cooked and could be heated up in the microwave. This also worked very well.

Arthur McDonald was talking to his manager and pilot for his private plane. He was expecting one of his ships to arrive overseas in port to unload some cattle. He had a new manager and pilot as the one he trusted to mind the cattle station with his wife. Did not work out well as the wife was not the honest person she was supposed to be.

Stan, the new guy, and excellent pilot for his plane and his helicopter. He was single and had no plans to have a girlfriend. They are just trouble.

Arthur was able to contact him, and the news was all good. No cattle had been hurt and all arrived in good condition on the airconditioned ship. Plenty of food for them and the crew kept them clean.

Arthur was in an excellent mood so decided to share his engagement and wedding plans with Stan. "That is great," said Stan. "I wish you all the happiness in the world." Stan paused for a second "How about I throw you a bucks party?" He suggested.

"Well, I would not say no," came the delighted answer.

"Great," said Stan. "I will organise it as soon as you tell me the date, so let me know."

"I will be in touch next week and we will set a date."

Bruiser contacted Mogo with a message to meet him in the café. Mogo presumed that it was to pay him, but it was more than that. After the money, four times the usual amount was passed over, Bruiser raised the subject of the cocaine.

"I have the outlet," Bruiser said. "Better set a price and some conditions. I recommend not to send it all at once."

"Best I trust you to do this. Just give me a time allowing for me to get it and I will supply it. How about two kilos at a time?" Mogo hesitated. "What price?" Bruiser leant over to Mogo's ear and whispered to him. Mogo's eyebrows shot up and a smile came across his face, his head nodded, and Bruiser continued to whisper in his ear.

The headlines in the paper were put in front of him while he was still waking up in bed, by Arthur. "Someone," said Arthur to Tristan, "is looking after us," he said.

Tristan could not believe his eyes. So, the hitman got Harris, he thought. Pretty sure about this because there were two shots to the head.

He turned to Arthur and said, "Arthur, are you thinking what I am thinking, that this is a job by the hitman. It seems to me that as Harris was under suspicion, he would not want Harris to identify him, and as they think the gun found in the tank was police issue from the Bay station, it looks like Harris was responsible. So, now should I see my lawyer?"

"Not just yet," Arthur replied. "Let us wait until we see what comes up first, just for a day or so. Then I will come with you. I want to be there for Christina."

Tristan nodded.

Stan Marshall was not only Arthur's pilot and manager; of his cattle station he was also looked on as a good friend of Arthur and knew Lydia quite well. Stan Marshall was also a drug dealer. He used the plane and helicopter often to deliver drugs or pick them up when he was not wanted to work for Arthur. Arthur knew Stan used the plane and helicopter for personal use but having no idea of what was going on, this never worried him. He knew Stan was an excellent pilot and would not risk the plane or helicopter.

So, because of his drug business, Stan ran into Bruiser often. Bruiser used him as a courier on pick-ups and deliveries by air. When Bruiser rang him and arranged to meet him at a small bar near his motel for little homeless girls, Stan was ready to go.

It was mid-afternoon when they met up. Stan landed the helicopter nearby in a paddock.

"So, I have forty kilos to offload good price and in two kilo plastic bags," said Bruiser.

"Ok," replied Stan. "Details please."

They worked it out and the first shipment of two kilos were to be delivered to Stan the next week when a ship was to leave for overseas, with a load of cattle. Stan was to be on that ship to escort the cattle and make sure they were well cared for by the crew.

The 'Ocean Princess' was a large ship built for the transportation of animals. Large, crated pens were in mid-ship crew's quarters, captain's quarters and the bridge were all in the bow of the ship, and in the stern were the fodder for the cattle. Bales of Lucerne hay, Stan organised the loading of the hay and always spent time on his own tying-coloured ties every so often marking the amount to be used daily on the trip for the cattle.

All the ties were different except the last two days which were always red ties. He told the crew never to touch those bales as he needed that to identify when they were running low on cattle fodder. He checked this daily, so the last bales were never interfered with.

There was always a couple of days left on every trip, so no animal went hungry. The days of hay left over were always reported to Arthur, so he knew the cattle were just fine. The amount of water left was also measured as more was used in the summertime.

Stan took his backpack down to the hold where the hay was stored and tagged for each day's ration. He went to the end at the red tag. The crew took no notice of him as he was often down there supervising. The two crew were checking the water levels as they knew Stan would check the levels before they left port.

He took out a matching piece of baling twine and placed that around the bale, then cut the tight baling twine that held the bale together, then pulled out the centre biscuit of hay fluffed it up a bit and made room for the two of the one kilo bags. Then he tied the bale tightly together again, flattened the hay around the disturbance rolled another bale on top of it, and removed the cut piece of twine.

As soon as Customs and Immigration had cleared the ship and the crew gone off on shore leave a very large limousine pulled in beside the ship, and Stan went over to meet the large Arab the struggled out of the car. The Arab nodded at Stan and followed him deep into the hold of the ship. A large canvas bag was unfolded out of the Arab's pocket and flattened out and unzipped. The bale of hay was pushed into the bag, and it was rezipped.

"For my camels," the Arab said. Stan did not answer, just nodded. The Arab left, holding the heavy bag beside him like it was full of feathers. They returned to the limousine, the Arab pushed the bag onto the backseat climbed in beside the bag and left. Stan knew he would get a phone call in about half an hour on the quality and price offered also if they wanted more of it. This was the usual procedure.

Stan received the call half an hour later asking when the next delivery could be made and a better price than he was hoping for. It must be top quality, he thought to himself.

Chapter 17
The Bay Police Station

Mendez was shocked at the Phillip Harris' shooting. His brain quickly worked out that as Harris was a suspect in the Paravoni murder that the hitman did not want a witness against him. The two bullets in the head were the same man. Harris was at his apartment's door, obviously he opened the door to someone he knew, and the time of death showed late at night when there would still be a bit of noise to cover the shots.

The hitman had guns that were unregistered and untraceable, this would show up in the forensic report. As opposed to the fact that a hitman shot the victims on that day of the Paravoni death, and the Paravoni death had a police officer suppled handgun that came from the Bay Station. Will this clear the suspected men that were supposed to be with him? This also means that the Thomas family can come out of hiding.

His next thought was would they want to. He would wait until they called him on the phone, and he would then fill them in just in case they had not seen the headlines if they were over the border.

Alan Davis was devastated. Such a good man, always ready to help him or anyone. His sergeant was dead. It was too much for him to handle. He sat at his desk with tears rolling down his face.

The other three, Bret McMillan, Roger Dixon and Barry Nicholson, headed for their lawyer's office together. They were shown chairs in front of Marty Mitchell's desk, and he walked around and sat to face them.

"Well, guys better fill me in and we will find out what bothers you to come and see me. Sounds like trouble as I am a criminal lawyer. So, tell me the truth and you know that it will go no further. So, who is going to start and tell me your story? I think as there are three of you one should start."

Bret started off their story from being asked to aid in getting rid of three or four drug dealers by Phillip Harris.

Marty interrupted saying, "The sergeant that just got himself shot?" The three of them looked at each other. "Go on," Marty said.

So, they told the story in as much detail as they could. They also told Marty about the rumours around the station that Detective Mendez was investigating.

Marty nodded and thought about what he had been told.

"Who started the rumours?" He asked.

"Don't know," they chorused.

"See if you can find out. In the meantime, I will pay a visit to the station and have a word with Mendez. If he knows, I doubt, he will tell me who it was. I will not mention any names or anything. I will check with you if I hear anything and if any of you are arrested say nothing just ask for me. Ok?"

They all nodded and filed out with worried looks on their faces.

Marty was concerned about them. Were they as innocent as they said and just wanted money? However, they did not know there was any money involved before the execution.

He rang Mendez and asked for a time to see him. While he was waiting on the phone, he cleared his desk ready for a fight if need be. Once he found out what was happening, he could attend to any impending cases, although most of them were almost under control and should not take long. If this got serious, he would have to call his brother in on it. No problems that he could see at the moment.

Mendez made a time with him for that afternoon. Marty decided he would have to be careful as he did not know how much Mendez knew.

When they met up, Mendez asked him if he would like a coffee as he needed one at that stage as he had no lunch.

Marty said that would be nice as usually it means a relaxed conversation sipping away on a coffee and they both did need to relax at that point.

Mendez did not know what Marty wanted and was a bit surprised that he wanted to talk about the death of Phillip Harris. He did not expect that at all, and he wanted to know why Marty was interested.

"Ok, Marty," said Mendez. "Just what would you like to know and why?"

"It seems there was a rumour around this police station that Harris had something to do with that missing Thomas family and the death of Christina

Paravoni. If you know who started this, I may be able to help him or her," said Marty.

"In what way?" Mendez asked.

"I would just like to talk to him as I think there maybe someone who could back him up. Sorry, that is all I can tell you for now, of course if any information relevant to the police I shall report to you immediately," explained Marty.

"I will talk to him and ask him to ring you," said Mendez. "I will do it now, just a moment." And he left the room. He rang Troy Bennet and told him the situation. Troy said he should talk to Marty, and they made a time that Marty and Troy would meet. Mendez planned to be there.

Marty was in his office when Troy came in. They shook hands and Troy was shown a chair near the desk. Marty then realised that Mendez was at the door.

"Mendez," he said, "this conversation will be private between Troy and myself. I am afraid you cannot attend."

"It is alright," said Troy. "I do not mind him being here."

"You may not mind that, but my client may object, and I feel this information apart from the name can be forwarded to Mendez later."

Mendez left the room, not happy about this situation.

After the door was shut, Troy said, "What is this about?"

Marty replied, "I have to ask you to be quiet about this because I have had three young constables very worried about their future. I think there was a fourth involved with the execution of the smith family. You had the foresight of asking the locals about what had been going on at the marina."

"Now they think the Smith family were the ones who were taken out on the boat for the burial at sea. They watched the hitman shoot the victims and search for the fourth victim. Who we now know is in hiding with her grandparents!"

"Mendez found them you know, and they ring him once a month. When they ring next time, he will fill them and make sure they know the circumstances," said Troy.

"Now the reason I do not want their names known is that the hitman who was the executer may come after them. They are witnesses to what he did. They will be easy to track down, if he knows their names."

"I understand that, but that has to come out sooner or later," said Troy.

"I think that it is a police matter now and an internal inquiry, we will wait and see. I just wanted to keep you up to date as you found the first clues and will be involved in an enquiry."

"Thanks," said Troy. "Will you represent me also if I need you?"

"Of course, that is no problem. I will keep in touch." Marty thought for a moment and then added, "You know that there was a fourth constable there that thinks that Phillip Harris could do no wrong."

"I know who that could be," said Troy. "He was basically Harris' pet. He did charity work for him, BBQs with him and really looked after him and his family. Alan adored him."

"What was his name?" Marty asked.

"Alan Davis, always taking Harris' coffee and hanging around him. You could not miss it."

"Ok," said Marty. "when he finds out what really happened, he may need me and the others."

He showed Troy to the door where Mendez was waiting, and they all shook hands, and Mendez and Troy left while Marty stood at the door wondering what was going to happen to those young constables. This could end their career or send them to jail. He would contact Superintendent Harvey, Troy's stepfather.

Mendez was keen to find out the reason Troy was asked to meet with Marty and who else was involved. Troy was waiting for it, the question from Mendez so he jumped in first.

"Marty knows who was involved with this execution. The reason the names will not be revealed is that they are afraid of the hitman that did the job. Word soon gets around a station like ours and the hitman would soon find out who was there. I think he already knows what they look like but if he knew their names, he could get their addresses and find them and their families fast."

"Marty wants to talk to the police internal enquiries and see what they say. He feels they would get a better and lesser punishment. He also wants to talk to Superintendent Harvey about the danger to Troy involving the hitman."

Mendez understood and went quiet.

Mendez thought about this hitman and how he could find him. He was not sure where to start. The facts were that the constables were not armed, Harris was, now that fact had come clear. The unarmed constables must have been thinking this was ok to go to an execution, why? Did Harris have something over them?

Harris must have been friends with the hitman. Best I start with the friends of Harris as someone must know who Harris hangs about with. He decided he should first start with Constable Alan Davis. Then he thought that the Thomas family, although were afraid of him, may know his friends and they were due to ring him. Mendez made some notes.

Did the three young constables have a description of the hitman or did he wear a balaclava or mask. The phone rang and he answered it, waited for a moment for the caller to speak. It was Bill Thomas. "Read the paper," he said. "Is that true, is he really dead?"

"Yes, he is," replied Mendez. "Looks like he was shot by his hitman. Also, we have more information about your daughter and grandson. We think they were executed and put on a boat for burial at sea. Hope this does not distress you too much but at least you know what happened."

"We have four constables here who we believe were present at the time. They were unarmed so they will be referred to police headquarters. We need to find that hitman, so can you tell me if you know of any friends of Harris or anyone you may have seen him with at any time?"

"No," said Bill. "I never knew him at all. We did not know he was in the Bay until Marilyn saw him there at the station. The fact that he was a policeman shook her as he was in the Airforce up north. We never saw him up there as we thought he mistreated Marion and he hated the kids."

"You may have just given me a clue," said Mendez. "What do you now about him in the Airforce? And where exactly was he stationed and when he was there?"

"Well, let me think about that for a minute. Marilyn may know more so, I will hang up and see what she knows and ring you back. Maybe our girl used to confide in her mother more than me. Marion used to tell her a lot about her life with him, but it was never passed on to me. I will get back to you as soon as I can."

Mendez hung up and had much more to think about. He was wondering if the hitman was in the Airforce too. Maybe someone up there knew them both and the connection. If only he could put the two of them together, he would get somewhere.

Bill Thomas rang back sooner than he expected. He had lots of information about Harris. The time and date and address in the Airforce compound. Two of his friends' phone numbers and addresses, his superior's names and the fact that he was often sent overseas to work for months at a time. Harris had organised to be there for the birth of his children, and both times had walked out of the hospital because they were not good looking enough babies.

One thing that did come across in this was the fact that everyone in the Airforce that he knew thought he was the greatest guy that ever lived. Mendez was very happy with this information and applied for leave to follow it up. Leave was granted.

He would take three days to get there, unknown time to find and interview his friends, then drive three days to get back to the Bay. He was not sure what to pack as this would be an unknown amount of time. If all went well, he would not be too long and then he could get back to continue his investigation at the other end back in the Bay.

Next problem was if he had the name of the hitman, where would he be? Not the Bay or in the Bay? Maybe the friends, if he found them, would have some idea. At least he had somewhere to start looking.

His first night stop was a motel that was close to the highway and was noisy, but it was clean and had ice in the small refrigerator. The next night, there was no motel, just a hotel and only one at that. It had a small room and all that was in a motel, so he thought it could be alright; however later when all the patrons came in, the situation changed. Gradually the noise got louder, the more they had to drink the louder it got.

By midnight, he had enough and left. He promised himself he would have an early night when he arrived at his destination, hopefully by the end of the daylight. He made it as the light was fading and he was able to find a large motel and ask for a room out the back away from the road noise. The one he was given was just what he wanted, so informed them he could be staying awhile so please keep that room available. They were happy to do that.

The next day, he went searching for the friends of Harris. The first one had moved to another Airforce base, so he went on to the second friend and found him on the base in the jet plane repairs hanger. He asked for Clive Jones. The call echoed around the hanger and a fellow appeared from behind the wing. He was an older man but had a smiling face, and walked up to Mendez with his handout stretched.

He introduced himself as Clive Jones and asked how he could help him. Mendez introduced himself as Detective Mendez and he was investigating the death of Phillip Harris. "Oh My God!" A shocked Clive Jones yelled. "What happened to Phil!" He was devastated.

Méndez replied that he would have thought as it was in the national papers, he would have known and was sorry if he shocked him with the news. He went on to explain that Phil had been shot and explained that they thought that he was shot by someone he knew. "Not me," Clive said angrily.

"He was my best friend. I loved that guy, he helped me with lots of stuff and my wife. She just thought the world of him he was so good to her and my kids. Played with them in our backyard and we had BBQ's nearly every weekend. The kids loved to see Phil, always had gifts for them he was an amazing man, I am not the only one he helped everyone. We trusted him with everything. No one on this base would hurt him I can tell you that!"

"Your name was given to me as his best friend, so you are not on my list of suspects.," Mendez lied. "What I want is you to tell me who else did he have close contact with, they may be able to help. I had to start with someone, unfortunately it was you! Now can you help me find out who shot Phil?"

"What do you want to know?" Clive said calming down.

"Well, as he was everyone's friend, did he have any hobbies or sport he liked to play, go to the gym, anyone off the Airforce base that I could ask a few questions; anyone who had a grudge that he thought he had settled with an apology? Just trying to get some clue as to where to start."

"Well let me think on that," Clive said. He turned his head and looked back into the hanger. "No, I don't think so but you can ask Malcom; he did meet up with him on the odd occasion. I never asked where they; went none of my business. They used to just wander off somewhere." He turned the other was and yelled out Malcom as loud as he could.

A man appeared from around the hanger side and headed over to them. Hand outstretched and Mendez stepped forward to greet him. "Hey," said Malcom, "need anything?"

Mendez replied, "Yes, I am Detective Mendez and I need information. Do you have a minute?"

Mendez headed off in another direction to leave Clive behind as he did not want him to hear this. When he felt he was far enough away, he told Malcom of the Harris' death and asked him a few questions. Then he asked, "Where did you go with Harris on the days you headed off the base? Sometimes he called in here at the hanger and picked you up."

Malcom hesitated and dropped his head down to look at the ground. "Do I have to tell you? I really would like to keep this private, don't want it to get out. I am ashamed about it."

"Better tell me, it will go no further, so nobody else knows about it. Just the two of you?"

"Ok, but please don't let this get out."

"No, it will not get out." Mendez was curious about this and wondered what was coming. He was ready to expect anything at this stage Malcom lowered his head further. "Well, a year before Phil left, I went home after consuming a bottle of rum. I had never done this before and was late home and my dinner was not on the table. As usual I did not look in the oven where it was."

"I was so angry that I beat my wife up so badly I put her in hospital with broken teeth and nose, black eyes and a broken arm. Can you believe she forgave me, and dropped the charges? Police said they would too as I had never done that before. Because she dropped the charges, I said it would never happen again and I joined AA and anger management classes."

"Phil took me to the classes so I would not change my mind and not go. After Phil left here, I continued classes though. My wife still loves me and I love her right back. I am sober for life, I can tell you."

Mendez said, "You are a good man," and Malcom smiled and brought his head up.

"Can you help me with anything Phil may have done to make someone shoot him?" Mendez asked. "Seems like he was everyone's friend."

"He was popular because he helped the guys with anything, even money and then tell them it was not a loan it was gift. He bought them new refrigerators and washing machines, whatever they were in trouble with. He had the most beautiful wife and two kids. Oh man was his wife beautiful!

"However, none of the men on the base ever approached her out of respect for Phil. He did have another friend; he did not work here. I think he knew him from their service overseas, not sure though. They used to meet up at the shooting range for practice. He often told me how his aiming with a pistol was better than a rifle."

"He did not say rifle though, I think he said sniper gun or something like that. I was never in that sort of thing, I hate guns. Phil's death is another reason to hate them."

"I can understand that," said Mendez. "You are being very helpful; can you get time off for a coffee and we can chat a bit more?" Mendez felt if he chatted more with Malcom, he could get more information.

Malcom gave a wave at the hanger and got a wave back from somewhere and nodded at Mendez, and they set off. Malcom knew where there was a quiet coffee shop and it was before the lunch rush, so they headed there. After ordering, they sat at a small table for two and relaxed.

"You have been very helpful," said Mendez. "So do you know anything else he may have been into. Seems Phil was a busy man helping the staff at the Airforce base."

"They sent him overseas a lot sometimes for months. He used to bring back little things for our kids but his were never around with anything new. Made me and the others wonder a bit. They never had anything new come to think of it, his wife either. Other wives would mention that she was in the secondhand shop that day or last week."

"I think they felt sorry for her as Phil would have made more money than they did, you do for living way from home. Marion drove an old bomb of a car that should not have even been on the road. He had a fancy job that was locked up in the garage. And I bet she did not have a key as that door was never open. I have only seen that flash expensive job once when we called in on the way to AA as he forgot something."

"They lived in a house on the base opposite the hangers, so he just had to walk over the road to work. Then all the time he was away, he had no use for the car. Never saw her in it." He thought for a while and said, "He had another friend too off the base. He spoke of him a bit as he was in a wheelchair; ex Airforce, I think. He used to cut the grass for him and his wife. Always doing good for others. I feel for his family though."

With coffee over, Mendez said, "You have been a great help and I cannot thank you enough for that. By the way, his mate at the shooting range, would you know his name or where he lives?"

Malcom thought for a minute. "I think it was Steven but he called him a short nickname, 'Monty' or something. Can't remember, it has been a while you know."

"Yes, I know," said Mendez. "You have been very helpful, more than you realise. So, thank you very much. Here is my card should you think of anything or get any information off your friends as you all seemed to like him."

They parted with a handshake and a smile. Malcom went in the direction of work and Mendez headed for the shooting range wherever that was. The coffee shop waitress pointed in a vague direction. He found it ok as it was signed at every turn on the street corners.

Large colourful signs out the front of the carpark and plenty of room to park. He jumped out of the car and headed for the office. He asked for the manager and explained who he was and why he was there. The manager went to get the records from the archives as it as not a recent enquiry so would not be in the office with current members records.

"What name was it again?" The manager asked.

"Actually, there are two names one is Phillip Harris, and the other is Steven, and the last name is a puzzle but something like Monty," said Mendez.

"Oh!" The manager said, his eyes lit up. "You mean Steven Montgomery, our champion for a long time. Sorry to lose him, won a lot of trophies, used to go into competition with Phillip. Steve always won though."

"Would you know where I could find Steve?"

"Not a clue," said the manager. "But he left soon after Phillip. I believe Phillip went down south so would not be surprised if Steve went with him. I believe Steven had a nickname too, but do not think it was Monty but something similar. If I could think of it, could make it easier to find him. Give me a minute."

The manager went over to a couple of members of the club they pointed to someone else who did the same. The manager stopped the next group of members, started nodding and then returned to Mendez.

"Old Joe knew it. The nickname was Mogo." The manager seemed quite pleased with himself. However, no one knew where either of them had gone. The phone rang in another room and the manager excused himself.

Mendez went over to 'old Joe' and introduced himself, and asked if he could join him for a chat. Joes face lit up and pointed to a chair for Mendez pull up. Mendez thought maybe Joe was lonely, he was so keen. But not so, Joe wanted to give him more information and was ready to talk for an hour to fill in his day.

"I hear you knew Steven and Phillip," said Mendez. "Want to fill me in?" Old Joe smiled and began his news.

"I knew them both well," began Joe. "I used to watch them compete, don't think they knew." He chuckled away. "Mogo was the best, but he always fired two shots into the target and Phil would only shoot one. Phil used to go off at Mogo for wasting bullets; quite funny really as he used to say fire two to make sure. Phil would say one should do it if you hit the head in the right place."

"The two of them worked overseas together then Mogo got sick of that, said he wanted a home and settle down. He said it was alright for Phillip, he had a wife and kids, so he wanted the same. Then Phil lost his wife, she left him. So, Phil left the Airforce and joined the police force. He went up the ladder there fast."

"Did not take long for him to become a sergeant and he headed off to the Bay. He told me that is where he has going. Said there was a station there that he had applied for and they accepted him. He was very happy about that. I don't know why though."

"So, tell me about Mogo," said Mendez. "How did they know each other?"

"Well as far as I know, they met overseas that is why the guns I suppose."

"Do you think that Mogo went to the Bay with him?" Mendez asked.

"Well," replied Joe. "They were always together so would not be surprised."

Mendez handed Joe a card as he stood up. "Thanks, Joe, you have been a great help."

Mendez headed for the door, turned to wave to Joe who looked disappointed that he left.

He headed back to the motel so he could sit and think in peace. If so called Mogo was in the bay, he was not sure how he would find him. He had done all he could do here; it was a successful trip he felt sure this Mogo had shot the family and Harris had shot Christina Paravoni while or after the execution of the Smith family.

He would head south in the morning and not stop at the town that had the hotel.

Back at the station three days after, he rang Paul Harvey. He wanted Troy there as well. Paul was glad to see him. He greeted Troy glad to see he was there.

"I have news I think is fact. I found out about Phillip Harris and his home life, about his friends and his Gun Club Shooting skills. I also found out about his shooting practice buddy who could beat him in competition and the fact that the shooting buddy. aka Steven Montgomery, always fires two shots."

"So, I am having a good guess that this Mogo was the executioner and Harris shot the Paravoni girl outside in the yard with his handgun. The constables at the scene will verify that. They did not see it but heard a shot and there was no dead dog at the scene as Harris said. Ok, so now my concern is if this Mogo gets wind of this and that there are four constables at the scene and one at the boat salvage all with knowledge of the execution are in danger. Although, we don't know where this Mogo is."

Mogo was in his unit surrounded with money and the last of the cocaine that was going that night. He had no idea they were trying to find him. He would exchange the drugs for money that night and then go home to his love. He could not wait to hold her and gaze at his schoolboy son asleep in his bed. His next day's school uniform laid out ready for when he woke up.

Felicity was an amazing mother. He decided that tomorrow he would contact Bruiser and see if he wanted or knew someone who wanted to buy his untraceable guns. He was going to retire and spend the rest of his life caring for his little family. He had plenty of money to do whatever they wanted.

He made a time to see his lawyer, Jonathon Mitchell, to get some of his affairs in order. Jonathon welcomed him into his office and showed him a chair. Mogo explained that he wanted his will altered as he had a unit that he wanted his wife to inherit.

"What can I do for you, Steven?" He asked.

"I want to include a unit I have had for a while into my will to go to my wife."

Jonathon tuned to his computer and looked for the will of Steven Montgomery. He found it quickly and said, "You left her the house and now you want to leave her a unit."

Mogo replied, "Right, and there is money in the unit. She is to have that as well. We have a young boy and he needs his mother to take care of him and see he gets everything he needs."

"Well, it will all go to her anyway if the money is in the unit and I will include the contents of the unit as well. Anything else?"

"Yes, there a motorbike in the garage and any car I own."

"Well, they are all your assets, they should all be covered in the will."

"The money is important as I know that legal things take a while to go through. Probate seems to hold up heaps of things. I had to wait for ages to get my parents' money."

"Ok," said Jonathon. "Give me a list of everything and I will itemise it all, so you are happy. Keep in mind that as next of kin, she will inherit everything anyway."

Mogo sat there as Johnathon went through his last will and made notes of the unit address and bike make and registration, that made his eyebrows shoot up.

Mogo gave him an amount of money but not the true amount in the unit and seemed happy with what the new will would contain. He then asked Jonathon how long before he had to come back and sign the new will. He was asked if he could wait as he was already on the computer, he would have it printed, and he could sign and not have to return.

While Mogo was waiting to sign the new will, his mobile phone rang. He answered and heard Bruiser say, "Coffee shop now!"

Jonathon seemed to be forever getting this new will drawn up and he just wanted to leave for the coffee shop. Finally, he returned and Mogo signed it. He thanked Jonathon, shook his hand and just about ran out of his office. Wishing he had come on his motor bike and not the car.

On arrival, he parked the car a good distance away as usual. The supermarket car park was always a good place, so many cars around no one should take any notice of his.

Quick walk to the filthy laneway, picked his way through the bins and saw Bruiser through the dirty windows. Glad to get in away from the smell outside. Bruiser pointed to the only chair available beside him and said, "I have heard rumours about you."

Mogo froze to the spot and then said, "What rumours?"

"Seems that stories are going around the local cop shop that you are a wanted man. The words were a hitman shot the three of them and polished off Harris." He continued, "I don't think they know, your name that was not mentioned."

"Do you know anything else?" Mogo said, "or should I just lay low for a while?"

"I know heaps," said Bruiser.

"Fill me in," said Mogo.

"Well, as I have heard that there are four young constables that have been found to have attended the execution of those three drug dealers who were not dealers at all. It was just a family, so Harris lied to you. Another young fellow was on duty when the boat that was used for the burial at sea was salvaged, and he chatted to the locals and found out heaps. Three of the young fellows got together and found out they were conned; however the other one believes that Harris could do no wrong so, defends him.

Three of them have seen a lawyer and I think he is referring them to the police internal investigators. Now, my concern is that I do not want them to get on to you because I need you, and I think they will as that smart arse detective has been up north looking for you; think he got some information."

Mogo sat listening and Bruiser thought he could hear the wheels turning in his brain. Mogo said nothing for quite a while. He straightened himself in the chair. "Looks like I had better disappear for a while then."

"Good idea. And when you return, contact me. Or better keep in touch."

Mogo jumped up from the chair. "How long have I got to disappear?"

"Not long I would say," returned Bruiser.

"Ok, I am off," said Mogo. "Thanks for the tip." He walked out as if there was no hurry and drove to the unit.

Mogo made the unit ready for him to leave. Packed his guns carefully in the big steel box in their correct places and locked them down. Put the ammunition in their boxes and place then in the area made for them. Then locked the box with a doble lock system. He packed and counted the money in several boxes.

He had no idea where he should stash it but decided in the top cupboards in the kitchen. No one should enter his unit while he was away, it should be safe here. He had no way to get his motor bike into his unit, but it would be safe in the garage. He hung up his clothes neatly in the walk-in robe and shoes placed in a row on the floor.

Wiped down everything in the kitchen and bathroom, door handles and window locks. He had all his expenses for the unit on direct debit at the bank so he would never owe anything. Finances taken care of. He went out to his car and home to his wife and Christian.

He had texted Felicity and informed her he was on his way and had a surprise for her. He went into the house and the two most precious lives in the world to him and hugged them tightly.

"Hey, my darlings, I have something special to tell you," he yelled happily. "Come and sit down on the couch and I will explain it to you, so listen carefully." Christian pushed himself between Felicity and Mogo to get closer to him. Mogo smiled.

"Ok, it is like this. My government department has given me a lot of time off work. I have long service leave and holiday leave and sick leave days that I have never taken as I never have a day off work and they want me to take this time off from tomorrow. So, I think we should take a trip; what do you think?"

Christian piped up. "What about my school?" He was very bright at schoolwork and Mogo did not want him to miss any.

Mogo said, "I thought of that we shall take a tutor for you that will teach you your schoolwork just the same."

Felicity could not stop smiling. "This is a dream," she said.

Mogo hugged her tight. "We will go overseas and discover the world."

"When can we leave?" She asked.

"As soon as we can get everything sorted. You do have a passport, don't you?"

"No and what about Christian?" She looked concerned.

"We can get a passport in twenty-four hours for emergency, and we can put Christian on yours or mine. I would prefer yours as you are mother," said Mogo. "Let me make a phone call and then we will know." Mogo left the room with his mobile for a long time. "Ok," he said. "I will go and get the forms and while you take Christian and get passport photos."

Both headed off on their missions. When they returned, Mogo had the forms and she had the photos. They sat and filled out the forms, photos attached and signed, and Mogo took them in to explain any questions they may have, and he was totally relieved when they said come back in twenty-four hours. He smiled and nodded and thought, "It's not what you know, it is who you know."

Passports picked up the next day and off to the travel agency to plan a trip and leave the next day. Mogo hoped this was quick enough.

"Don't pack much, we are buying new clothes as we go as the weather could change and we do not know what we need." Felicity thought that was a waste of money but complied, and the next day they flew off to see Disney Land as Christian had asked for as first stop. Next on the list was a tutor for Christian and his world was in order. He had enough money to travel forever and give his family the best of everything.

Chapter 18
Bruiser

Bruiser was a murderous thug who happened to like motor bikes. With a drug addled set of parents and five siblings, it was amazing that he survived. On the street at the age of seven, stealing food to survive and rarely sharing it with his brothers and sisters, he managed to learn street smart early and was pleased that he grew tall and muscular so he could push anyone around.

He had stolen his clothes as well by just putting what he wanted in a bag and walking out. He was rarely challenged at the door but the look of defiance that was aimed at anyone was enough to back off and leave him go. They knew if the police grabbed him, he would be back for revenge.

When he was a lot younger, he would put on filthy torn clothes and steal just a pair of shorts so the shop attendants would look away and not do anything as they felt so sorry for him. He had it all under control.

At sixteen, he stole his first motor bike. Police caught up with him; unregistered, uninsured, no helmet, no license. First offence so no charges and got off with a warning. He took a lesson from that made sure the motor bike had a registration plate and a helmet on the handle. Keys in the lock, owner in the shop it was in front of.

He headed for the hills to a small town where no-one would know him and parked it in the back street while he went into the main street to get some food. He had managed lately to pick a few pockets so could pay for food now.

He went to the next town and repeated that procedure. It worked well but then he saw a bigger motor bike that looked a lot faster than his. He thought about this and returned to the bike in the back street he had stolen and took off the plates. He returned to the bigger bike in the main street and looked for the owner.

There was no-one in sight so he must be in a shop or store further along to road. He pulled out his pocketknife and sat beside the bike then fitted the knife in the slot. The screw turned easily and fell out on the number plate, and then he repeated this, so the plate fell off. Still no-one in sight. He then replaced the plate with his own.

Still no-one in sight except for a woman pushing a pram up the top end and could not see what was happening. He jumped on the bike tried the keys from the other bike and it started. He headed off around the corner and hid it in the bushes of a house that looked deserted. Then he strolled back to the main road to see what had happened.

A young fellow was running up and down the street in a panic. Bruiser approached him and asked the problem. The young woman with the pram walked down to see what was wrong. She told him that she had not seen anyone near the bike in the street and if she had, she would have thought the owner was riding it.

The young fellow was really upset and panicking, so Bruiser said did he see which way he went, and as the fellow could not speak properly, he pointed in the direction that Bruiser had taken the bike.

Bruiser had a suggestion for him. "I have a motor bike at my place you can borrow, I will bring it around and you can chase him up." He did not mention that the bike was unregistered.

"You would do that for me," the young fellow said.

"Sure, just wait there." Bruiser raced around the corner and mounted the bike and returned to him.

The young guy mounted the bike and took off to see if he could find his bike. The lady with pram told Bruiser what a good soul he was. Bruiser headed back to the newly stolen bike and headed in another direction. His next project was to get a legal motor bike and a license. Next plan was to sell the newly stolen bike to get there.

There was a motor bike shop in the next local town. He headed there. Walking into the shop, he saw his first Harley Davidson and he smiled and knew that what was he wanted. The price was proudly displayed on a card on the seat. He looked for the salesman with an idea in mind.

His first idea was that he would like to trade in his bike for the Harley. So that was ok, and a price was suggested and accepted, so next step was the salesman looking at his bike to see if it was what Bruiser had described. It was, so back in the office for the paperwork. Bruiser looked much older than his sixteen years and had a fat wallet the salesman noted. The fact that it was full of stolen money did not occur to him.

Bruiser asked if he could test drive the Harley and the salesman agreed that would be a good idea. Together they wheeled it out of the showroom, Bruiser mounted it and took off, loving it. The salesman returned to his post in the showroom and wheeled Bruisers' trade in out the back for the mechanic to assess what was needed to put it in the showroom for secondhand section for sale. Then they discovered that the trade in bike had no number plates.

Bruiser got his nickname from the fact that he was a thug and if he did not like you because of what you said, you would soon be covered in bruises. He was at peace and kept riding until midnight. In the morning after sleeping by his bike in a cow paddock, he found himself in the Bay.

His first thought was he had to make this bike legal, so cruised around the bay looking for another Harley so he could swap plates. Took a while before he found one, but the owner was nearby. He stalked him for the day until he left the bike on the side of the road and went into a diner.

Bruiser saw him through the window and found that he could not see the bike from that position, and he had left the bike between two four-wheel drive vehicles that were very large. The pocketknife as the screwdriver trick worked easily and plates swapped within seconds.

He felt he should skip town quickly, but he liked the place; the beach, the coffee shops and the tourists busy little place to get lost in.

His family would never care where he was, so it did not matter where he settled for a while. To his surprise, he got a job!

He liked his job because it gave him a social contact with men who could feed him information on what was going on in town, and the surrounding area. He also learned the art of bricklaying. He never rode the bike to work, he left it at the small studio apartment that one of his co-workers managed to get him. There was a small shed came with it so, the bike was locked up in there.

The work was good and outside where he liked it, money in his pocket and his Harley in the shed ready for night-time rides. Yes, life was good, and he felt it had turned around. He was happy and the guys he worked with liked him and all were friendly.

It was a pleasantly warm night with a gentle breeze drifting across the bay from the southeast. He sat on the sand enjoying the night when a voice behind him startled him.

“Like your bike,” the voice said.

“Me too,” replied Bruiser.

“Want to make some money with it?” The voice said.

Bruiser did not bother to look around until this stage to see who he was talking to. The voice came back strongly. “Don’t look at me,” it said. “Or the deal is off.”

Bruiser turned his head back to the waves. “Ok,” he replied. “What’s the go?”

“Interested in some delivery work,” said the voice.

“Delivering what?”

“Oh! you know little white parcels.”

“What’s the pay?” Bruiser said. He was feeling excited about this. In on the drug trade excited him, that made big money and he wanted to be in on it.

“You could just about name your own price,” he said, “and the work is as night and permanent.”

“Can I think about it?” Bruiser said.

“Ok, meet me here same time tomorrow and no tricks,” said the voice.

Bruiser heard the man scramble away and thought he heard someone else scramble away with him. So, he had backup and how many were there. He never heard any form of transport, so no car or motorbike, pushbikes? He sat thinking for a while and feeling tired mounted his bike and headed back to his small apartment.

He spent what was left of the night dreaming of making piles of money and lots of excitement making getaways and being chased by the cops while on his Harley and they never caught him of course. Drugs were the answer to a lot of money, but he had to check out this guy who would not face him and had backup.

The sun came up as usual in the morning and he headed off for work and had a spark in his step, feeling good, and greeted his mates with enthusiasm. Nobody noticed any difference in him as they set about the days’ work. He was happy holding his secret and looking forward to a new adventure and probably making his Harley legal or just buy a new one.

He had his motor bike and thanks to a member of the crew, his car’s driver’s license. He was eighteen years old the next day.

He sat on the beach again, weather the same warmth and gentle breeze no rain forecast. He waited for the voice it did not come at the same time, but he waited. He was starting to get impatient when the voice came. He did not turn around.

"Got your backup tonight?" Bruiser said. The question went unanswered.

"You made a decision," said the voice.

"I'm in," said Bruiser.

"Good lad," said the voice. "Thought you would be so, have your first delivery here. You will have to remember the address as nothing goes on paper got that?"

"Right," said Bruiser.

"They are expecting you," said the voice. Time place and description of the recipient was given. Instructions to wear his full-face helmet and his leathers as well. "Make sure you have a full tank of fuel as that was our last guy's big mistake. He ran out on a chase and cops got him. But he did not spill his guts so we were safe, anyway he could not identify us either."

A bag of white powder fell into Bruiser's lap. He did not know which direction it came from.

"Meet here tomorrow night same time for your pay," said the voice and he heard the scuffling in the sand and grasses as more than one of them scuttled off. Bruiser realised they may not know what he looked like either. They did know his Harley though.

The following night, Bruiser was there, and the voice was heard, and an envelope of money came over his shoulder. He grabbed it and emptied it into his hand. More than a week's pay.

"Ready for another drop," said the voice.

"Right," said Bruiser. His brain took in the place, description of the recipient and time. All different to the last drop. This time it was an address of a very wealthy area of very large homes, most of them palace like to Bruiser.

"If you do this right for week, we can up your drops if you want," said the voice as another bag fell into his lap.

Bruiser did not answer and made no move to get up until the scuttling had stopped and he thought about the money he had made in a short time for one delivery.

This procedure went on for the rest of the week. Bruiser hid the payments in his small apartment. It made him feel good to have spare cash laying around. His wages were reasonable, and he managed to save a bit as his rent was low but he did not cook and went to takeaways most days.

He kept his expenditure the same as a big spend may lead to suspicion as to where the money came from. He was lucky he had never been pulled over by the cops or he would be in trouble. Still, he felt he could outrun them.

The next week, the process with the deliveries doubled. He was more alert and careful as he had a lot to remember as that doubled the information he had to follow. The pay packet doubled too, so he was excited about that.

Bruiser continued with this delivery service for one year, he remembered because this started on his birthday. Now he was nineteen and wanted more of everything. He had studied the tones of the voice so knew that if he heard it anywhere else, he would not let on that he knew who it was but take notes and maybe stalk him, so he had more information on him.

He was always on alert when in the street or any gathering as luck happened, he heard him at the Bad Boys Motor bike club that he had just joined. He was sure of the tone and manner of speech as soon as he heard him. The voice showed no recognition of Bruiser he was sure of that. So now to work his way up in the club and be the boss. That was the next ambition.

Grog, guns, drugs and women were what it was all about. Who had the best and fastest bike, who took the most risks and survived it, who had spent the most time in the slammer was also on the list, the most tattoos were not high on the scale? The cops could identify you by your tattoos and had photographic records of them. Very handy if you would not give them your name.

Bruiser did not have any tattoos as he felt they were incriminating and identifying if they got arrested or under suspicion of a crime. He was the only clean skin in the club and planned to keep it that way. He also had never been arrested and planned to keep that the same way as well.

From his first night at the club, he planned to take it over and be the leader. He had heard on the grape vine that the club had a protector. Bit of insurance by the name of Phillip Harris. So, he made time to see him and make sure he was the guy to see about continuing his protection and what else he had under his protective wing. He also wanted to know who protected him.

He had only been in the club for a week when he made the call and asked to see him, but not at the station. Was there anywhere would be more suitable? He received directions to a coffee house but not the one Harris usually went to. Harris wanted to check him out first. The meeting was successful. Bruiser introduced himself as second in command of the Bad Boys bikie club.

Harris knew this was not true but said nothing. After a talk with this youngster, he knew he would be the leader very soon. He listened to Bruiser's spiel and told him that they would meet again soon at a different coffee shop and told him how to get there and the coffee was good.

They met up a week after up the lane coffeeshop. Bruiser stepped between the smelly rubbish bins and what looked like dead rats and unwanted junk that had been thrown in there. Careful where he stepped because Bruiser had been able to lift himself up and was clean and neat; a long way from how he was kept as a child. In fact, he thought he had developed a fashion sense. Harris was waiting.

After exchanging greetings, Harris ordered coffee and Bruiser was happy in the coffee shop as the aroma was delightful and took away the stench from outside that lingered in his nose.

"I think we can help each other," Bruiser started. "I know a drug runner in the Bay, and you can grab him, make you look good."

"And what do you want in return?" Harris said.

"A hitman," replied Bruiser.

"Tell me what you know first," said Harris.

"Ok, there is a drug runner in the bikie club. I know all the address and descriptions of nightly deliveries over the past year. I can give you all that information. The drug that they were dealing in is cocaine."

"Now that is a prize for me," said Harris. "How do you know all this information? Were you the delivery man, Bruiser?"

Bruiser did not answer, just smiled.

"So, who did you want eliminated? The leader of the pack?"

"That's right, but he is also the drug runner."

"Do you have any idea how to work this as I cannot arrest him if he is dead."

"I was thinking you could get the others and let him sweat as you get closer."

"I have a better idea," said Harris. "I will have him eliminated. You will not have to pay for the hitman. I can fix this. I can arrest him and have him done in. I get the prize and you get the job you want. My hitman only likes to eliminate the bad guys, I get 'mates' rates'; deal done. Now some names and addresses please."

Harris could not believe he had confided in Bruiser but felt they could do well together. He sat there patiently while Bruiser made up the list of nineteen drug dealers and their ringleader.

"I know a lot of these guys, suspected, but could never prove it. Well done."

Bruiser collected his motor bike, mounted it and rode it home, locked it in the shed and went into his kitchenette to make coffee and wished it was as good as the coffee shop up the lane.

He slept well that night and so did Harris.

The next day, the 'voice' was found dead at the front door of his house, two bullets in his forehead. This was sooner than Bruiser expected but Harris must have wanted it that way.

As the Bad Boys Bikie Club had no leader, he put himself forward and was voted in. The Bad Boys were back in business. Bruiser laid out his plans for drug dealing, setting up or buying two brothels to start with. The members put in their ideas, some good some bad, but at the end of the meeting, they were all happy about the result. Bruiser was their champion.

Within six months, he had the brothels running legally in an area that was industrial factories only. The police and council approved of this set up. Harris as sergeant had it approved, and he was their protection for more money than before. Not that he needed it.

Then Bruiser contacted Harris about Billy, the bastard, who was sleeping with an underage girl. Harris introduced him to Mogo. It was the perfect time to do it as the court would give a light sentence to Billy. Harris had a good reason to tell Mogo of the problem with Billy and hook him up to Bruiser. It was up to Bruiser to pay Mogo, his one hundred thousand bucks.

Bruiser was happy to do that. It meant he would not have to do any of that dirty work. The execution was done.

The money rolled in for Bruiser. He kept his club members under control mainly by his size.

***

Stan Marshall was a bad man and a con man and every other sort of nasty anyone could think of. He had charm that could get him anything he wanted and talk men into doing bad things for him as well. He was very good at this, so he took advantage of it.

His charm and experience of flying helicopters and small airplanes got him the job with Arthur McDonald. This also gave him a good reason to run drugs and get in with the drug lords flying cocaine and other addictive drugs all over the world via planes and ships with McDonald's aircraft. Arthur McDonald trusted him and let him use the aircraft whenever he wanted to if it did not interfere with the helicopter duties rounding up cattle on his station, the management of the station, check fences or his trips back to his station from the Bay, sometime including Lydia who was now his fiancé.

Stan Marshall was looking to extend his money-making ventures and as he had a motor bike for when he was in the Bay, kept in the aerodrome hanger when not there, he went to visit the biggest Motor Bike club in the Bay and met up with equally bad boy, Bruiser. The best thing about it was that Bruiser had an outlet and Stan had a way to get it overseas via a ship.

Teamwork. Stan would fly wherever the ship was and tell McDonald that he was checking his cattle was being shipped in the correct manner, and that really pleased McDonald to think that Stan would do that without even being asked, even checking where the fodder was stored in the hold in the ship. Stan would ring McDonald and tell him if all was well, or the water or fodder was not enough. He even checked the air conditioning was working for the cattle on board.

This was a big load off McDonald's mind and a big lump of cash in Stan's pocket. Stan liked animals so he was happy to do this, and he liked being boss in the ship yelling at the crew who had not checked these important supplies to keep the cattle healthy and arrive in good condition, so McDonald's name was well up the list for export quality.

Stan had been told by Bruiser about his motel and invited to visit there. Stan knew what was going on there and flew over it in the helicopter checking the position and security. The motel was set off the main highway and a tree lined drive that was a good distance from the highway. This ran into a carpark surrounded by trees and a steel sheeting fence with a gate to match.

No one in this area at this hour in the morning. He flew over the swimming pool that was the same sort of layout. Trees around the fence line and inside the fence also the steel sheeting. The gate was hard to see as it blended in with the fence line. It looked like strings of lights draped over the pool for night-time entertainment.

He looked at the main building that seemed to be in good repair, the signs of 'The Little Girls Club' were bright and colourful, easy to see except from the highway.

He planned to make a time with Bruiser to visit the motel as soon as he could as he could maybe use this as entertainment for his friends and get in on the act of making more money. He met up with Bruiser in the coffee shop that day as he had to take the helicopter back to the cattle station for the management people for some reason, he was not sure what.

Bruiser was waiting for him. They made a day and a time the next week to meet at the motel. Surely, the helicopter would not be used for that long as it was not round up time for the cattle and he just had a shipload go on its way with a load of cocaine hidden in a bale of hay that he had put there. The station only needed the helicopter for one day to take guests of the station to the Bay airport and pick up some paperwork for the next trip to the Red Sea at Ah Mohka Harbour.

So, Bruiser and Stan met up at the motel, both arriving within a minute of each other. They did not go into the carpark but stopped at the front door and office of the motel. Stan was impressed at how neat and clean it was. The paintwork in very bright colours and potted plants around the main door. There was no sign of anyone.

Stan queried this and was told that at this hour the girls are in school. "We have an older lady who has been with us for years as she is also a nurse and checks the health of our girls. Cannot have any STDs in our brothels. She does that every week and the rest of her time is schoolwork for the girls and their health check. Her sister does the meals for them and snacks for the men if they ask for it. Her sister also checks that the girls have cleaned their rooms. It works out well."

Stan then asked if there were any others employed.

"Yes," said Bruiser, "two armed guards and their dogs."

"So, you make enough money with the girls to finance all of this," said Stan knowing he would of course, or he would not do it otherwise.

"This does not cost me anything," said Bruiser. "The government grants pay for it and I still make a profit on that bit. I must fill out forms to get my grant, tax dodge and inspections by appointment. Works well for me. But I cannot have the girls not being able to read and write or unable to do arithmetic. There is always a chance they will ask them to write their name or spell something. Do not want any problems."

"I am impressed," said Stan. "How does the night-time work with the men?"

"Mainly same as the brothels, in fact when they get to sixteen, that's where we send them if they don't want that we get them a job somewhere else. We really do not want them to rat on us. Mind you, we can deny it, and the little ones here would back us up. They really do not want to leave after what they have been through. Back on the street is not a good option."

"Remember most of these have been abused sexually by fathers, uncles, brothers or someone, they know what it is all about but here there is no physical abuse, no broken arms or pain for days. It is the one rule here, the girls must be happy. The best thing they will tell you is they get to dress up."

"Better fill me in on how I can get in here one night soon. I rather fancy a night with a little girl from this club."

Bruiser laughed at him and said, "Just a phone call, you know my number. We only have twenty-five girls a night. Five spares in case of a hiccup. Five spare rooms if needed. So, get in quickly, I am booked out next week. You have no idea what these guys will pay. They love to get hold of a youngster!"

"Right, I'll get back to you. I have a 'Bucks night' to put on in a couple of weeks. I may just book for me first so I can see what goes on and give the guys some idea of how it works. They may even be able to help fill seats for you as well. Well, maybe I will book now for next week if you have spare girls, you could fit me in for sure."

Bruiser waved him goodbye and thought that he would just love our little girl auctions by the pool. In his brothels, you go in and chose a woman and off to the room. It is a set price unless you want an escort for a party or to spend the night with her. This was a bit different in that the girls came out one at a time on a boardwalk beside the pool and the men bid for her.

The highest bid was the one who takes her to her room and does what he wants or get her to do what he wants. The men sitting around the pool in comfortable chairs munching on caviar, olives and various cheeses makes them feel at home and the wine, whiskey or cold beer put bravado into them. They often started singing and telling jokes as they paid over the money with a grin and fondle the little body that they had just purchased. Bruiser made a mental note to put an extra chair in beside the pool.

Stan Marshall was looking forward to the night with the Little Girls Club, very much so. He would wear casual clothes so not to get his choice afraid that he was an official and take her away.

He fronted up at eight o'clock that night, drove up the long driveway and the gates to the carpark were open with one of the guards handling a large German Sheppard dog on a leash beside him. He emerged from the car slowly always watching the dog. The dog looked at him and them turned his head to the handler to see if there was a command.

Another car pulled in and then two cars followed each other into the carpark. All vehicles were of the most expensive kind and that amazed him as, although they could not be seen from the highway if someone happened to come in by foot there may be questions asked. Having just thought about it, these two older cars rolled and four men tumbled out laughing and joking headed for the pool gate. The dog took no notice. Stan joined the laughing group and joined in with them.

Cars kept rolling in and soon the chairs around the pool were full. Stan counted the chairs and as there was an extra one, he knew his booking had been taken care of.

Wine and snacks were coming from outside the pool gate. Wine beer and whiskey were flowing, and all twenty-six men were having a good time. Music started and the show started. Bruiser put himself at the front of the boardwalk and started the bidding war for the first girl.

"Gentleman, I hope you are having a nice evening. As the auction starts, be ready to bid on the one you want. They will come out one at a time and you will have time to look closely and bid slowly."

The first girl appeared. Stan judged her to be about twelve years old. Dressed in a sparkling fabric G-string and matching bikini top she walked the boardwalk in small high heeled shoes like a professional, smiling at all the men in all directions. Stan looked at her eyes and thought that she had been drugged, in fact he was sure of it.

He did not care as it would mean he could do what he liked as long as he did not leave a mark. She would not remember. She went for five thousand dollars to an old fellow that was well drunk. Stan was waiting for something younger.

They came out in various fancy dress, all trying to look sexy as they would have been told to do.

Stan bought the first ten-year-old in a sheer mini dress for seven thousand dollars. He planned to get his money's worth out of that one. She was small with long blonde hair and a cute smile. Stan had bought his camera so he could get some 'kiddy porn' photos and sell them for big bucks. There was always a good market for that. The internet was great.

After Stan paid for the child, she was handed over to him to sit on his knee. Yes, she was drugged; they all were. The other men would lean over out of their chairs for a closer look or touch her hair. One told him he did well with that choice and hoped he could get one at that age as well. Stan stroked the child on her back and then let his hands wander. Stan never knew what the other guy got; he was too interested in what he had on his knee.

He left early next morning, leaving the child sleeping in the big king-sized bed. She would be tired after posing for photos for hours and then giving him pleasure. There were no guards on the carpark gates and most of the cars had left. He had hired a car for this adventure as he did not want to ride his bike or borrow anyone else's car.

This venue perfect for a 'Bucks night' entertainment spectacular. He must tell his friends to bring their cameras. If they did not need the photos, he would buy any good ones that he could use for the guys on the internet.

Stan was so looking forward to phoning Arthur to get a date for the 'Bucks night'. Hope he had the wedding organised so he could book a night for the Little Girls Club.

The morning passed quickly and then he rang Arthur who had set a wedding date and was happy to talk to Stan about details of his 'Bucks night'. Stan just told him it was a surprise, and a date was set.

Stan rang and booked the night in question and then set about calling his friends, the wealthy ones only. He had booked for ten men to attend the 'Bucks night' with his eight friends, Arthur and himself. He never asked Arthur if he had anyone he would like to invite, that could be trouble at this place. He did not have to tell his friends what went on as they would be into anything like that.

Two of his mates were the usual drug runners that used Stan at times to help, three of them had brothels and the other three were lawyers who knew all the tricks of proving the guilty innocent. The lawyers had learned lots of nasty stuff, and how to get the thugs off who committed really bad crimes, usually against women and children.

They had been able to get them off with no jail time and no conviction against them. Stan knew all of them very well and had been to parties of theirs that would shock the average bad boy. He thought they had never been to anything like this so would enjoy it.

Bruiser was pleased that Stan's booking booked out the night of twenty-five guests. He organised everything for the night issuing orders to everyone as usual, but they all knew what they had to do. They did this work every night except Monday because that was the day off. Bruiser had takeaway bought in for the girls, much to their delight and the others as well.

Early Wednesday morning, he knew the government inspector would come on the usual three o'clock Wednesday afternoon appointment once a month. This was to check all the girls were happy, healthy and doing their schoolwork. He would also bring the paperwork to continue the government payments. At five past three, the phone rang. It was the office of Children's welfare that Bruiser deals with for his grants and payments.

The message was simple that the inspector's car had broken down on the way. Bruiser assumed that the inspector would not be coming as the voice on the phone did not say he would be late or delayed. So continued with his work making sure the guys that come would have a good time.

None of the 'Bucks night' guests lived in the Bay. They all flew in using their owners or their own plane picking up the others on the way. Stan also did not live at the Bay; he only kept his motorbike there in the hanger. At the airport in the Bay, they hired cars to travel to the motel arriving at eight in the evening, and following directions from Stan, drove up the long tree lined drive behind the motel into the two-meter-high fully fenced carpark.

They all scrambled out of the car and went through the high steel gates towards the motel. Bruiser could hear them coming, laughing and joking and obviously looking forward to the night ahead.

They were shown into the pool area and the wine, beer and whiskey along with the snacks appeared. The alcohol was working well, and they were having a great time waiting for the guest of honour.

Stan arrived in a rented car on his own and Arthur followed not far behind in his Rolls Royce. Various others, some who had been before and were returning for another session with the little girls and the rest of them, came on recommendations from their friends. Possibly not having any idea what this was all about.

They all joined in with the drinking, eating and singing and getting very drunk including Arthur who was thoroughly enjoying himself with this happy band of fellows who wanted to be his best friend, so he thought.

While this was going on and no-one was taking any notice, including Bruiser who was making sure his guests were have a great time, a car drove up in front of the office. A man in a grey suit got out and the first thing he saw was two little girls dressed in sparkly bikinis and feather boas headed towards the fence around the pool. He stopped and took in this situation and immediately realised something wrong was going on.

He got back in his car to drive out and was fronted by two guards with two large dogs. He had to stop the car or run over them, and they angrily approached the car.

"What are you doing here?" One said in a menacing manner.

Quick thinking in this situation was easy for a fellow who had been in this sort of situation as it goes with his job.

"I think I am at the wrong motel, there must be another one near here. I am very sorry."

"Move on out of here or else," said the other guard not realising who the grey suit belonged to.

"Thanks, the motel must be further up the highway."

"Move it then," and they both stood aside so he could drive out. The two dogs wagged their tails as he drove past and out the driveway. The guards did not report this to Bruiser as they thought it was ok. Bruiser would have told them if he was expecting someone to come to the office.

The man in the grey suit drove further up the road. He rang his office and explained what he saw. He also checked on his paperwork and contacted the head of his department and the government minister in charge of child welfare. Then he rang the police. He was put through to Detective Mendez.

He explained what he had seen and what he suspected, although he did not know exactly what happened there, but knew by what he had seen that it would be exploitation of children. He did not know if there was boys and girls. However the place was called the 'Little Girls club', so presumed it was only girls. He had only seen two little girls about ten or twelve years old dressed in a sexual manner.

He estimated there would be about thirty men having a party around the motel pool. He gave Mendez the phone numbers of his superiors and the Minister of Child Welfare.

Mendez was having trouble taking this all in so fast. He was silent for a few seconds then said that he would get on it right away. He organised a raid with Paul Harvey, stating this was urgent as the call had just come in and children were involved seems to be very young girls being exploited. Paul was ready for action as this sort of thing would be urgent.

He put the call out for enough men to handle thirty violators needing riot squad and vice squad and policewomen to look after the victims. He summoned his stepson, Troy, and his son, Hunter, told them what he knew and asked Troy to contact Mendez and Hunter to stand by his own phone in case he needed Hunter to contact any others needed on sight that he may have overlooked. He took his police supplied mobile.

Mendez asked the man in the grey suit if he was still on site and if he felt safe to investigate a bit more without putting himself in danger and giving him a very good description of the area where this was all taking place. The man in the grey suit said he would get back to him but there were two guards with large dogs; he would have to watch out for. Mendez said to be careful as they could be armed and hung up.

Mendez felt that his instructions would be ok as that man would be always investigating child abuse and was used to crawling around in the bushes. Mendez smiled to himself.

The man in the grey suit had realised that there was a carpark further up the drive as all the men here had to park somewhere, they certainly did not walk there. So, he kept in the trees that lined the driveway and made his way up the long driveway. He saw the steel fence, it was green, so it did blend in a bit. He then found the big double gates and the large lock so pushed the gates closed tight together and put the large padlock on, and to his amazement there was a key in the lock, so he put that in his pocket.

He then rang Mendez so he could pass that message on to the police. He then returned around to the back of the motel. Looking through the restaurant window, he saw a woman sitting on her own eating off a large plate. The front door of the restaurant opened and the man in the grey suit ducked his head and then after a few minutes, peeped over the windowsill again.

It was one of the guards, he had both dogs with him. He must have been hot as he took off his coat and revealed that he had a gun on his hip. The woman rose and went to a cupboard and pulled out tins of dog food. She proceeded to feed them. The guard left the dogs with her. So, the dogs were not savage.

He returned to the trees and passed this information on his mobile to Mendez. A woman, dogs tame and armed guards. Mendez thanked him and again told him to be careful.

Arthur was tipsy when the parade of the Little Girls club started. He was beyond horrified. He looked at Stan in fury, Stan just grinned at him. "Enjoy yourself," said Stan. "You may really like it."

Arthur really did not like it. "They are just babies," he yelled.

"Maybe but they are happy and very co-operative. Better pick one or you may miss out on what you would like," grinned Stan. The rest of the guys there were bidding away on their choice. Then they got the idea that Arthur was not happy.

"Come on, Arthur, don't be like that, join in the fun." Arthur was afraid of them getting angry with him as they were chanting 'Join the fun' over and over. The next girl up was dressed in fishnet stockings on a garter belt, strippers' pasties on her flat chest big rabbit ears on a headband and nothing else looked about sixteen. He had to bid ten thousand dollars to get her. He thought she would be able to understand he was not happy with this.

The auction had just ended and while the men were scrutinising the other men's little girls, Bruiser headed for the restaurant. He did not hear anything further up the highway, but something caught his eye, he had a second look and saw the red and blue flashing lights. He ran to the restaurant and called the nurse. "Gail, move it quick and follow me out to the bike, the cops are coming."

She moved quicker than he thought she could and ran down to where he hid the bike. She mounted the back as soon as he mounted the front, it started immediately. He left his lights off and headed down the track through the trees to a hole in the fence through to the next property, on to their driveway and out to the highway.

He turned his lights on then and headed into the heart of the Bay. He let Gail off at her home and headed for the Bad Boys Club. They would deny he had left the place all afternoon and well into the night. He now had to think of the investigation that would take place starting tomorrow.

Back at the motel, the riot police surrounded the motel. The police vans were ready to take prisoners. The men were arrested and the ones that took off to the carpark, found it locked. They could not get their cars out to escape. The little girls thinking they were in trouble, started to cry and those near the dogs went to them and hugged them. The dogs wagged their tails and seemed to comfort them.

The police who thought they were savage and were about to shoot them, put their guns away. Policewomen and councillors moved in to calm the girls and assure them that they were not in any trouble. They wanted Miss Gail, where was she?

The media arrived and started taking photos of the naked or near naked little girls. Most hurried up with their story so it would come out as a scoop in the next morning paper.

The three lawyers started reading the police their rights and what they had rights to. They objected to their clients being handcuffed and put in a van. They never gave up pleading their innocence and where was their warrant, they could not just come in anywhere when they pleased. The three of them all came up with threats to the police and in the end, Mendez set them straight for the charges they would get when they returned to the station.

When they had all been taken away, Mendez gathered his men together and they searched the place. They were still there gathering evidence until daylight the next morning. Before they left, Mendez notified the car rental place that their cars were locked up in the motel's carpark and gave them the address. Mendez had been given the keys by the man in grey suit when they arrived. He praised his actions and thanked him for everything h had done.

They then went to an early morning coffee shop and sipped coffee together and talked until the sun was fully up. They were very pleased about the job that had been done and how observant the man in grey was. If he had not realised something was wrong, this could have gone on for years, wrecking children's lives. He was a hero in Mendez eyes.

The man in grey said it was his job to protect children from that sort of thing. He admired Mendez for getting on to this so quickly and made it clear that he would be there for the court case. He also hoped that justice would get the job done. He wanted them all put away for life.

Chapter 19
The Wedding

Tristan's salesman had been with him a long time. He had bought a house not far from the showroom and every morning picked up a newspaper for Tristan and one for himself. When he arrived at work, he would put the paper on Tristan's desk for when he came down from his unit that was above the showroom. He did that this morning.

He then went into the tearoom that was always his second stop and made two coffees, one for Tristan and one for himself and put them on their desks. His salesman then did a quick check of the showroom to see all was well to start the day, returned to his desk for the paper and the coffee that should have cooled enough to drink while he read the headlines of that day's paper.

He rolled the paper open, flattened it out as usual and took a double take at the large photo on the front page. It was Arthur with a very young almost naked young girl on his lap. *Cattle Baron in porno ring*. It went on to say that Arthur McDonald self-made multi-millionaire caught with sixteen-year-old girl almost naked girl on his lap that he had purchased for the night at a Little Girls Club auction.

It made him physically ill. He had to fold the paper and put it down, he had read enough.

His next thought was how would Tristan react? Worse still Lydia who he thought was the most gentle and lovely lady he had ever met. Should he tell Tristan before he looked at the paper? Or say nothing, just let him find it.

He had to tell him, to warn him of the bad news. This was worse than bad. Poor Lydia, the worst thing that could happen to her. What was Arthur thinking. He could hardly believe that this was happening. He decided to tell Tristan before he picked up the paper on his desk and then heard him coming down the stairs.

Tristan gave him the usual morning wave and headed to his desk, picking up his coffee first. His salesman took long fast strides to get to the desk at the same time and looked Tristan straight in the face. Tristan was quite taken aback with this and stopped his coffee in midair.

"Tristan," his salesman said. "There is a frontpage story in today's paper that will upset you and your mother."

"Can't be that bad," replied Tristan and rolled open the paper to see the front page. His face went white, and he plopped down in his office chair. He looked at the paper aghast. "No, no…"

"So sorry, Tristan, I hope your mum will be ok."

Tristan sat in his chair for quite a while. He did not know what to do about this or how to tell his mother. He got out of his chair and went out the back to his workshop where his men were already on the job. He stopped at the door and was not sure whether to go in or not.

The men looked up as usual for their morning greeting that did not come. His face must have told them. They asked him what the problem was, and he called them over to him. He asked them if anyone had seen the morning paper; the answers came ack negative. After telling them to wait, he returned to his office and got his paper to show them.

They were all shocked and stood silently before him. One of them spoke up. "Tristan," said Mal, "I may enlighten you on something if you would like me to."

"What is it?" Tristan said.

"Before I left for work this morning, I received a phone call from Lydia, your mother. She asked me to get her red Maserati ready and have it at the door as soon as I could. I left immediately and came in. I checked tyres, fuel and oil, started the engine as it has been a long time since she had been on the road."

"I checked the brakes, battery and lights and anything I could think of. Her car was spotless and windscreen clear. Inside was perfect. I would not want anything to happen to her your mother is one special lady."

Tristan knew that all his men knew cars inside and out and it would most certainly be roadworthy, and that was good of Mal to help like that, but where had she gone. Why so early and how did she find out. Too early for the paper to be out as well.

Lydia was ahead of them. She had heard part of a conversation between Stan and his mate, and they were laughing. Most of the conversation was not in her hearing range but the words about paedophiles raised a red flag in her brain.

Tristan returned to his desk, picked up his phone and rang Mendez who to his surprise, answered the phone.

"Mendez," said Tristan. "I am sure you are busy, and I hate to ask but this is about the story in the paper about the arrest of some men last night. Did you know Arthur McDonald was amongst them and if so, where is he now?"

"Oh! Tristan," said Mendez. "I thought that was him at the porn show, he is here in jail. I doubt he will get bail when they come up before the magistrate later this morning. This was the worst case of child abuse have ever had to deal with. He had his phone call, made it last night. By the way, the girl on his knee in the photo was only fourteen years old."

"What time will he appear before the magistrate? I would like to be there," said Tristan.

"Well, I think late morning as he has a lawyer lined up, but most of the others do too. Here were three lawyers on site enjoying the show, so they will probably try representing themselves or each other but they are all in jail now, all twenty-five of them. We are on the trail of the leader of the gang. Believe there was a woman involved as well."

Tristan hesitated before he said, "I am interested in this case because my mother was engaged to be married to him."

"Shit," said Mendez. "Your mother is a lovely lady. I don't understand this why would she get mixed up with him?"

"I do not know what to think," said Tristan. "I am totally confused about this. I know he was excited about his 'Bucks night' but I would not have thought they would even have organised a stripper. Just does not make sense."

"Well, he was there," said Mendez, "and there is a front-page photo to prove it. Hope your mother gets over him as he will be put away for a longtime."

"Can I ask who his lawyer is?" Tristan asked.

"Sure, it is Marty Mitchell, but he will not be in his office. He asked permission to look at the site of the offence and I gave it to him, but I am not sure if they will let him in on the crime scene."

"Thanks," said Tristan as he left.

Tristan did not know where to go or what to do. He drove around town for a while trying to let it sink in. He rang Trevor, his salesman, and checked everything was ok in the office and told him he was not sure when he would return. He also asked Trevor to let him know if his mother returned or rang the office and to try and ask her where she was.

Tristan left a message for Marty Mitchell to contact him as soon as he could. It was a short message that included the fact that his mother was missing.

A flash of an idea hit him, and he turned his car around and headed for his home in the unit above the showroom that he shared with his mother. Trevor saw Tristan arrive and race up the stairs to the unit. He followed him. Tristan yelled, "I just thought Lydia may have left me a note, come and help me search for one."

Mogo and Felicity had the same thought at the same time. "Do you think we should go home soon?" Felicity said.

"You just read my mind," he answered.

They arranged to leave for home the next day. Christian was happy about the decision as well because he was looking forward to seeing his friends at school and tell them of all the countries he had been to and how other people lived. Both Felicity and Mogo had spent most of their time researching the countries they had been to and their culture they considered it part of his education.

They also home schooled him with a tutor, so he would not fall behind being so long away from school. Later, it proved to pay off as he was dux of the school; his school marks were so good.

They arrived at the small airport at the Bay and while waiting at the carousel for their bags, the three of them stood together. Sniffer dogs checked them out, but they were also checked out by Lydia Paravoni. She was heading out to the departures when she thought she saw Tristan, so did a double take.

She stopped as near as she could when she realised it was not him but a teenage version that she had raised. The call went out for her flight, so she had to leave but at that time she felt in her sorrow about Arthur, a ray of light that baby James was alive and well and now a teenager.

Lydia boarded her plane with the thought of baby James being alive and well. She should have stood back and used her mobile to take a photo. Damn, damn, damn. She took comfort in the knowledge that the Bay was not so big, and Tristan and Marty Mitchell would find him. Then the thought of what if they were only passing through? Should she ring Tristan now and tell him or not tell him at all.

Arthur had rung Lydia at eleven o'clock at night, waking her up from a deep sleep. She mumbled, "Hello," and rolled back on her pillow. Arthur's voice came through loud and clear and that made her sit up and take notice.

"I am in trouble," Arthur said. "Just listen and do not say anything." She did not answer so he went on. "I am in jail because Stan who organised the Bucks party, took me into a child porno den with a heap of paedophiles and got me drunk. There was a police raid and I was caught up in that, get me Marty Mitchell and tell him to get me out of here. I have not done anything wrong."

These were orders and did not go down well with Lydia, and what he had said so far did not go well with her as well. He should not have spoken to her like that, even though he had never spoken to her like that before. Was this the way he would speak to her when they were married.

"Fill me in," she said quietly.

"Well, Stan took me to a motel where they auction little girls for the night. There were twenty-five of them. I did not know this and was happily drinking and then the show started. I bought the last girl hoping to save her from this place. She was supposed to be sixteen but turns out she was fourteen. There was the media there as well. I hope they do not put my photo in the paper."

"Why did you not leave?" Lydia quietly asked.

"Because they were all asking me and chanting as me to buy one," he tried to explain.

"You took the Rolls by yourself and listened to a bunch of paedophiles, abusers and did not walk out as soon as you knew what was going on." She hung up the phone and turned her mobile off.

She then rang Marty Mitchell and told him that Arthur was in jail, and she did not think he would be able to get him out and hoped he could not. Marty was really taken aback and wondered what Arthur had done to upset Lydia so much.

He found out when he got the early edition of the paper. "Shit," he said to himself. "Stupid bastard."

Mogo and his family arrived home and were pleased that the gardener he had hired to look after the place had been very busy and had the place looking immaculate. He was pleased and thought he should give him a bonus.

The house inside was just as they had left it, and he knew within the hour Felicity would have it back to normal. Christian was busy putting his souvenirs away and helping Felicity unpack her and Mogo's clothes. He knew she would go out into her garden then.

Mogo had a few minutes to himself, so he rang Bruiser to see what was going on about town. Bruiser only said, "Meet me at the coffee shop," and hung up.

Lydia boarded her flight and slept all the way there. She was exhausted and did not want to think of anything. On arrival, she went to the hotel that had been booked for their honeymoon. It was her choice to go there so she thought it would be just as good on her own.

She explained she was early and hoped if the room they had booked was vacant or another room would be ok. The room she had chosen to stay in was vacant. Lydia had chosen the destination and hotel as a surprise for Arthur, and he did not know where it was. If he was to guess there was no doubt, he would think the last place she would go was their honeymoon destination.

Tristan had organised most of this for her, so he knew where the honeymoon was to be but not that is where she was going. She would ring him later and tell him her plans when she had made them.

Bruiser was sitting in the coffee shop when Mogo arrived. He went straight to him grabbed a chair and sat.

"What's happening?" Mogo said.

"Have you seen today's paper?" replied Bruiser.

"You in it?"

"No, but I well may be soon," said Bruiser.

"Fill me in," said Mogo.

Bruiser filled him in trying to make out that he was really a good guy as he knew Mogo hated scumbags and that is what he is. He went on how he saved these girls from the street and educated them. However, Mogo was a wake up to him and all the posing made Mogo angry. He felt that if Bruiser was caught, he could get away with this in court and that was not right.

He felt Bruiser must go. This was disappointing as he had really retired. He had eliminated so many bad guys and that had made him wealthy, but they just seemed to keep coming. The only way to stop it was to get rid of his guns and not associate with bad guys. When it came to Bruiser, he knew too much about Mogo, so he had to go. He went home with a plan.

Tristan and Trevor found the note on her pillow, pinned there so it would not get lost. It explained briefly what happened with the phone call from Arthur and asked him to cancel all the wedding plans. Arthur would be in jail she hoped, and she was going on the honeymoon by herself. He could join her of he wanted a break but never tell anyone where she was.

Her Maserati was in the long-term car park at the airport if he wanted to retrieve it. He could pick her up at the airport when she returned. *I think I have had a lucky escape*, it read. It went on how she loved him and hoped he was ok with this.

Mogo went back home and was trying to think the best way to eliminate Bruiser. Then the way to get rid of his guns. If he had the guns, he would be tempted to use them, and he certainly did not need the money; he was having trouble spending the interest. Their overseas trip heled that a bit but the money kept rolling in. He had thought at one stage he could sell them to Bruiser but now that was off the cards as he had to eliminate him. There was no doubt of that as he hated paedophiles.

As he headed for home, he turned off to his unit. He took his guns out of their steel box and set them out on the floor. The time had come to get rid of them, but he must choose the best one for the assassination of bruiser and decide how and when to use it. He carefully disassembled each one and cleaned it. He could never replace these as they were all made up of pieces of other guns and were untraceable.

Seemed a shame to sell them as he would not get in cash what they were worth. He also thought of all the bad guys he had taken off this earth and in doing that made life so much better for others. However, bad guys are always around and would always take their place so he would always have a job.

He was sure he did not want any more money, especially as Felicity was careful with every dollar. Another reason for his love for her. Christian was his other love and to go to jail would not be good, as he was so smart and would have a wonderful future. He did not need a dad that would drag him down in whatever profession he chose.

He chose a pistol with a silencer. His favourite as it was small and light.

Chapter 20
Trials

Mendez had a lot on his plate. He had four constables who had really stuffed up and twenty-five men all accused paedophiles in the cells. Paperwork up to his neck! He had already decided with the help of Superintendent Paul Harvey to hand them over to the police internal investigation department. They would sort it out or put them through the usual criminal investigations and possibly all have their own barrister.

He did not think there was one in the Bay, let alone four of them. Looked like they would all have to go to the big smoke, but they would have to anyway to face the Police Internal Investigations. Could be away from their family for quite a long time, especially if there was jail time.

The twenty-five in the jail cells were his next problem. He had to have his paperwork for the night magistrate who had to get out of bed to put this lot away. He did not think this would take too long as he was mainly looking to keep them in the cells, and not get bail. He did not want any of these guys out on the street or trying to get out of the country.

They all had enough money to get a private jet to escape and a lot of them had their own plane anyway, so would head straight for the airport that the planes or helicopters were at the ready.

If they did get out of the country in these times, they could run their business by the internet or get high paying jobs, it would just mean a hic-up in their career. Then there was Arthur McDonald. What a grub! He said in his defence he wanted to save the last girl. Why not the first one or just walk out when the first one came on the catwalk.

Mendez was on the trail of the so-called school teacher. However, he did not know about her sister as neither of them were in sight that night. What happened to the two guard dogs? The guards had no interest in them so, maybe they did not belong to them but someone else involved in this horror. Back to the paperwork.

The night magistrate sat at the bench and the twenty-five men filed in, most had their heads bowed. Mendez spoke to the magistrate, putting his case and requesting that no bail be given. It did not take long for the magistrate to take in the situation and realised that they possibly would all try to flee the country.

He listened to the three lawyers putting their case forward, but no reason was good enough and they were pilots or had pilots that flew them around, so escape was on the cards. Arthur McDonald had Marty Mitchell put up his case of he wanted to save one of the girls, but to no avail, he was also denied bail. The magistrate then said no matter how high he set the bail, it would not impact any of them, so bail was refused to all. He went back to bed.

Marty Mitchell went up to McDonald as he was escorted out to the cells, and said, "I can get you a good barrister, but this case is not for me. I will give the details to Tristan; he can pass them on." McDonald gave a slight nod but held his head up as though he did nothing wrong.

They were all taken to another city hoping that from a great distance they would get a fair trial. While they were all together, they started cooking up stories that may get them off. McDonald thought he had the best chance and if one of them backed him up, he could get through alright as well. The armed guards were listening to all of this and shook their heads as they usually did when men like this were in denial.

Most of these guys were single. The ones that were married or engaged, as Arthur McDonald was, knew that their partners would never get over it and forgive them, even if they said the whole thing was not their fault or they did not know about it, was drunk or some other excuse. Maybe some wives would be glad to get rid of them with a divorce and most of the money.

Lydia was enjoying her time in the sun with a waiter bringing her drinks, not all alcoholic, to the beach, and could not believe her luck that this happened before the wedding. There was only a very small number invited to the wedding and she hoped that Tristan had contacted them and that this would not make the paper. She could either go back to her previous life or begin a new one.

She had seen the front page of the paper at the airport and decided not to buy one. To call the wedding off three days before the wedding was not a good thing to have to do but she did not expect Arthur's sins to be the reason. She lay back on the towel in the deck chair and drifted off to a light sleep. It was late in the afternoon when she woke and decided to ring Tristan. She went back to her hotel room and dialled his number.

"Hi," said Lydia. "What is happening back there?" She smiled at the sound of her son's voice. It was so great to hear him. It made her feel that all was right with the world.

"Hey," he said back. "You ok?"

"Sure," said Lydia. "All is well in my world now I hear your voice. I am enjoying a relaxing holiday and I will stay until I have used up the honeymoon time and then I will return to my suite, and we shall return to our life as we knew it before Arthur tried to ruin our lives. Where is he by the way?"

"In jail, no bail, that goes for the twenty-five of them. The reason they were refused bail was that all of them had the means to fly out of the country and most of them would never need to return," explained Tristan. "The two guards with the dogs that were not theirs are out on bail as they did not join in the fun, and they tracked down that woman that was the little girls' teacher and she is on bail but they think she is ok because she said she only taught school there, and was never there after school time at three-thirty."

"She went home. I think those two dogs were very friendly and the girls used to take them into their rooms at night after the men left. They also think the dogs belonged to Miss Gail, the teacher. Seems they all liked their teacher who to her credit, taught them all to read and write and do arithmetic."

"Dreadful for those little girls. They will never recover for the rest of their lives."

"Yes, I know," replied Tristan. "By the way I have your car."

"Ok, I will let you know when I fly in, and you can pick me up. Can you get rid of anything in our apartment that may remind me of Arthur, Tristan? Please do not worry about me. I feel I had a lucky escape; you can save the paper for me. I will read it when I get home."

"Bye bye, my beautiful mother, see you when you decide to come home. I love you."

"I love you too, my son, and thank you understanding."

Mendez went to Superintendent Paul Harvey's place and knocked on the door. His wife, Helen, answered and seeing Mendez, broke into a big smile. She knew Mendez and Paul worked well together and Mendez would call in to update Paul whenever he was working on a big job.

"Hi, Mendez," she said. "Do come in." As he entered, she continued, "Paul will be back in a moment. We ran out of milk; can you believe that. Come into the kitchen, the boys are there." They entered the kitchen and Mendez saw the kitchen table covered with Law books and notebooks. Troy with pen in hand, writing something and Hunter beside him, guiding him how to term the words.

He looked at these young men and thought how great this household was. So happy and busy. He hoped his household would look like this one day. Troy looked the policeman by his neat clothes and navy trousers, and Hunter looked the university man with his long blonde wavy locks and trendy clothes in pastel colours. He must be the ladies' man, not Troy.

Paul Harvey let himself in the front door and headed for Mendez with his hand out, ready to shake Mendez's hand in welcome and friendship. Troy was his stepson but in their police clothes, police hairstyle and same colour hair, you would think they were the father and son. Their actions were the same as well. Police training Mendez put that down to.

Helen made coffee and the four of them had a chat about the boy's study, life in general and then Mendez and Paul left for his study, a room Mendez was beginning to know well, and Mendez caught Harvey up with the latest case with twenty-five paedophiles involved. He had tracked down Miss Gail and the two guards they were out and the rest no bail.

Paul knew they had been taken outside the Bay so they would get a fair trial. Mendez also asked if he knew that he had tracked down a man known as Mogo. All this was a good while ago. Troy was still working on it for Mendez but there had been no luck. Troy seems to think that he had fled the country.

"So, Troy and I are thinking of contacting Interpol and see if they have any murder victims with two shots in the head, and never any footprints made with shoes just a toe or heel print in soft earth, never a heel and toe together so you could match up the size of a shoe." Paul answered that he would contact the federal police and sort it out with them.

Hunter went passed them as they headed to the front door. He was dressed in more formal clothes just as trendy as before.

"Well, looks like you have a hot date," said Mendez.

"Think he has," said his father. "About time too!"

Hunter let out a laugh. "Yep," was the reply as he headed for a little red convertible sports car half out the garage ready to go.

"Your boys are great," said Mendez.

"I agree, how lucky am I," said Paul.

They shook hands at the front door and Mendez left with a wave from his car.

Mogo had thought about the best way to eliminate Bruiser. It would be his last job before he gave his guns up. He decided the best way was to get him at the club house early morning when no-one was there. He had a few options like in the lane to the coffee shop, outside the clubhouse or. He stopped in mid thought.

There was a room in the club house that he presumed was an office. He had never been in it, but it had it be so. He had only been in the club house once when he assassinated Billy, the bastard. He saw the door on the back wall and at the time thought that would have been a bedroom to take that young girl into as she was living with him.

Or was it the office; he had to have an office somewhere as he was running the club. An office would be good if he was sitting in his office chair, good height for a shot or two in the head.

Mendez arrived back at the station to receive news from the Internal Police Investigation. Constable Alan Davis was found guilty and received four years jail. He was found to be financially involved with Phillip Harris for financial gain and for not making enquiries as to the reason for the assignation.

Constable Bret McMillan was ordered back to the police academy for retraining. The reason was that he was the one who questioned about the assassination after the fact and possibly McMillan went along with his superior's orders as he was taught.

Constable Barry Nicholson was also ordered back to the police academy for retraining. He encouraged McMillan and agreed with him that this matter should be investigated. Also, he had obeyed a superior's orders.

Roger Nixon was dismissed from the police force. Reasoning that he was curious about what Nicholson and McMillan were up to. He did, however, agree to join them when the facts were made clear. No charges laid.

Mendez thought they were all lucky. They would not get off so light if he was in charge.

After two weeks, Lydia flew back home to Tristan. She was happy to be home and was singing away as she unpacked her bags. It had been a while since Tristan had heard her singing happily away, so he knew she was at peace with herself.

At dinner, she raised the subject that had been on her mind. Tristan knew something was coming and he hoped it was not too drastic. He felt guilty that his thought was that he hoped she did not want to involve him in anything too much as he was never so busy. Seems everyone had decided to restore a vintage car and he had to find one or the Arabs decided to update their Rolls or Bentley.

Trevor had been sent overseas to Oman or Dubai, keeping them happy and ordering what they required. The Arabs really liked him, and the service he and Tristan provided he did wonder, however what Trevor would say if they offered him a twelve-year-old princess for a wife. He smiled to himself as it was a problem for him. Eventually, he had convinced them she was not for him.

"Tristan," she started, and he braced himself for what was to come. "I have been very upset over those little girls at the motel. I have been thinking that maybe the child welfare system is so busy, they really do not check out others as well. So, I thought I could volunteer to help this department and fill in some of the cracks in the system; just fill in for someone who has experience will have more time. They may not want me, but I can ask. Now at the same time I have my work with you, so I will catch up having been away for two weeks then go and see about this. I know you are busy so if you need me, I will give this idea away."

"No, you will not," Tristan said. "We will try this and if I cannot keep up and you can help children, I will get a part-time person in and we will see how that goes." He was about to add to that decided to leave it.

"Thank you, Tristan." She smiled. "I knew I raised a good man, but let us take this one step at a time."

They cleared the dishes and Lydia went to her room; Tristan went down to his office. Both content with their decisions.

Chapter 21
Hunter Harvey

Hunter Harvey had style. He was well into his university years and loved it. He loved his family and admired his brother immensely. His father was proud of Troy as well, and Troy being a bit older, had helped Hunter with his studies before university; however now was a bit beyond him. Hunter stepped up to the plate and was able to help Troy with his law studies.

He really wanted Troy to make his goal and become a detective. He was able to get law books from the library of the university that really helped him.

However, Hunter had a secret that he kept to himself or so he thought. Helen Harvey as a mother knew what was going on. It never occurred to him how she knew what clothes to buy him for one thing. Helen never told Troy or his father that Hunter was gay. That was up to Hunter.

So, when he went out at night, she worried about him until he was safely home in his bed. He had won a lovely red sports car in a raffle at the university on his twenty-first birthday. The family was happy for him, but Helen had her doubts that she never spoke about.

She never worried about Troy as he could handle himself and she knew he usually hung around with his police mates in the places they always went. This made sense to her as they always had things to talk about, whether it was work or play. She had a feeling he had his eye on a certain policewoman a bit younger than him. That pleased Helen.

It was not called 'the Bay' originally. Had some long fancy name that nobody could pronounce or remember. The Bay had a wide mouth of six sea miles with a large island in the mouth, causing shallow water and deep channels all over as the tides changed the seabed. However, it had beautiful light-coloured sandy beaches, wide and well protected from the elements. The perfect place for families to bring children to play in the shallow water at the edge of the water.

The Bay's main street had most of the pubs, motels, clubs, big shopping centres, doctors and lawyers, just about everything was along the main road with a few side streets coming off in various places. Next to the cinema was an exclusive club that had a doorman at the entry. If anyone insisted on coming in, the bouncers were called in and one look at them, you would change your mind quickly.

There was a carpark off the side street, well lit up, parking for the patrons of the Gay Bar.

Hunter wheeled his red convertible sports car into the rear of the carpark, put the top up and locked it. There was security on hand at this time as it was dark, and they knew who owned the car. Hunter entered by the rear entry of the club as he always did, in case his father or Troy should drive past and see him enter. Worse would be one of their colleagues telling them where they had seen him.

He headed to the bar for a drink and settled on a stool where he could see the front door, the main entry. He was looking for a man over fifty years old, very handsome and strongly built. The man that gave him the red car for his birthday, bought him men's expensive jewellry and hired a bank security box to put it in. Hunter had stopped on his way here to get some of it out of the box to wear for him tonight, as he had not seen him for a few weeks and wanted to please his lover.

Steve was twice his age and adored Hunter. Would buy him anything and was in the process of buying him a unit near the university, so Hunter could leave home and be independent. Hunter thought this man was the love of his life and it would last forever.

Steve entered the club and headed for Hunter for an embrace Hunter hoped would go on forever, he had really missed Steve but never asked where he was over the weeks he was missing. Steve would tell him when he was ready.

"I really missed you," smiled Hunter.

"Not as much as I missed you, I can tell you that," said Steve. "Now before anything else, I have something to ask you." Hunters heart sunk. "It's ok. I know you always go home for the night as your mother waits up, but I was wondering if, as I must go away again, you could spend the night with me and not race ff to go home."

"Ok," said Hunter. "I will go now and see what I can do." He pulled out his phone and rang his mother as he walked to a quiet corner, as the club by this time was getting noisy. "Hey, my dearest mother," he crooned. "I will not be home tonight, but not to worry, I will be in a very safe place and see you in the morning."

Helen did not know what to say but knew this day was coming, so said, "Ok, my darling, I will see you in the morning." She was worried. She had a feeling of doom as many mothers do. She did not sleep that night. Paul Harvey asked her what was wrong and she told him.

He laughed it off. "He is not a teenager, my sweet, and if he said he will be in a safe place, he will be. Seems to me he means her father does not own a shotgun." He laughed.

Hunter returned to Steve and said, "All sorted." Steve grinned. This made him very happy and had something to look forward to. A night with his angel.

They left the club at one thirty in the morning and headed out in the red sports car. Steve would get him to drop him back to his motor bike in the morning. The Harley was safe in the care of the Gay Cub boys in security. Steve suggested that they open the front gates of the Bad Boys Club yard and park the red sports car out the back of the club. Best out of sight.

No-one would touch a motor bike out the front of the club, but he was not sure of the car. They went in the back door of the Bad Boys Club that led to a large bedroom. The door to the office led off to the right and the next door in the office went onto the club rooms.

The bedroom had an ensuite off it and the room itself had two large comfortable chairs and a small bar in the corner. The room was very modern and comfortable. Steve had a special reason for bringing Hunter here that night and opened a bottle of champagne to celebrate.

"What is this about?" Hunter asked. "I love this room but champagne?"

"I have something special for you and I want to give it to you now as I may have to go away again in a few days."

"Ok," said Hunter. "What is it?"

Steve went over to a large modern painting on the wall and took it down revealing a safe. Hunter thought that was the most obvious place for a safe in the room and told him that was not a good idea.

"I know," said Steve. "I have another safe in here that no-one would ever find, but this one is just for overnight or a few hours and that is the case here." Steve drew a large envelope out of the safe, shut its door and turned to Hunter. "This is for you."

Hunter opened the envelope and found the title of a property. Reading, he found it was for a penthouse with an amazing view of the ocean. The first bit of paperwork was photos of the penthouse and the views, the second part was the title in Hunter's name.

"You need your own place and I need a place to see you that no-one will ever know about. I also need to know that you have a safe place of your own. You can live in it permanently or just when we get together. If anything should happen to me, you have this, and I have peace knowing that you are safe."

"The 'Body Corporate' fees will be paid from a bank account set up for you that will automatically direct debit from, so no expenses for you as well. Just live in it and enjoy it when I am with you or if I am not."

"I do not know what to say," said a stunned Hunter. "Can't you and I live permanently together in it?"

"No," said Steve. "I am afraid not." He smiled at Hunter trying to take this all in.

"Bedtime," said Steve. Hunter's head hit the pillow dreaming of his new apartment.

Mogo was ready to go. It was just on first light when he rolled his motorbike silently into the street and brakes on outside the Bad Boys Club. He had his pistol so he could get it easily but if he should run into Bruiser, he would take no notice of the gun as he knew Mogo usually carried one.

Mogo saw that there was no motor bike in the front so had a quick look around the back to see if Bruiser's bike was there. No bike but a red sports car, a convertible. Bruiser's life must be looking up, he thought. That would have cost a bomb, he thought. Doesn't matter, he won't be driving it again.

Mogo entered the club and headed for the door on his left. As he entered, he could see it was the office; the door on the other side could be a bedroom. He slowly opened the door thinking of a good excuse for being there.

Bruiser was half sitting up asleep with his head on a huge white fluffy pillow. There was a big white fluffy doona bedspread over the bed and all this dwarfed the large man sound asleep in the very large bed.

Pop, pop into his forehead, the blood splashed onto the whiteness, and then to Mogo's horror, the doona bedspread moved and a cascade of blonde hair fell across the other pillow and as the head turned towards him, he saw a young man's face. Too late; pop, pop and Mogo turned around and left the club house, mounted his bike and roared off.

It was almost lunchtime when the bodies were discovered by a member of the bikie club. He had been drinking at the bar in the club with another member when the question was asked about Bruiser's where abouts. He was usually around at this time and there was a red sports car in the backyard they had never seen before. So, they went looking.

The fact that Bruiser had a man in bed with him overtook the shock that he was dead. They started trying to make excuses for this one being here with him. He must have had a long-lost son and no other bed to put him in. Other stories came to mind, but they had to face facts and ring the cops.

Bruiser had been a good leader and they all liked him. There were no arguments with him, and he settled any between the members quickly, quietly and fairly if anything arose amongst the men.

Mendez was the usual detective to start investigations of homicide. However, he was in his office when the call came through and Troy Harvey was on the road, so Mendez directed him to go to the scene and he would leave now and see him there. He did not for one moment think Troy Harvey would be faced with the victim being his dead brother shot while in bed with another man. Worse still, the other man was the one suspected of running the paedophile ring at the motel outside of town.

Troy had seen his face in a mug shot of him as a wanted suspect. Troy Harvey could not hold a brave face and became distraught. Fortunately, one of his police buddies that knew him reasonably well got out his mobile and rang Paul Harvey and asked him to attend the scene of a murder that had upset his stepson. Paul Harvey left his office immediately.

The scene was not as he had imagined he would have to face ever in his lifetime. He took Troy home and had to face Helen at the same time as grieving himself. Too many questions in his head.

When the information came to light at the Bay police station, a councillor was sent to their home by Mendez. The paramedics had not even loaded the bodies yet. Mendez had taken over the investigation and was taking his time to make sure that nothing was done to destroy any evidence, as he felt this was the work of the one known as Mogo and that meant he was back in the Bay. He did not need that.

Mendez looked from one body to the other and shook his head. He wondered what they could see in each other at first, then of course thought about money and youth; the older man to care for him and buy him anything he wanted; the rough tough Bikie with a young fellow to be his trophy when out with the gay community. He doubted they were deeply in love with each other but who knows.

Both had two bullets to their foreheads, so he guessed that Mogo had struck again. It had been a while and he thought that was over.

Mendez had been in touch with Interpol and found that there was an assassin in Europe at work in most of the countries, seems the name was Mogo. It did not surprise him very much as this guy was good. Sniper or pistol, none of them were traceable, except for the bullet casings that told forensics if it was a sniper rifle, had a silencer or a pistol of a certain size.

Just things that would fit the obvious size or type of firearm. When he finished his work there, he went to Paul and Helen Harvey's home. He wished he had not when he saw them with Troy. The two men were sitting on a lounge with Helen waiting for an ambulance to take Helen to the hospital as shock had set in and she was a mess. She had stopped screaming at last.

The councillor that had come from the police force had ordered her to go to the hospital for treatment. He feared she could end up in the mental ward so needed help quickly. The ambulance arrived soon after Mendez did, and the councillor left to go with her. He told Paul and Troy to ring the hospital in two hours and asked if it was ok to visit if they wanted to.

Mendez sat in silence with them for a few minutes and no-one said a word. He conveyed his condolences, made it clear he was working hard on this case and also made it clear that if they needed him, he was there for them. No words were said so he left them to grieve the loss of a son and a brother.

He wondered if the biggest shock was that Hunter was dead or that he was gay. Maybe it was that he was with a Bikie that they were looking for that was a paedophile as they suspected in the motel saga.

Mogo arrived home in the morning. He had decided that would be his last job here or overseas. He decided to hand his guns in to the police and just keep one pistol with a silencer for his and his family security. Problem now was how to hand them in without being traced to all their origins. The parts were all army, as the guns would be tested, and the bullets identified to each one. At the breakfast table, he formed a plan.

He had his favourite gun on him as he had just used it on Bruiser and his gay friend. Shame about that, he was so young. Wrong place, wrong time.

He saw Felicity and Christian out in the garden, so he went to his car and took it out, still in its box and put it in his safe that was a wall safe in their bedroom. That would be the safest place and Felicity knew the combination. He decided to tell Felicity about it being there as he did not want her to find it and get a shock.

She may even ask Christian to get something for her out of the safe and then he would find it. That should never happen as he did not know the combination as Mogo changed it regularly, in case Christian happened to find out the numbers and letters to open it.

As Felicity came back into the kitchen, she was alone, Christian was still outside.

"Honey," he started. "I have something I have to tell you and I do not want you to be afraid."

She stopped and stared at him. "What is wrong?" She stammered.

"No problem," he answered. "I must tell you that I have bought a pistol; perfectly legal, my darling, so I have protection for the two of you. I do not think or hope, I will ever use it and I am only telling you so you will not worry or get a fright if you find it."

"Oh! That's ok," she said. "Is it well hidden?"

"I hope so, it's in our safe in the bedroom. Just make sure Christian does not go there. I always tell you when I change the combination but never let him go to it for any reason."

"Ok." Then Christian entered the room, so they went silent.

"I have to go and see someone tomorrow early so will be out most of the day," he said.

She smiled back so he knew she was ok with it. He left early in the morning for his unit and the rest of the guns.

Mogo went back to his unit and checked he had packed the rest of the guns and ammunition in the steel box. As all the guns were disassembled, they did not take up much room in the steel box, so it was easy for him to attain a cardboard box to put the steel box in. He then rang an interstate motel and booked in for one night in two days' time.

He then rang an airline to book a return flight for that date and a courier for an address of the coffee shop a few doors down stating that he would be on the roadside to hand the parcel over, and it was to be delivered to the motel at the address he had booked for. He also checked the date and time that the parcel would arrive as he knew that the parcel would be taken to another courier to deliver it interstate. He had also worked out that his only problem would be a delay of the delivery to the motel, but he could always get a later flight back.

As soon as he arrived the motel, he would get another company to take the parcel back to the bay with the name and home address of Mendez on it. This company would also change couriers near the border of the two states. He then bought a mobile phone and put Mendez mobile phone number in it.

Mendez was busy working on the murder of Bruiser and Hunter. He started by contacting the woman know as Gail. He went to her home as he had that address, and she was in and helpful.

She told how it as her job to teach the girls. The two dogs were very gentle and loved the attention the girls gave them they would ever bite anyone. She did not know the guards, except for the fact that they were supposed to be taking the dogs for a walk. She did have another job for Bruiser and that was to check on the heath of the sex workers in the two brothels.

If they did not look well or said they were ill, she drove them to the doctor and had them seen to. She had at times had to leave the other girls reading or occupied as she took any of them to the doctors. If they had a health problem.

"Did Bruiser interfere with those girls at all in any way that was inappropriate?" Mendez asked.

"Never," she replied. "He really looked after them. It was like he would never have any children of his own." She thought for a moment. "He received grants from the government for them to pay for everything for they needed, like their uniforms and schoolbooks. They had good food as I cooked it, and fruit and treats. They were good girls as well."

Mendez knew that so the night-time tortures were for the big money.

"Can you tell me anything else?" Mendez asked.

"Only that I am quite sure that Bruiser was not a paedophile as they said he was"

"Who said that?"

"The police that came here," she said. "That, I cannot believe."

"Thanks for your help," said Mendez. "But before I go, did you ever see Bruiser with that young man with him when they were shot?"

"No," she replied. "Never." She had lied most of that time but not at the last one.

Mendez said, "Thank you for the information; you have been a great help."

He left wondering where Hunter came into this. At least his parents would know that Hunter was not a paedophile and was only really with a gay man who was not a paedophile, just a money-grubbing mongrel. He drove to the Harvey household to see them.

He was welcomed into their home. Helen was obviously drugged to ease her pain. He gently told them of his information about Bruiser and Hunter. That neither of them was paedophiles, just gay lovers. Still a shock for Troy and Paul but not for Helen. She told them of her feelings that Hunter was gay, but it was his place to tell them not hers, and she only suspected.

Chapter 22
Guns

Mogo did not tell Felicity of his plans. He did tell her he may have to go away for two or three days. She understood that this was his life, so she was used to it but did query that surely, he was retired. He explained that he was and would be often asked to be an adviser to the ones who took his place. That this would be on-going for a little while. She nodded and was satisfied with this explanation.

He waited outside the coffee shop with his parcel and a new disguise that he recently purchased so that no-one would recognise him as it was possible because he only lived nearby in his unit. Although, he was not friendly with anyone around here; it was best not to take a chance.

The courier came on time, so the heavy parcel was handed over and a paper signed, cash given to the driver, no receipt required. The truck disappeared down the road. Mogo went to Felicity as he had an early flight in the morning. Before he left, he rang the interstate airport and booked a hire car for the next day the time of his arrival for pickup.

Back a home with Felicity, he told her of his early flight and set the alarm to make sure he made it.

He made the flight easily and went to get his hire car, they did not accept cash and wanted his credit card. He had one in another name that he had kept active for years for just such an occasion. He kept another one like this when nobody asked questions and did not check up on anything, just lend them the money. Times are different now, he thought to himself.

He drove himself to the motel that was under another name, and he wore his disguise of only a cap with red hair sticking out the back and heavy dark rimmed glasses that made him look almost blind.

He gave his assumed name different than the one on the plane and went to his room. He was delighted when the courier delivered his overnight parcel arrived at the time estimated. He rang the second courier to take it back to the Bay and said the parcel was ready to be taken, and waited for him or her to come and pick it up.

This did not take long and again the parcel was loaded in a van, and he watched that one disappear up the road on its way to be changed to another truck and delivered to Mendez at home. He then sent a text to Mendez. *Mogo has retired, to prove it, his guns will be delivered to you tomorrow afternoon.*

Mendez received the text and thought it was a joke. He just dismissed it as such and deleted the text. That night, he thought about it and wondered if it was true. "Those sorts of guys never retire," he said aloud to himself.

The next afternoon when Mendez came home, he found a courier at his door, he had been knocking and no one was home. He was glad Mendez came home and could sign for the parcel. He told him he was pleased that he did not have to come back later. Mendez signed the paper and the driver left.

He remembered that this afternoon was the children's swimming lessons so no one would be home for at least an hour or so. He loaded the parcel in the boot of the car and opened it to check what it was. Sure, enough there was keys to a steel box under the cardboard and they fitted the lock on the steel box. He opened the box and there they were all laid out neatly ready for assembly and the shelf in the box was loaded with ammunition.

Everything cleaned, neat and in order ready to go. "Wow," was all he could say. He repackaged the guns as they were, locked the box and put the keys in his pocket. The evidence room will love to see this. He could not sleep that night, he paced the floor and thought about those guns. At four in the morning, he made a decision to keep them.

He spent the rest of the night trying to work out here to hide them. They should be safe in the boot of my car for tonight and tomorrow, and no one knows I have them. No one saw the delivery and Mogo will not ring the station to see if I got them because he sent them here. Maybe he meant me to keep them. He slept well after that.

The next afternoon, he knew it was judo lessons or maybe tennis lessons, there was ways something on for the kid's sport. So, he took the hour off work and went home. He had thought the best place to hide them was up in the ceiling. It was unlikely anyone would look up there. He drove the car into the garage and parked it under the manhole.

He found the step ladder and opened the boot of the car, climbed up the ladder and slid the manhole cover across leaving enough room to push the parcel through onto the ceiling rafters. Down the step ladder and put the parcel on the roof of the car under the manhole, climbed up the step ladder again and lifted the guns into the manhole and slid the manhole cover back into place. He was happy with this as a temporary solution he would do better later.

He went to step back onto the ladder and missed his footing. It seemed like slow motion as he flew through the air and as he hit the ground, his head hit the garden shovel and landed on the garden pick that went through his skull.

He wife came home a bit earlier than usual. She would return to her kids later as they were happy with their friends and opened the garage door with her remote. The door went up to reveal Mendez car at one side of the garage and on her side was Mendez in a pool of blood. She stopped, pulled on the hand brake and got out the car, turned to grab her mobile phone and approached his body.

She rang the ambulance and then felt for a pulse. He was alive but the ambulance had better hurry as his pulse was barely there. She could see the point of the old metal pick was right into his skull and vomited. She could then hear the siren. Thankful that the children would not see their father like this.

She ran out the front of the property to guide the ambulance in. They were unsure what to do as they had never seen anything like this, and if they had they had been trained to not pull it out of the wound. After asking for assistance, they decided to get the stretcher to him, ready for assistance from the other paramedics.

It was decided that one would support the pick and get him on the stretcher and get him to hospital as soon as possible. One of them notified the hospital what was coming so they could arrange a surgeon and theater for the operation if he survived. He died twice in the ambulance, but they bought him back both times. The hospital was ready for him.

Sandra Mendez sat beside her husband every day from morning to night.

Her sister, Sally, cared for the four children as well as her own two little ones. Sally's husband, Brent, loved having six children in his house. He had wanted more than two, but Sally said no. He had to accept that, so to have four additions pleased him greatly.

The four cousins got on well as they had known each other since birth. Sally lived just around the corner. This made it easy for her husband to take the six kids with him to keep the Mendez home neat and clean up the bloody mess in the garage. He wondered how Mendez had survived, although at times he thought Mendez could not survive this and come out normal. The children felt happy that their house was still there waiting for daddy to get home from the hospital.

Sandra had watched her husband recover from six brain operations and skull repairs and five months in a coma. Still, she sat there and waited, read books to him whether he ever knew that was not known. She told him of the children's progress and anything else she could think of, just in case he could hear her or understand what she said.

The doctors finally told her that he would never be the same. How he came out of this was unknown, however they did not think he would be in a vegetative state as the rest of his body was working. The best she could hope for was that he would know her and his family and would have speech that was slow. She was thankful that he was still alive and maybe any memory that had been lost would return in time.

Mendez did come out of it gradually over time. He seemed to know her and nodded when she spoke of the children, Sally and her family which was encouraging. He never spoke a word though, and it seemed that he could not even try. He would be in the hospital for quite some time yet.

Mendez laid in his hospital bed that was just outside the nurse's station. He heard lots of conversations from the doctors talking to each other and talking to the nurses. One day, he heard two doctors talking about a young man who needed blood as he had been in a road accident. The problem seemed to be that the young fellow did not have the same blood as his father or his mother.

They had tested this twice but had to get an entirely different blood from blood donors. His parents had both given a blood donation for which they were grateful but testing this, they could not use it. He thought to himself that the fellow must have been adopted, funny they did not think of that. It was strange the things he saw and heard from that position. It kept him amused. He could not talk though, but it did not bother him.

The day came that Sandra leaned over him and asked him a question. "Darling, what were you doing in the garage that made you fall. Did you trip on the step ladder while you were putting it away or what about the shovel, did that get in your way?"

Mendez did not say a thing, but his brain went into overdrive. He could not remember. That night he could not sleep, he was wondering what happened. Did someone attack him, or did he trip or fall. It was a problem for him and he could not solve it. Maybe if he ever went home, it may come back to him.

His thoughts were interrupted by a lot of talking at the nurse's station. Someone was going home. He opened his eyes and looked around him. A wheelchair was on its way down past the wards and he felt he recognised the young man in the chair, but he could not remember where.

"There you go, Christian," said the nurse. "No more accidents on the road please, you really upset your mum and dad." She smiled.

"No, I will be more careful next time," he said. "Thank you for looking after me." The wardsman appeared and pushed him off in the direction of the end of the ward. When the doors opened, two people were there, he supposed his mum and dad.

Mendez knew him, but from where.

The next day, Sandra went to visit as usual. As she entered the room, Mendez looked up at her and said, "San." She burst into tears. He did not say anything else all day, but she chatted away as usual and the next day, he was sent home as there was nothing else they could do for him.

Sandra thanked them all for their excellent care and devotion to making him well and he did appear happy. He was wheeled to the car by a wardsman, and they helped him into the car. Sandra drove carefully home. Before she left, she rang her sister and her husband, told them she was bringing him home and could they meet him in case she needed help to get him into the house, as she did not know what to expect.

They were at the gate and so were the six children, so excited that he was coming home. The excitement continued inside the house; they were so happy to have him back with them.

Mendez looked at them all, they were strangers. He thought for a while and of course he knew Sandra, then he thought that he knew Sally. He kept telling himself he must know them all. His two eldest children he knew, he even remembered their names, no recognition of the other two and he did not know the man with Sally. He hoped he would know who they were soon, as they were all confused that he did not know their names, worse than that he did not speak.

Sandra shuffled them all out of the house as she could see that her husband did not know some of them and did not seem to know their names; did he even know where he was?

Mendez sat and thought of where he was and was that his family. Slowly he remembered things. Yes, he had four children to his wife, Sandra. He remembered Sally and that fellow was her husband. That must have been her two children with them. Right? Things were coming back to him.

That night in bed with Sandra, he thought he should hold her to him to reassure her that he knew who she was. However, family was not really on his mind. He was thinking of what happened to him. Did someone try to kill him? Did he try to kill himself? Was it just an accident?

Too many questions for his brain to cope with, so he fell asleep. Probably because of the medications he was on.

When he woke in the morning, he turned to the woman beside him and said, "I love you, Sandra." She burst into tears and held him tight. He responded by gently kissing her. "Who are the other kids?" He asked. She laughed and made sure he knew all the names he should know. He repeated the names and told her he hoped he could remember them. She laughed again, she was so happy.

His speech was slow, but he was remembering things like the doctor said he would. He had told her none of this was unusual with a severe head injury. She was getting her husband back. She rang the Bay police station and asked for Troy Harvey.

Sandra told him what was happening and keeping him up to date, and keeping the police in the station informed as they were always wanting to know how he was going. It was a happy report.

Mendez greeted his children, but when he spoke, they knew all was not right. Sandra told them he was still getting better so they must help him remember things during the day. The eldest told him he promised him a dog! "If I said you could have a dog then you can have one," answered Mendez. Sandra was horrified but said nothing, but took the child into the other room and gave him a good talking to about taking advantage of his father, as his father had never told him that he could have a dog. Of course, he had his chores doubled and more punishment to come as soon as she could think of some.

After the children went to school, he asked Sandra to come out into the garage and show him where she found him. He had to work out what had happened. They went out and she showed him where his car was parked, not in the usual position and where the shovel was, the rake and the pick that was now missing. The ladder was on the concrete in a strange position.

It was in its bracket on the wall now so, Mendez took it down and put it in the position she found it. His detective mind was kicking in. Sandra went inside the house.

Mendez backed Sandra's car out of the garage. He found his driving was still good and that was a relief. He wondered if he still had a license. He then repositioned his car in the position that Sandra said it was. He walked around the car, looked at the ladder. Sandra had told him that it was an accident with the ladder, forensic testing had proved that by the angle of the injury.

So, he was not attacked or try to do himself in. It was an accident. Sandra believed that as, she had asked him to put the ladder away after he had cleaned the gutters on the house, she thought that maybe he did not do that. She presumed that he then was putting it back in the garage the next day, when he came home after lunch time. So, what was he doing?

He was looking around and then up. Directly above the roof of the car was the manhole to get up into the ceiling. He took the ladder to the car and climbed it to find that on the car roof, he could reach the manhole easily. He slid back the cover and there was a cardboard box there. He pulled it towards him and pulled open the lid to expose a steel box.

He found the keys to the steel box and opened it. There were guns in it. So why was he hiding it, as that was obvious, but he had no idea. He locked the steel box and put the cardboard lid over it. Slid the manhole cover over the hole and carefully climbed down.

The shiny roof of the car was slippery, so he was careful. That verified it was an accident; getting down from the roof of the car he had slipped and fell. So, what were guns doing in his ceiling over the garage. He would have to think about that.

Chapter 23
Court

The courthouse was busy with people, all wanting to get in and see the trial of twenty-five men up on child sex abuse. The crowd was shuffling and pushing to get in as they all knew there was only a certain number of seats for the public and they did not want to miss out. Not many relatives of the defendants were there as they did not want to b associate with the type of person who would abuse a child.

Some of the wives appeared as the solicitors had told them that their husband was innocent, and it would look better for him if they appeared at the trial. As the man was usually the bread winner in most cases, and in this case, they were all wealthy and the wife did not care about the fact that he was guilty, as she knew or suspected such things from him in the past. The main concern from all the wives was that they would lose the lifestyle that they had become used to.

To lose the great mansion, flights to all over the world, pampering at salons and fancy clothes and shoes seemed too much to bear. Of course, they would all say that he was innocent as she had never seen anything to make her think otherwise.

The three lawyers all had an excuse for being at the Little Girls Club. The first one said he was writing a book on the abuse of children and was on a fact-finding mission.

The second lawyer said that he was studying this so he could help change the law to a stronger and longer sentence for men who did this abuse. He could not present a case to the government unless he had the facts.

The third lawyer said he was going to work with a 'Government Child Abuse Program' to help victims of child abuse and their families. He needed this information so he could deal with the child the parents or other relatives or neighbours that had abused a child. This was an essential service to bring the family together to help the trauma of the child and to protect the child from further abuse.

They had chosen to come up before the judge together as they would look supportive of each other in their innocence. The judge ruled that they should have a separate trial with their own lawyer and sent them back to the cells with remanded in custody.

The next few were also sent back to the cells with a date to appear before a jury. They all had their own barristers or lawyers.

Stan was next who pleaded innocent as he was attending with Arthur McDonald and was told it was a buck's party. It was his word against Arthur's. If Arthur said the opposite, neither would be believed. Back to the cells for Stan with a date to be set for his trial.

Arthur McDonald was next. He had heard what Stan said so sat at the desk in front of the judge. His lawyer said the opposite to what Stan said and Arthur being the older of the two, knew he was sunk.

Suddenly, Arthur stood up, vomited all over the papers on the desk, shit himself and fell down dead.

The court was closed and the rest of the men on the charge were sent quickly to the cells and an ambulance was called. The court was closed, and the judge returned to his chambers.

The judge later rang the hospital to check on the dead man and was told that he had a fatal heart attack. He hung up the phone and thought that maybe that was a good outcome for McDonald as he really had no excuse for being there except for child sex abuse.

This news was national and in every newspaper in the country. So, Lydia found the newspaper at the breakfast table with the headlines *Heart attack stops trials*. She read the article and said, "Well, at least he did not die in jail."

Tristan had read it and was on the phone when Lydia came in to see him. "How did you feel about that?" He asked her.

"I feel nothing," she replied. He dropped the subject.

"So, what is on today for you?" He asked. "Back to your new profession saving little children? I am so proud of the work you are doing. You really are special."

"I love my work," she said. "It brings meaning to my life, and I feel good about what I do. I have a new idea of how to help the little ones. I want to start a new department to assist the mothers of these babies. The majority are so poor and no idea of money management."

"So, a lot of the money that they receive from working or government money is wasted. If they feel they are gaining on their income, they would be happier in their life. When you have the time, I would like to talk to you about it."

"How about right now over breakfast," he said.

"Ok," she said. "I am very busy at work, and I am finding it difficult to come here after that and on weekends doing your paperwork. So, I have found a bookkeeper and wondering if you would do an interview tomorrow afternoon at some time so they can take over my job, and that will leave me free to get out and about to these families."

"Now, what happens if they are not suitable?" Tristan asked.

"Just tell me and I will find someone else," she said.

"Fair enough." He smiled. "I am sure you would not send me some dumbo who cannot add or subtract. Alright, how about three in the afternoon tomorrow?"

Lydia smiled, finished eating her breakfast as they sat in silence.

A peck on Tristan's cheek and she was off to work or 'to save every child on the earth' as Tristan would say. He was very proud of her and the way she involved her friends that she had lunch with every month or so. She had a regular little army going there.

Tristan went down to his office by the showroom. Trevor was here and Tristan informed him that he had an order for a Citroen 2CV from 1948. Seems it was for a young woman's father as a surprise birthday present.

"These odd ones are always for someone's surprise birthday present; I sometimes wonder how much of a surprise it is. Could be more of a shock!" Tristan said.

Trevor laughed. "Well, I think I can outdo you. I have just had a call from someone, sounded like an elderly gent wanting a Goggo mobile," said Trevor.

"You win," laughed Tristan.

They returned to their offices and back to their computers. Working to import both the cars with their agents. Tristan thought about Arthur and how he died and how his mother handled the situation. He thought about it for a while and then realised that Lydia had never got over his father.

She was still in love with him. The more he thought about it, the surer he was. What a great love that must have been. Although, he still thought about

Christina on the odd occasion; he had often thought about having another go at having a wife and a family. He often felt sad about his situation.

The day went quickly as days seemed to past so fast these days, and while he was daydreaming about how his life should have been, he heard the clip clop of high heeled shoes on the marble tiled floor of the showroom and a low woman's voice asking Trevor where Tristan was. The high heeled shoes neared him, and he closed his laptop lid down over his work as he usually did when a stranger entered his office, then he looked up.

Starting as she walked to him at the delicate feet in the high heeled shoes, magnificent legs, perfect body dressed in red and then almond eyes, kissable lips, shiny jet-black hair framed face, he stared. Trevor was close behind her. "Y…Y…Yes, Trevor," Tristan stuttered.

"Nothing," said Trevor as he turned to go.

"I have found the car you wanted," Tristan managed to stammer out.

"No, I did not want a car," that low toned voice cruised.

"Oh! Then how can I help?" Tristan regained his composure.

"Your mother sent me as a bookkeeper. I am Chonnay."

"I forgot," he blurted out. "So sorry."

"That's ok," she replied. "Your mother said you were always very busy."

"Take a seat," he said as he leaped to his feet to help her with the chair.

"My mother would only recommend you if you could do this job." Tristan smiled. He could not believe his luck. *My wonderful mother*, he thought and then checked Chonnay's fingers for rings.

There were none.

They sat and talked for a long time. Seems Chonnay could not handle working with the child protection agency. The stories that were told or discussed in her presence were too distressing for her to handle. She was a very gentle woman who loved children and the thought of them getting abused and bashed when they were so defenseless, gave her nightmares, so Lydia thought dealing with the books on cars and importation and exports would be a good job for her.

Lydia was right. However, she set Tristan on fire like he never knew possible.

After Chonnay left, Trevor came into his office and said, "You like her, Boss?"

"Sure do," smiled Tristan. "Why?"

"Because if you don't, can I have a shot?" Trevor grinned.

"No chance. She is in my office so I can see her all day!" Tristan said.

“I was only asking,” laughed Trevor.

Lydia came home after work that day. “How did you go with Chonnay,” she asked. She knew what the answer would be as soon as she looked at Tristan.

“You could have warned me, naughty mother,” smiled Tristan.

Lydia laughed. “I wanted to surprise you.”

They settled in to make dinner together, both so happy and Lydia hoping Chonnay would be a good choice for Tristan to fall in love again.

Chapter 24
Christian

Troy Harvey called in to see Mendez with a plan. He wanted Mendez to return to work and hopefully, his memory would be jolted back into his life. He knew that Mendez could still not remember his youngest child, for the life of him where did that child come into his life. He did not ask Sandra as she may be upset about it. He remembered the three kids now but not the youngest. That fourth child had him puzzled.

When Troy asked him to come into the station, Mendez was delighted. To get back to work may help him remember lots of things.

Troy started to give him the Mogo file that was large and covered not only local searching but also Interpol enquiries. Mendez thought this was too big a file to start on. However, Troy thought it was the best one as Mendez had worked on it for years. As he read it, Troy was hoping that Mendez would pick out some things that Troy would be able to comment on and memories would come back.

Some things did come back very plainly like going interstate to find a family that was hiding in fear of their lives. Dreadful stuff.

Mendez read over and over the Mogo part of it. He was the one that internet had an interest in; he was trying to see the reason he always fired two bullets. No reason given. In the end, he thought he should read the file from the very beginning. What about that baby that was taken?

The lady caring for him was shot twice in the head and the baby never found. Was that investigated enough? Why was that not the most important matter in the murder. It is not easy to steal a baby. This baby was only a few days or weeks old a newborn and never found. They must have needed food and clothing for it.

A bag of baby things was stolen at the same time. So, if it had food in it for a few days, someone needed to buy more. If a baby needed food, it would at that stage be on a bottle, so some sort of milk or formula would be needed. Did any baby food supplier notice a strange woman or man come in and buy some?

It was a bit difficult as the Bay was a tourist town, so a traveller going through or staying for a holiday could call in and buy baby food. Did anyone report anything as it must have made headlines in the paper or on social internet or television. No-one reported anything at all according to this report. Who was the father? Who was the mother?

He looked further into the report and found Tristan Paravoni. That rang a bell very loudly in the Mendez brain. He decided to call in and see Tristan Paravoni. Did he remember Mendez? He would go and see.

Tristan was in his office when Mendez walked in. Tristan greeted him warmly and said that he was pleased to see him back on the job. Mendez started to stare at Tristan. "I am not really. They are trying to get me back on the job, but my memory has not returned to normal. They have me reading up on the Mogo file as, that was the one I spent most time on."

"I am sorry I keep staring at you, I do remember you but while I was in the hospital, a young man was discharged and he looked just like you. Now I have caught up with you, I can remember that clearly."

"Really?" Tristan was puzzled and not sure what this was about. He invited Mendez to sit down, and they could have a talk about this. He made Mendez a cup of coffee and they talked for an hour and a half. When they parted, Mendez remembered so much more of the Mogo file and Tristan's distress losing his son. They vowed to keep in touch regularly.

Mendez was pleased with his progress with his memory and returned with new hope that he would get back to his normal self sooner than he thought. He relayed the visit to Troy who was pleased he had brought Mendez back to the station and his detective brain had snapped back into place.

When Mendez went home, he found his mobile phone and checked all his text messages. They went back for about a month where he had copied the previous ones onto a computer and deleted them. So, he had one month's text messages still on his phone. As he read through them, he copied them also onto his computer and deleted them off his mobile.

Then he came to the last few days and one message jumped out at him. *Mogo has retired, to prove it his guns will be delivered to you tomorrow morning.* "Well, there you go," he said aloud, "that explains the guns." He thought about them in his roof and wondered why he had not handed them in. *Too late now I suppose, I don't want to be investigated over this. Deal with them later.*

Mendez was back on the trail of a missing baby. He headed off to the hospital and asked for the medical records department. Of course, he could not really access the records, but he could get a name from the head of the department as part of an investigation.

A bright young woman came to the front desk, and he explained the situation quietly to her and asked if he could just have the young man's name.

"I will have to ask my superior but as it is a police investigation, Detective, it could be ok. Can you give me the time and date of the discharge and I will go and see what we can do?" Mendez gave her the information that he had.

A very official looking middle aged man approached him with the young woman this time. He doubted he would get information from this guy. After introducing himself to the man, he asked how he could assist. Mendez explained that he only needed the young man's name so he could see him and ask him a few questions. That his name was Christian.

He would also like to talk to one of his doctors if he could. Not to access his records but to ask about blood and parent's roles on passing that on to their offspring. The head of the department was helpful and said that, as it was a police officer, he would give him the name of the doctor and the young man's full name.

Mendez received the name of Christian Montgomery and the address. He saw the doctor first to ask about baby's blood. The doctor told him that babies usually have the same blood type as their father, however it was not unknown for the baby to have the mothers blood type, but rarely. Of course, you get the variations of what is known as a blue blood or other problems.

If you say the baby was stolen at a few days old, it would still be in the hospital or died soon after it was stolen. Mendez thanked the doctor and headed around to the address he had been given.

He waited in the car up the street about four houses up and retrieved his long-distance camera with the big zoom lens out of the glove box. No one appeared from the house or going into it. He would just have to wait. He rang Sandra and told her he was on stake out. She was surprised but was pleased he had become a detective again. Mendez arrived home about one in the morning and climbed into bed with his wife.

Mogo was in bed with his wife. He adored her and sometimes watched her as she slept. At two-thirty in the morning, his phone gave a buzz and he caught it before she awoke. He slipped out of bed and went into the lounge room to answer it.

He knew by which phone it was that it was in Europe, probably France, as that time was the usual time they rang. He was right but this time, it was the Vice President Marcel Joubert. He had spoken to him before but usually someone else rang first to inform him.

Marcel spoke urgently to him about a job he wanted him to do as soon as he could. It was so important that the target could bring down the President and cause riots in France. Mogo listened and took it all in. He would come on the next flight to France and ring Marcel as soon as he arrived to get the details of the job he had to do. Mogo would need time to get this target.

Mogo was able to get an early morning flight. He woke up Felicity and told her he had to leave immediately. She understood but did query why now he had retired they were still ringing him. He explained that it was government information, and he could not tell her anything in case someone came here to ask questions; she would not be able to tell them anything except that he worked for the government.

He had told her this a few times and she always said she understood. Mogo added that she was safe if you do not know anything.

He left for France and rang Marcel when he arrived for the appointment to get the information and to see what arms he had available for him to execute this assassination. He must have a very accurate long-distance rifle. As the victim was well known, he would not need a description but he would need some type of timetable for this man so he could check up on his routine.

Also, he would like to get him in enclosed areas so he would not have to worry about wind direction or resistance. Bodyguards could be a problem. Marcel knew these possible problems, so had made a list of the target's possible destinations and where the bodyguards would be most likely to be with him. Mogo looked at the paperwork and was pleased.

The target lived in a mansion surrounded by a high rendered block wall. Trees surrounded the outside of the wall enclosing a large backyard that was barely visible to the outside world. Heavily armed bodyguards patrolled the interior of the back yard but no-one on the outside. No savage dogs. The target did not go for walks in public as he was well known, and people tried to stop him to talk politics.

In the walled back yard, he had gym equipment to keep himself fit. He used it for one hour everyday no matter how busy he was. He would even cancel appointments to keep up his exercise. He felt if he ever changed the time, he would put it off and stop using his gym equipment so often, or just give it up.

The bodyguards at that time had one hour to eat and have their food and coffee or tea as they relaxed from the day's duty; the next night-time shift would join them and take over until the morning. The target did not want his guards to see him on his gym equipment as they would probably laugh at him.

Mogo had been given a hand drawn map of the property marking out the back yard, gym equipment and house also a rough diagram of the trees that overlooked the yard as requested by Mogo. This was accurate as it was drawn by one of the bodyguards who did not agree with the target's views on politics and thought that it would cause riots and death if he was not stopped. This guard also knew that the target had already caused two deaths already.

Mogo was pleased at the two guns, both rifles with sights and loaded, were exactly what he had asked for. He arrived at the destination fifteen minutes before the target would be in the back yard. His information was accurate. No bodyguards in sight. He chose the tree that would be easy to climb and directly in sight for the shots.

He was pleased, this would be easy and it was. The target came out right on time and headed for his exercise bike; he settled on it and concentrated on the digital read-out right in line with the rifle sight. Pop, pop and he fell off his bike dead. Mogo carefully descended the tree and walked away; no sound came from the property.

He placed the two guns in the back of the car and sped away to return the guns from where he had picked them up. Handed them to their user and drove to the airport. He then changed his mind and decided to go to a nice hotel he knew, and ring Felicity from there. He checked in and turned on the television to see if his work had been discovered. Not yet. So, he would have a drink, relax, eat dinner and then ring Felicity.

Mendez had been on watch from seven o'clock. He figured the boy called Christian would be headed off to school around that time. He was but his mother was driving him, so Mendez thought he should follow and get a photo then. He followed their car for quite a way until the pulled up at an exclusive private college.

That made Mendez's eyebrows shoot up. Money in this family. He pulled out his camera but by the time he set it up, Christian had joined his friends who were happy to see him and gathered around, so a photo was impossible.

He would try later. He returned to the school later and was able to get a photo of Christian to take to Tristan.

Tristan looked at the photo and was silent. His mother came in then and he past the photo to her. Lydia took the photo in her hand and said, "This is an old one of you, where did you get it from?"

"It is not me," said Tristan. "It is a boy called Christian." He sat quietly thinking how this had happened.

Lydia whispered, "I think I have seen him before, at the airport, a few years ago. I just did not believe it so; I did not say anything."

Mendez, Lydia and Tristan just sat there looking at the photo for quite some time.

Mendez decided that he should knock on the door next afternoon when the young man was at school and ask her a few questions. At that time, he did not know what to ask but a plan was forming in his brain, and he felt he was becoming a detective in pursuit of a crime and that made him happy.

Felicity opened the door to face a large man who introduced himself as Detective Mendez. She was immediately alert, something about him said danger. He asked to be let in for a moment, she hesitated but she opened the door further so he could enter.

She motioned to the lounge, and she took a large, padded chair. Mendez took in the comfortable scene of a family home for some reason that surprised him.

"I want to talk to you about your son," said Mendez.

"Has he done something wrong?" She asked with a worried tone to her voice.

"No," he said. "I was wondering if you could tell me where he was born."

"We did not live here at that time," she lied. "We were interstate, and he was born at the Women's hospital in Mayfield, why do you ask?"

"We think you have the wrong baby," said Mendez looking her directly in the eye.

"Impossible," she lied. "There were only two of us in the labour ward and she had a daughter. I saw my son before the cord was cut so no mix up there. You have the wrong baby and family," she snapped. "I think you had better go," and she rose and went to the front door then opened it. Pointing where he should go.

Mendez left. He thought she was not telling the truth, but he could check up on the Montgomery family from that hospital. He drove off thinking he maybe should have put that question another way so she would not be so upset, then he could have asked her more about her son. He went back to the station to talk to Troy Harvey.

Mogo had been watching the television to see if his handywork had caused any problems. It did not hit the headlines until the next morning when there was a report that the well-known Communist Rebel rouser causing all the trouble with marching and fighting in the streets of Paris was dead from an aneurism of the brain.

"Well, that was a good description of a bullet or two."

A phone call followed from Marcel. "Excellent job and apart from your fees, you will now be under the protection of the French government. You will be unknown as far as the police and Gendarmes are concerned; your existence does not exist. You will not even be known by Interpol." Mogo was pleased and thanked him. It was also left open if Marcel needed his help again in the future.

Mogo rang Felicity in the morning. She told him what had happened and how the detective was quite pushy. "Can he come and ask me those questions?" She asked.

"No," Mogo said. "That is an invasion of privacy. Felicity, I feel you could be in danger and Christian also. I want you to do some things for me, my darling, so you and Christian will be safe. I am not sure what is going on, but I want you here with me in Paris. However, the first thing you must do is put Christian on that four o'clock flight to France in the morning."

"That is the one I caught and there will be no problem getting him a seat on it. Pack him a backpack, wake him and leave now. While you are at the airport, book a ticket for yourself for the next morning. After you do that, drive home and I will ring you at five and tell you what to do next."

"While you are waiting for my call, pack a bag for yourself. Anything you forget we can buy here, so do not be too fussy."

He rang her ten minutes before five in case she was ready to leave. She was. She was not afraid.

"First thing to do is get the gun out of the safe and with it is a set of keys. Put the gun into your bag until you get to the destination, just in case you get pulled up by the police, they cannot see it, then take less than ten thousand dollars out of the safe leave the rest. Understand me so far." Mogo's voice was calm, so she felt safe now he was in charge.

"Yes, I do," and she repeated exactly what he said.

"Your destination is a unit on the beachfront in town. The keys will open the door. It is on the second floor the address is 569/4, The Esplanade, the Bay. Put the gun on a shelf in the wardrobe, the boxes there all have cash in them. Do not touch that money as you cannot take more than ten thousand dollars with you overseas. Then put the gun in one of the large carboard boxes with the money in it."

"Why did you not tell me you had a unit there? Do you rent it?" She asked.

"No," said Mogo. "I bought it for Christian in case anything happened to you or me, he would always have his own place." He lied, well not really, he had recently changed the title into Christian's name so did not think it was a bad lie just a version of the truth.

"What a wonderful dad you are, no wonder I love you." She gushed.

"Now go in your car and the unit has a garage under it, one of those keys from in our safe opens it. I also have a motorbike in there, just leave it and there is room to park your car beside it. Catch a taxi to the airport."

"Hurry, my darling, I want you safely here. I will pick up Christian at the airport and ring you when he is with me. After that call, get rid of your phone. If anyone asks you are on your way to South Africa. Got that? Be careful, I don't know what I would do without you."

Mogo made two more phone calls. One to a young lady called Monica who was the waitress at the coffee shop near his unit and where he met Felicity.

"Hi, Monica," Mogo said. "All well with you?"

"I am just fine," she answered.

"Monica, remember I gave you an envelope a few months ago. Have you still got it?"

"Of course, I have," she replied.

"Great," Mogo said. "Now I want you to get it and I am sure you know there is money in it and a key."

"Well, that is what it feels like," Monica said.

"I want you to open it and take out one thousand dollars for yourself and leave the other four thousand and the key in the envelope."

"I don't need any money from you," she said. "I am fine."

"Well, just buy yourself a lovely gift from me as my thanks for caring for the envelope."

"Thank you, you are so kind," said Monica.

She always bought him his coffee when he went back to his unit if he felt like a coffee before he went home or out on a job.

"Now this is important. A man will come this morning and ask you for the envelope, can you just give it to him. I owe him the four thousand dollars and need to pay him today," said Mogo.

There was a silence for a moment, and she said, "He is here now, do you want to talk to him?"

"No, my dear, just give him the envelope."

Silence.

"Ok, I have done that, and he has left. Sorry but he had to take the one thousand out for me, he knew to do that."

"Job done then and thank you again, Monica," said Mogo.

"Bye then," Monica said and hung up the phone.

With Christian already on the plane that morning, Felicity had no interruptions or distractions as what she had to do. She would be on the plane the next morning and soon be with them.

She retrieved the gun from their safe, put it in her bag as instructed. Next was the money. Felicity counted nine thousand five hundred into her bag as well and then the keys went into her pocket. She left the house at six o'clock and drove to the unit.

Twenty minutes later, she parked her car beside a motorbike in the garage under the unit. She climbed the stairs to number four and the key fitted the lock. All was well.

Felicity opened the door to the unit and stepped inside and closed the door behind her. She looked around at the apartment and was pleased at how nice it was. Sparsely furnished but tasteful, pleasant pastel colours and paintings on the wall. She went to the wardrobe and opened it.

Bit of a shock there. Hanging in the wardrobe were all sorts of clothes, wigs, shoes and scarves to start with. The she remembered that she at some stage she was convinced he was a spy, and these were his disguises. He even had bags, one was blue and like a sea farers type of soft canvas. No problem they were all for men, no women's clothes. She laughed out loud at herself. There were eight large brown cardboard boxes and a small grey cardboard box.

Felicity looked at the eight bigger boxes closed and taped up. They were all the same size, so her curiosity got the better of her, so she went to the kitchen to get a knife and levered one of them open, so was the next one. It was full of money, all one hundred-dollar bills and all looked new. After looking in the next box that contained the same, she counted how many bundles were in the top and guessed how deep the box was to give herself an approximate layer there.

Then calculated that there was about one million in each box. Before she retaped the boxes, she dropped the gun in one of them and left them there. Felicity knew she had the nine thousand five hundred dollars that was almost the maximum you could take out of the country.

Gun in the box, money from the house, basic clothes, shoes and her handbag and passport, she set out to catch a taxi. Very easy at that hour just before the rush hour that started at six in the morning. She headed to the airport and enquired if there was an earlier plane to France, but no luck there. Felicity decided she should go to the airport motel and have a sleep. She also thought she should ring the guys that cared for their house when they took Christian away for a great tour of the world. They did a good job and Mogo had given them a bonus.

From her motel room, she rang to see if the house sitters were available to care for their house, while they were away.

"Where are you off to this time?" He asked.

"South Africa," she answered. "So can you do it again for us?"

"Certainly can," he said. "Same arrangements for payment each month?"

"Exactly," she answered. "I think our bank still has our arrangements with you as we never cancelled that. However, I will check that as soon as they open today."

"Thanks," he said, "Have a great time."

Felicity lay on the bed and drifted off. She awoke when the sun was setting and knew she would have to stay awake until four o'clock in the morning. So, she went down to the restaurant for dinner.

At this time, a small furniture van pulled up in front of the building that housed Mogo's unit. Two men went up the stairs and entered unit four. They had a trolley to help them get the heavy boxes down the stairs. It did not take long to get the eight boxes on board the truck, and it drove off to the airport to catch a freight plane on its night run to Europe.

They put the labels and the key to unit four to their destination on each box. Couriers met the plane and delivered it to a small plane at the other end of the airport to Switzerland that left as soon as the boxes were loaded on board. The boxes were then collected by an official of one of the Swiss banks, and soon after in the vault below the bank with the rest of Mogo's millions.

Felicity returned to her room glad she had not seen anyone she knew. She was looking forward to her flight. Time seemed to go fast, and she was soon boarding the plane and then on her way to Mogo and Christian, who had not long before rang his mother and told her he was with his dad.

Then Felicity destroyed her phone with a knife and put the bits down the toilet, flushed it and checked that it had gone. The next night she was in Mogo's arms and Christian was by her side waiting for his turn to give her a hug.

Later that night, he told Felicity that he had been in touch with Oxford University and there was a place for Christian if he wanted it. He will do very well there as he wants to go into medicine and he is clever enough to do well in any field of that, if it is research or specialise in something else. *We have a very bright boy.*

Felicity suspected that a couple of million dollars thrown in the direction of any university would make that happen. However, Christian's school results were extremely high so maybe not. She said she would miss him greatly. So now she would only see him about three times a year. Christmas would be very exciting though.

She slept soundly in Mogo's arms that night. All was well with the world. Mogo felt safe too. He had just taken three phone calls, one from the furniture removals saying the delivery to the airport went well. One from the courier who confirmed the boxes were on the small plane, and one from the Swiss Bank confirming that eight boxes were in their safe keeping. Mogo felt freedom at last.

Chapter 25
Freedom

Mendez went back to the station to find Troy Harvey. Troy was sitting at his desk in the same area as Mendez. It was known around the station as the detectives' spot.

As he approached Troy Harvey, he was trying to remember the last conversation he had about the man called Mogo. He was sure that they had some sort of trail to follow him on. Then it struck him that it was the fact that Interpol had been involved as they had the same 'two bullets to the head shootings'. Mendez started the conversation.

"How is it going, Troy?" He asked. "I have just been to see a Mrs Montgomery to ask about her son. I think I stuffed it."

"What happened?" Troy asked. "She throw you out?"

"How did you know that?" Mendez asked.

"Mothers are very protective of their sons you know," smiled Troy. "Don't let it bother you, just tell me what happened." Mendez told him word for word.

"Ok," said Troy. "Start with the hospital and just keep an eye on the place now and again. You can soon find out if she was telling the truth and there was another woman in the ward with her. Only take you a few minutes. If there is any problem, take time off and go there."

"It is just she got so angry, and you never get any results when you upset someone like that."

Troy smiled. "Make that phone call now and we will talk about it in a few minutes to see our next step."

"Well, these days thanks to computers, I have found out that was not true. The funny thing is that at that time they had a run-on girl baby and no boy babies for over two weeks except two sets of male twins. I spoke to the midwife, could not believe she was still delivering babies. She remembered the long run of girl babies and her joke was there would not be enough husbands around when they wanted to get married. Anyway, there was no one under the name of Montgomery on the records for babies or injuries. So that settles that."

"I think I had better go back to Mrs Montgomery and see what she has to say now." He took off like a man on a mission as he was.

It was two days later when he knocked on the door. No answer. He would come back tomorrow and see if anyone was there.

He gave it another two days and felt he had to come home sometime. But no one was there. As he went to get back into his car, another vehicle pulled up. It was towing a trailer with some sort of machines on it. He walked towards them.

"Are you looking for Mrs Montgomery?" One of them asked.

"Yes, I am," said Mendez

"They left a couple of days ago," was the reply.

"They say where they were going?" Mendez asked.

"Yeah," came the answer. "South Africa; think they are taking the boy on a safari. Just guessing that bit." He laughed.

"Thanks, anyway, did they say when they were coming back?" Mendez asked.

"No, they could stay away for a year."

Mendez had a thought. "Well, how do you get paid? I take it you do get paid."

"Sure, we get paid," the voice was suspicious. He was not sure where this was going.

"How do they pay you?" Mendez asked.

"Why should I tell you that?" He asked.

"Sorry, I should have introduced myself. I am Detective Mendez, and I am looking for them. We are concerned about their boy," Mendez spoke as nicely as he could. He needed the answer to that question.

"Ok, money goes into my bank account at the end of every month. We cut the grass, empty the letterbox, well check it as there is never anything in it, do the garden, pick up junk mail and clean the windows."

The voice never told him that they also have a key to the house to check inside. That is not for anyone to know except them. This guy would bring a warrant and then they could lose their customer. He looked back at the other fellow with him, and his eyes told him to shut up.

"Can you give me any details about the bank account?" Mendez asked.

"Well, no, the money goes into our account, never late and always there."

"Well, thanks for that," said Mendez.

While the guys got there machines out of the trailer, Mendez took the name of the company and phone number. By the time he drove off, one of the men was pushing the lawn mower and the other was weeding the garden.

Back at the station, he went to find Troy. He came in soon after. "I think our bird has flown the coup," he said worriedly to Troy.

"Why is that?" Troy said. Mendez relayed the story of what happened and when.

"Well, he must be around somewhere and as Interpol has him on record. Perhaps, we should contact them again and see if he has shown up there or any other sign of him. He may still be here. Don't discount that and he has a wife and a boy. It, at this moment, is the boy we are looking for. If he is a stolen child, then that should be our priority."

"I tell you what, I will talk to my father and see the best way to go but, if wish to get in touch with Interpol ring or send them an email. That would be a good start. Better check airlines as well."

"I have done that, before you came in," said Mendez. "I think I should email Interpol that may get more of a response. They do keep you waiting on the phone at times, and it can take a while to get to talk to the right man."

"Good plan," said Troy. "I am off early tonight, and Paul will be there. We need to talk about mother as she seems to have regressed. I will ring you if he has any ideas. Don't like to bother you at home but this could be urgent."

Mendez left the desk and went to his computer to send an email to Interpol. He relayed what they had told him about having a man called Mogo who seemed to like to shoot people in the head with two bullets and did they have any other information or could they help with his where abouts at this time. They were interested that it could be him who stole a baby years ago, and a boy that has been seen to look the image of the man who had his child stolen.

He went on with a few more details that seem to be in keeping with the stolen child and would be grateful if they had any information at all.

He ended with *Regards from Detective Mendez.*

No immediate response but he did not really expect one. He would check later.

He went back to the staff room for a coffee, he was on his own, seemed everyone had headed out on some crime or other, so he sat down to think. As he sipped his coffee, it occurred that the house would be in Mogo's name. So, he went back to the computer with his coffee and looked up property registration. Then found the address.

The property was registered to Felicity Montgomery. He wondered if she had any other property as well. He scrolled through the Montgomery file and to his delight he found a property, a unit registered to Christian Montgomery right on the beachfront on the esplanade. He could not believe his luck. He kept scrolling but nothing else.

There were plenty of Montgomery people but nothing that could connect with this case. He was quite excited about this and was anxious to speak with Paul Harvey that night. Instead of waiting for the call, he drove out there around dinner time but remembered that Troy and Paul were going to talk about Helen, so drove past and went home.

The next morning, he went straight to his computer and checked for an Interpol reply. He received quite a shock.

Your query into a man named 'Mogo' is odd as we have no information as to anyone of this name. We also cannot recall any previous requests from you regarding any information of this kind by phone or email. We have checked, this has delayed our answer with everyone and even called international services regarding crime. Regretfully, we cannot assist in your enquires.

Regards.

Mendez could not read or recognise the signature, but Interpol logo was displayed, so he knew it was from them.

"In other words, you are on your own or he is being protected," Mendez said aloud to himself. He had the names of the property owners to go on and he was hoping to get a warrant to enter and check them out. He was still thinking about this when Troy came in.

"You will not believe this," Mendez before Troy even got to his desk.

"What's that?" He asked.

"Interpol now knows nothing of Mogo, denies our emails and phone calls and said they have been in contact with international crime investigation, and they know nothing!" Mendez said.

"You must be joking; they were the ones who said they had heard of him and put us on his trail," said Troy.

"Yep."

"Ok, so now what have we got?"

"I have found two properties; one, in the name of Felicity Montgomery and the other in the name of Christian Montgomery. Both properties in the Bay. I would like to check them out. We know the one in the suburbs but the other one is on the tourist strip. That is the one Christian owns. What I need now is a warrant to enter them."

"You had better have a good reason for the magistrate to sign off on that," said Troy. "Although, I know one who if you spin a good story on the crime, he will give you one. I will give him ring now."

"Before you go, how is your mother?" Mendez asked.

"Not good, we have to put her back into care. Poor Paul is in a state but does throw himself into work to forget a bit of it," said Troy.

"Sorry to hear that," said Mendez. "I am sure they will work with the doctors and fix the problem but mental health I feel is difficult to work with. Keep me informed though in case I can help."

"Will do," replied Troy.

Troy left to go to the phone on his desk and talk to the magistrate. Mendez could see him and by the look on his face seemed to be getting permission to search both houses.

"Ok, my friend, go get the warrant and sign off. Are you going now?"

"Will do," answered Mendez.

"Want me to come with you?"

"Sounds like a plan. Do you have the time to come now?"

"Sure do, I feel this is important to get onto quickly," said Troy. "If we have any problems, I will call Paul, he will back us up."

They headed off, both keen to track down Mogo, especially if Interpol denies any knowledge about it, when they certainly did a few months ago. Then suddenly, Troy stopped and turned to Mendez and said, "You know on the way we should go into the files office and check exactly what Interpol said to us as now they deny it."

"Right," said Mendez and he turned and headed in another direction. They asked for the file on Mogo and Interpol. The young constable disappeared into a room and returned quickly handing to them by putting it on the desk in front of him. The two of them perused it carefully and looked for the Interpol reply to their enquiry, and the answer they received.

There was nothing at all about either of them, it was like it never happened. They looked at each other, then searched further into the file from the beginning again. They shut the file and handed back to the young constable and thanked him and turned to head for the car. They never spoke a word to each other until they arrived at the house with the warrant. Mendez was hoping that the men who cut the grass and did the other jobs were not there, and they were not.

The house was securely locked. Mendez was good at picking locks but not dead locks, so they went to a window and was able to get in that way. Hopefully, no-one saw them as they awkwardly scrambled over the windowsill. The house onside was all in perfect order.

The only hope they had of finding anything was that the safe in the bedroom was not locked. The opened it to find five hundred and seventy dollars in cash. No paperwork of any kind, no jewellery or even a watch. So, they went back out the window and shut it, then rang the men who cut the grass.

The company receptionist answered the phone and took a message for them. Mendez wanted the men to check the window was locked again, and the police had searched the house with a warrant at nine-twenty that day.

They headed off for the unit on the esplanade in the tourist strip. It was a bit windy so not many people about at that hour. There were usually a few bikini bodies wandering throughout the coffee shops. It was too early for the bars and bistros to be open.

The view of the ocean was clear for a windy day and it as a most pleasant place to be. The sun was on them, and they both felt good. "Nothing like a nice day to cheer anyone up," said Troy.

They went up to the apartment and of course it was locked no way of getting through the deadlock or a window. So, Mendez rang a locksmith and asked him to come immediately as this was a police matter. The locksmith was there within minutes. Did not take him long to get the door open. Mendez paid him cash and receive a receipt in return to hand in at the station to get his money back.

They entered a modern, sparsely furnished apartment, spotlessly clean. "Batchelor pad," said Mendez. Troy nodded. They checked the kitchen, fridge empty and turned off, the door ajar. Bedrooms, two of them; one furnished, the other empty. The furnished one had clothes in the wardrobe that was very large and full length of the wall.

Troy slid the door back and there were clothes there. Men's clothes. There was also a grey carboard box. As well as this there were hats, shoes, wigs and bags. Troy picked up on one of the bags.

"That is a soft blue sailor's bag, that was used in the shooting of the man in the boat that was under water. I recognise it from the video of the night of that storm and there is the coat with the hood, and that is the walking stick so that should all say Mogo was here. I will look through the rest of the stuff. See if I can recognise anything else."

Mendez went for the grey cardboard box and opened it. "Woman's clothes; do you think he had a woman in this?"

"Don't think so, better look at what size they are as it is possible he used them as a disguise at times."

"You are right there," said Mendez. "All large size and large shoes. However, a small size set here a full set of lady's small size with the tickets still on, so they are new. High heeled shoes as well, also underwear, never worn."

"Makes you wonder," said Troy.

"Get out the camera and take photos of all this and get forensics out here, wonder if we can get a DNA of this stuff," said Mendez.

"With a bit of luck," said Troy.

The talking stopped then and the search continued, photos taken, and phone calls made. When the other departments arrived, they left to go back to their desks and continue with tracking down Mogo.

Mendez was on the phone tracing plane flights, none for Montgomery for the past week domestic or international. Then Christian Montgomery popped up as flying to France on the early morning flight, and the next day Felicity Montgomery same flight time same place. So where was Montgomery himself?

He informed Troy of his find, then said, "Impossible to go and find a taxi that took them somewhere, but I can check hotels where they maybe by phone or email, So I will go that way."

As the French are not so efficient, he discovered that no one of that name had been there. So, Mendez started given them descriptions of the trio. With no luck. Maybe they are staying at a private house, and they now have a car, he thought. They are probably in Spain by now.

He was not far wrong. The three of them were sunbaking on the beach, enjoying their time together as Christian was headed to study at Oxford in a few weeks.

Forensic reports came back with no result. They did get some DNA but that was of no use without something to compare it too. "What now?" Mendez said.

"We will talk to Paul and see what he thinks. We will do that as soon as we can, so he has time to come up with ideas. Other than that, I think we have been outsmarted. We can't let this murdering bastard get away."

Mendez had a headache. He had suffered with headaches since the accident, but they were getting worse. He struggles to remember things and still could not remember his youngest child. He never told Sandra that knowing she would really be upset. He knew the child was his otherwise; where did he come from?

Sandra would not try to fool him or trick him he was sure of that. It all made him unhappy, and he hoped no-one in his family realised that as they might want him to see doctors and specialists, and he did not want to go into that again, he had finished with them forever. He felt sad all the time and did try to snap out of it but that was not working, so he just pretended to be his normal self.

This Mogo thing made him feel a failure in his job. Maybe he should not have come to work early as Troy had wanted but he wondered how he would have been at home with nothing to do. Then there were the guns in his roof. He could not imagine where they came from, and this disturbed him greatly.

Were they Mogo's guns? The text message seemed to say so, but he could not imagine a man so fond of his guns and using a different gun for every occasion. He had not examined them thoroughly, but he wanted to keep them a secret because he had not handed them in, and he could be locked up for that. So as long as they were in the roof, no-one would ever know until they pulled the house down. It never occurred to him, he was suffering depression.

Troy and Paul Harvey were waiting for him when he came in the next morning. Neither of them looked happy. They were both of the opinion that Mogo had escaped them for now but an alert on the file on him should remain active. With two properties in the Bay, one of them at least are bound to return.

They could not do anything about Christian as they did not have his DNA and he was not guilty of anything. They just suspect that he was stolen. Felicity as well had not committed a crime; they doubted she even knew what he was up to. As his wife, they doubted they could use her as a witness to his crimes, as wives cannot testify against their husband in usual circumstances.

Mendez said he was going home. He had the worst of headaches and needed to rest. Defeat by a criminal did not go well but they would be waiting for him the day he returned, no matter how long Mogo stayed out of the country. They did not have his photo or DNA, fingerprints and going by the bullets, the guns were unregistered and untraceable.

Mogo was a cunning fox. He drove home in great sadness for Tristan who was denied a son and he had one he could not remember. He also thought of Lydia who was denied a grandson she could dote on him and spoil him. He would have a different name, not Christian. He remembered they used to refer to him as baby James; so sad for them.

When Mendez arrived home, he found himself alone; Sandra was not home. Sandra basically led her own life with the children as he was always late home or left early. Weekends studying files on cases that were current or cold. He was a busy man not much time for family.

He began to sink into a deep depression and lay on the bed. Maybe Sandra was not going to come back because I cannot remember the youngest boy. He tried to think what he looked like but could not. He cannot stand it.

He went to the first aid cabinet for his medication that he would probably have to take for life. The cabinet was up high so the children could never get to it. Lots of pills in there, bottle full of them.

Sandra arrived home late in the day. She had picked the children from school and gone on to their sports activities, dropping the girls off for dancing lessons.

Sandra saw Mendez car parked on the driveway so knew he was home. She parked in the garage after the remote opened the garage door. She got out of the car, hands full of parcels to put way before she went off to pick up the kids in about one hours' time. It was surprising that Mendez had not come out to greet her, but she thought that he was probably reading one of his files again.

She rarely asked what the crime was because most of them were horror stories. However, after she had put everything away she went into the lounge room and he was not there, so she left to pick up the kids and to see the results of the dancing lessons as they were a change from watching the boys with their soccer; both of them were pretty good at that so did not cheering on. She bundles them into the car, picked up the boys and went home.

The car was still in the driveway which was odd as he usually put it away for the night. She had left the garage door open as she was not away long, and Mendez was home anyway.

The children all ran into the kitchen for the fridge looking for something to eat as usual. As she did not see Mendez around, she quietly went into the bedroom in case he was resting. She knew his headaches were bad at times.

Sandra knew something was wrong by the way he was in the bed and the empty pill bottles on the bed. An empty bottle of water beside the bed. She touched him and no reaction so, got her mobile phone out of her pocket and rang the ambulance before she started CPR. Tears streaming from her eyes. Fortunately, she had closed the bedroom door behind her so the children would not come in as they were told if the door is shut do not enter.

The ambulance sirens could be heard a long way off, and the children were on to it. "Hope it is not for daddy," they whispered to each other. When the paramedics came in and took over, Sandra went out to the children and took them out into the back yard. She kept them there until the babysitter arrived so she could follow the ambulance to the hospital. She knew the way well.

Mendez was dead on arrival. "Why did you do this when you have a great family, why did you not tell me you were unhappy?" She said to the body. Sandra blamed herself. She knew she had to pull herself together for her little ones at home.

The news hit Troy and Paul hard. "Why did we not see it?" Paul said. "Now there is four fatherless kids and a widow. What a tragedy. Hopefully, the force will help her out. Oh my God." He put his head in his hands.

It was a dark and rainy day for the funeral. The children did not attend. Sandra wore black with a heavy veil over her face so you could not see her tears. Paul and Troy were devastated but held a brave face in the crowd that attended.

Tristan was there with his mother. They liked Mendez as he was so kind through their troubles. Always there for them and the time to talk to them, even took a photo of a young man they thought could be his; the photo sure looked like him. They will never know now.

Tristan was going to bring Chonnay but decided that may not be a good idea. His mother was there for him and involved in the problems and the theft of his son, so it was right that his mother was there.

Tristan and Chonnay were couple now. He had found love again. Lydia loved her and was hoping for this, so she was happy. Chonnay loved him back, she wanted to marry him and have a family. She did not tell him that but he was a gentle man and loving, and they had discussed moving in together.

Lydia was never there these days. She had inherited Arthur's cattle station, sold it and had a children's refuge built and staffed. Most of her time was spent there. She was happy to live there at the refuge as she had a large unit built there for her to live in should Tristan remarry.

Lydia would be happy if Tristan married as sometimes, he looked very lonely. Chonnay had filled his life and he was always happy these days. Fingers crossed, she thought.

Not only was Chonnay beautiful, she was smart and looked after the company finances better than anyone he ever had there. He would never tell his mother that as she did a good job too, but times had passed and Chonnay was more up to date on the computer and quicker at finding and solving problems too.

Two months after the funeral, there was a wedding. Lydia was delighted and moved permanently into the children's refuge unit she had designed for herself. This left her full time on the job to care for those unfortunate little ones.

Mogo and Felicity happily settled in a beachfront house, not quite a mansion but a large and with a pool. Felicity always counted in the maintenance of anything they purchased. Mogo had to maintain the pool, or they would not have one she told him. He loved her shrewdness, always looking after their finances as he worked so hard for them. Well, she thought he did.

They were sitting in the front of the house on their deck chairs when Felicity suddenly asked him, "You know when I went to Christian's unit like you told me to and put the gun in the box of money."

"Yes," he said, "and by the way, I popped into Switzerland and picked up the gun. It is in the house safe now; in case you need it."

"Ok, I wondered where you went on an overnight trip," said Felicity. "So, when I was in the unit, there were eight carboard boxes that were brown and one smaller one that was grey. Can I ask what was in the grey box? I knew there was money in the others like you told me."

"I was curious as to how much. But I did not look in the grey one, so what was in it? Will you tell me?"

"Yes," he replied. "As you probably realise as a spy, I need to have all sorts of clothes for a disguise so that one was full of lady's clothes and shoes. Most to fit me but one complete set to fit you in case you were in danger."

"Ladies clothes to fit you?" She laughed. "If I had seen those, I would not be here with you now." They both laughed and laughed. Life was good and they were free. He had not left a trail, that he knew of.

The End

CPSIA information can be obtained
at www.ICGtesting.com
Printed in the USA
BVHW051132070623
665543BV00008B/165